TRIPLE OVERTIME

A BILLY WINSLOW NOVEL

TRIPLE OVERTIME

C. JULIANO

Published by Penny Publishing

Paperback ISBN: 979-8-9860837-2-8
Ebook ISBN: 979-8-9860837-3-5

Cover art by C. Juliano

To Denise and Penny, and to the spirits.

CONTENTS

PROLOGUE

In a field, thick vines scale the side of an old, abandoned building, its pitted walls a diary of death and decay. Silence and stillness fill the empty spaces. Animals drift nervously through the ruins to feel a certain something, the absence of anything, a sign that it's safe to return.

The countryside holds secrets, and the structure memories of years gone by. Seasons change as time slowly wears the days away, but for some, they never end. For some, they go on and on, forever and always, in a field.

In the darkness the house seems to creak and moan. In the light, shadows flicker and fade. The discordant chime of a doorbell sounds. A door opens over and over again. Voices that won't go away sometimes echo into the living—into lives, to forever change and to alter their paths.

The earthly seldom cross over. Few get to enter the netherworld, but who better to go than someone who had nothing? Who better to tangle with the ever present than a man who'd given up everything? Who better to wrestle with the spirits than Billy Winslow?

While exiled in Mexico, Billy ate a plant. A cactus, so it seemed, at the Temple of Kukulcan. He was sick and then well, but it was the time in between that told the story. It was a tale of flowing robes and glowing apparitions. Voices came, forbidding, at first, and then more understanding as bright vivid colors pulsed through the dark, deserted night.

Billy was laughing and then crying. He begged for forgiveness while cursing his own existence. Never one to pray, he did now as it began to storm.

Different sounds came from the sky, rumblings, rain, and the unexplained. Blasts and cracks echoed from above: crashes of destiny, flashes of mortality, all things to be taken quite seriously.

Shimmering goddesses illuminated the darkest night. Celestial conversations occurred. From ancient voices came a thundering debate on whether to save a son or to reveal his fate.

ADIÓS, AMIGO

"To save a son, to save a son, to save a son," repeated Billy as he lay cold and shivering at the base of the temple.

The phrase ran through his head like an ancient, forgotten song as he slowly came to. Billy didn't seek any shelter. He took the full brunt of the storm exposed and vulnerable, hoping to feel the same pain he'd inflicted on others.

He wanted the storm to subside—in himself and in the sky above. He wanted to feel good again. And after a night of near-death experiences, the gods finally spoke. Billy was spared. But instead of jumping for joy, he simply laid on the ground, remembering the bitter dried fruit from earlier. Javier had handed him a piece and said it was good, that it was some kind of an edible cactus, harmless. Now that the storm had passed and the spirits were gone, Billy was left a tattered mess.

"To save a son," was all that he could recall. What did it mean? And where was the damn shaman? *What kind of a shaman leaves a ceremony?* thought Billy. It was supposed to have been a fun outing, not a full-fledged spiritual retreat. Billy had been promised some sights and sounds, not a voyage into the depths of his soul. But he'd gone, nonetheless, and now he didn't have a ride home; so he walked.

Shirtless, with thick blond hair, blue eyes and a determined stare, Billy's muscled torso flexed with every angry step. And where did his shirt go? He didn't know. At least he had his shorts and shoes.

As Billy continued on, he thought about dying. He'd heard death by dehydration was rather painful, but he figured the aftermath would go pretty well. The buzzards could pick his bones clean and he could return to dust, but that wouldn't happen today. Today there was something else going on so as he trudged along, thirsty and tired, Billy hoped there was something else going on or he just might die.

With no relief in sight, it was already hot and Billy didn't have any water. Thoughts of the supernatural began to swirl as heat rose from a distant road. A tiny black dot broke the horizon and moving steadily closer, it was a farm truck with an empty seat, so Billy hopped in.

"Where you headed, amigo," asked the driver, thankfully in English. Billy's Spanish wasn't too good.

"To the nearest cantina, my friend," answered Billy.

It was early, but he needed a drink. He also needed to make sense of what he'd seen, if that were at all possible. But at the moment, the whole thing seemed rather senseless, just like the gravel peppering Billy's face through the broken passenger window. Rattling along through the countryside, one thing became crystal clear: he wouldn't be heading back to the temple.

Finally in the parking lot of a rundown bar, Billy gave the driver a few bucks and headed in. Smoke wafted through the relative darkness as the locals cautiously turned away. This wasn't the place for idle chatter.

Spying a pay phone, Billy called for a ride and then ordered a beer. Following his first sip, the hallucinations returned, so he walked outside to wait. It was sure to be an interesting day.

As his friend Felix finally motored up, Billy got into the car only to hear Felix ask, "What the hell happened to you?"

"I spent the night at a temple."

"With no shelter? What, did you get abducted?"

"No, I went to Chichen Itza with Javier and ate some cactus."

"I told you not to go anywhere with Javier. And you didn't just eat cactus, you ate peyote."

"Hmm," muttered Billy, "so that would explain the bright lights and vomiting I guess."

"I guess," repeated Felix. "Where's Javier now?"

"I don't know, but he left me to die, so I'd better not see him anytime soon."

Silence followed the grim statement as they clattered through downtown Cancun. Finally at Billy's place, Felix casually said, "See ya, Billy, and stay away from the cactus."

"You bet," replied Billy, "and thanks for the ride."

Felix was a good friend, and Billy was going to miss him.

Walking gingerly down a cobbled walkway to his secluded villa, Billy was glad to be home. Pink oleanders pierced the pale blue sky as Billy nervously felt for his keys. The beauty and the sky were the same but beneath it, something had changed.

Sparse, orderly, and unresolved, Billy's apartment was also the same. Mementos cluttered the shelves, but it wasn't home. Women stopped by, but they didn't stay. And as a stiff gust of wind pushed through an open window, Billy instantly felt the winds of change.

But he wanted to stay the same. He wanted to stay hidden so he couldn't do any more harm, but that wasn't part of the plan. Maybe he wasn't meant to be an exile in a foreign land or a hermit on a distant shore. Maybe he had more to offer. Maybe Billy needed redemption too.

Thoughts sped anxiously through his mind as he finally laid down to rest. The room then started to spin as the chant *To save a son* sent Billy back into the beyond.

In a chaotic dream, storms raced tragically through the countryside as a lone car sped down a thin highway. There had been a fight, unresolved. It never would be resolved, because in the opposite direction came a truck. Just over the center line, with the rain heavily falling, two vehicles collided and shot out in different directions. One in the truck survived but three in the car had to be rushed to the hospital. It took a while to free them from the wreckage, and as an ambulance began a long, lonely wail toward the emergency room, Billy woke up.

Twisting his way back into consciousness, he was again left with the words *To save a son.* It felt like an order or a command of some sort. It seemed like he needed to go, but where to? And following another stiff gust of wind, a map of Florida was torn from Billy's wall and plastered onto his face. *Guess I'm going back to Florida,* thought Billy.

As Billy carefully extricated himself from the map, first the dream came into focus and then the hallucinations. The good news was that his life hadn't actually been ruined when he fled Florida. The bad news was that it might be ruined now. Between the cactus, the voices, and the winds of change, Billy was feeling a little out of whack.

It wasn't so long ago that he and his ex-girlfriend Rita sped toward Orlando International Airport for a one-way ticket out of town. One step ahead of the law, the sexy Rita Polli flew him down to Mexico and then stole the notes for his first novel. Finishing the book on her own, she named it *Kidnapping Steve,* and as one might imagine, Steve got kidnapped. Billy got banished; Rita got published and then married the publisher.

She was now called Rita Flake, as Billy learned from a subsequent letter. From R. Flake, somewhere in New York, came a heartfelt message with a duplicate deed to a property in Florida. She'd bought him a house in lieu of payment for his book. He'd refused the cash; after all, how can one mend a broken heart? He was also cleared in the kidnapping, which was good to know, since he hadn't kidnapped anyone. But Billy was now being forced back to the scene of the crime, and he wasn't quite sure what to expect.

Billy was once a respected member of the community, or at least a member of the community. He was on his way up before he met Rita, or on his way somewhere before he met Rita. Truth be told, he'd never been completely stellar, but he could be now. There was something in the air, and instead of scared, Billy felt empowered. With a pair of scissors firmly in hand, he began ceremoniously shearing his long blond locks. It was time for a change.

With strong, determined swipes, Billy's hair fell to the floor as his face slowly reemerged. Now down to the scalp, he looked every bit the all-American boy—the same one who'd pledged allegiance to the flag in a little beachside school. But this was a new journey, so he'd need a new approach. There were things to do before he went any further: tickets to buy, jobs to quit, and of course, good-byes to be said. Billy hadn't been in Cancun long, but it was where he'd regained his strength, and for that he was thankful. If he were ever in trouble again, he knew where to go.

In a foreign land, with close to nothing and nowhere to stay, his first few weeks were rough, but Billy eventually settled in. Without any reliable transportation, he walked almost everywhere and had even started running. Playing basketball with the local kids, he'd also regained his form. At six foot five and with a good outside shot, Billy was headed to college before becoming a beach bum.

While playing in rec leagues, lettering in high school, and eventually being recruited by some top colleges, he liked the sport—but not the structure. Tired of the coaching, the yelling, and all of the other expectations, Billy chose more joyous pursuits. But in Mexico, the court once again called, and Billy answered. He'd arrived in decent shape, but he was now a physical specimen.

So, with the fatigue from the last couple of days wearing off and his confidence on the mend, Billy strolled into the Seadust Cancun looking for Carlos.

Surprised by the new and improved Billy, Carlos asked, "What's up, Señor Bill? You putting in for a promotion?"

"It's time for me to go, Carlos," answered Billy with a heavy, but determined heart.

Carlos had been there from the start. He'd watched a weary American wander in and ask for a job. The front desk waved Billy off, but Carlos called him back. He saw something in the wandering spirit, perhaps a need for salvation or possibly a second chance.

"You sure you're ready to go back, amigo?" Carlos cautiously asked.

"No," answered Billy, "but I've got to."

Carlos was a good boss and Billy a good worker, so eventually a friendship grew. A little rough around the edges, Billy worked hard, and unlike the other gringos, he never missed a day.

Billy found peace in the landscape and solitude in his work. He was popular around the resort but had never shared anything personal. Reserved to a fault, Carlos wondered what Billy was really doing in Mexico. Some came to explore and others to party, but Billy did neither. It almost seemed like he was doing time—or paying a penance.

Carlos had seen people on the lam. He knew their wary movements and guarded expressions. Some told him and others didn't, but Billy was different. He had a spark, almost like a ruler in exile.

After a few drinks one night, Carlos asked, "Hey Billy, what's your story?"

"How do you know there is a story?"

It was a fair question. Tall with long blond dreadlocks, it wasn't likely that Billy could be completely anonymous, but he tried. He stayed mostly to himself, but Carlos had taken a chance on him, so Billy took a chance on Carlos. Deciding to lay it all out, Billy told Carlos of his gorgeous girlfriend Rita and about the botched kidnapping. He explained how he'd written about the ill-fated abduction under the pseudonym "Flash." He talked about his old friend Van, who'd first suggested the sinister scheme. He mentioned Edwin and the young bum and how they were supposed to be the specialists. He told of how it was supposed to be a laugh—until a criminal named Keller got involved and left a guy named Steve bound and gagged at his doorstep.

"I never kidnapped anyone," said Billy, "nor brought about any harm. I never would have. I was simply trying to impress a girl."

"Sounds like you messed up, amigo," replied Carlos.

"I sure did," agreed Billy, "but I'd appreciate it if you didn't call the law. I'll move on if you want, but I'd sure like to stay."

Carlos liked Billy, and it sounded like one hell of a story.

"Absolutely man, just don't write any more of those kinds of stories in Cancun. You might not get out so easily."

That's why Carlos was sad to hear Billy was leaving when he asked, "Is it safe to go back?"

"It's safe," answered Billy. "I've been cleared."

"You sure?" said Carlos. Mexican justice wasn't quite so forgiving.

"Yup, got a letter from Rita the other day. She said it's safe to come home. She got the book published. Married the publisher and bought me a house on the beach, I guess."

Billy declined to tell Carlos about the cactus, the hallucinations, and the winds of change; that could wait. He'd simply come to say thanks and good-bye.

"You bailed me out, Carlos, and I won't forget it. The apartment's clean, and the key is under the mat. I'll see you again soon, my friend," said Billy with an outstretched hand.

Carlos had heard some crazy stories, but this one had taken the cake. When Billy told of what he'd done for a girl, Carlos was a little suspicious, but Rita was obviously no ordinary woman and Billy wasn't an ordinary guy. It was farfetched, to say the least—a best seller and a house on the beach—but, for some reason, Carlos believed him.

There'd usually be closure when someone left, but not today. There was a new, crackling energy in the air and Carlos knew to let it be. He instead took Billy's hand and in a stern, understanding voice said, "Adiós, amigo."

BILLY'S BACK

Leaving town, Billy gazed toward the crystal-clear waters of the Caribbean and felt a strange kind of sadness. It seemed like he was losing something, like he was losing himself. The days of meandering would soon be gone. The time of aimlessness was coming to an end. The simple life was fleeting, and he was leaving.

In a bumpy cab on the way to Cancun International Airport, Billy was going back to Florida. It wasn't good. A lot had happened there, and he wanted to stay gone for a while, maybe forever. Billy needed to turn the cab around, but as he reached for the cabbie, the car hit a bone-jarring pothole and threw his hand quickly aside.

Guess I'm going back, thought Billy.

With a one-way ticket to Orlando, Billy would arrive as he'd left, carrying a backpack and little more. He had some money saved, but he'd still have to work—unless of course, the spirits had a plan for that as well.

He owned a house, but what to do with it? Sell it? Rent it? Live in it? And what did he need to do? Maybe he wouldn't even be staying. And what about the guys who were waiting for him? Billy wasn't exactly going to announce his arrival. If they wanted him, they were going to have to come and get him.

Boarding the flight, Billy had more questions than answers. Who was the son he was supposed to save? And where was he? It obviously wasn't going to be straightforward. If it had anything to do with Billy, there was sure to be more pain than pleasure. Hopefully there'd be some joy as well, but at the moment, the only certainty was a long walk home from the airport. He didn't have a ride.

Reluctantly shoved into a window seat, Billy gazed at the ocean while the flat blue of the Caribbean stared back. Then, curiously magnified in the crystal clear water, he saw a car tumbling tragically along, end over shattered end before slowly evaporating into the sea. Billy rubbed his eyes and refocused but the lines were gone. He saw the light of day, the clear of the sky, and the emptiness of the water, but there was no vehicle. But it was a familiar sight. He remembered it from the other night, from the nightmare. It was a car crash, and Billy seemed to be heading straight for it.

It wasn't a stunning image. It should have been, but Billy had come to terms with the fact that things were going to be a bit different. He'd actually come to expect it. He wanted it; purification in the sense that he wanted to change. He wasn't certain that he had.

Sure, he'd left town. He'd found peace in the quiet contemplation of his work, but was he different? And when he got back, would he fall into the same insanity? At thirty thousand feet, Billy finally let go. There was a plan, and he was part of it. He'd pierced the thin veil of sanity, and it felt good. He couldn't fail. He just needed to keep moving and when the plane touched down, Billy was ready.

Grabbing his carry-on, Billy exited the plane like an athlete on the way to a big game. Where was the game? He didn't know, but he was going there.

He looked every bit the part. Square shouldered and tall with close-cropped blond hair and sparkling blue eyes, he was a new man. It wasn't so long ago that he'd been at the same airport with a tear in his eye, leaving Florida, and leaving Rita as well. But that was then and this was now, and coming home, he wore a look of ferocity instead of sadness.

Passing the people and the cars and the captains and crews, Billy had finally hit his stride. The pretty girls took a peek, but he didn't notice. He was on a mission. Through the glass doors and away from the cabs and shuttles, Billy set a course due east. He was going back to the beach.

It was a dangerous forty-mile jaunt down a busy highway to the coast. Cars streamed by in frantic packs, but Billy continued on. He wanted to take it all in. He wanted to see where it went and as the sun rapidly set, it seemed to be going into darkness. With the sky nearly purple above a fading marsh, a black car pulled to the side of the road and waited.

Nice, thought Billy. Getting into strange cars on interstates is basically a death sentence, so it seemed like the perfect way to begin a journey.

Idling suspiciously quiet, the car looked like a space-age station wagon in metallic black—of course. As Billy clutched the handle and pulled, the door swung open to reveal a hulking black-haired chauffeur wearing a black suit with a red rose in the lapel. Billy thought him a fitting executioner as he plopped down alongside the specter and shut the door.

"Where you headed?" asked the stranger, motoring neatly into a pack of cars.

"To the beach," answered Billy.

The car seemed to glide rather than drive. Looking curiously out the window, Billy wasn't even sure they were on a road. In a quiet, flying car with a psychopath at the wheel, he said the only thing that could possibly any make sense. "Do you mind if I turn on the radio?" asked Billy.

The stranger instantly clicked it on.

"Not much for conversation, eh?" he continued as they drove quietly along.

"Don't get many passengers."

And just above the hum of traffic, Billy heard the chime of an acoustic guitar and a singer proclaim, "In my mind I'm gone to Carolina."

Great, thought Billy, *I'm going to be murdered to a James Taylor song.*

"Hey, um," stammered Billy, "what's your name?"

"Name's Ray."

"Well, Ray, you mind if I change the station?"

"Suit yourself."

Billy liked James Taylor, but not in a strange car on a dangerous highway. He needed something loud. He needed something to blow the windows out this death machine, but as he feverishly turned the dial, that same solemn voice returned. He went a few clicks right but to no avail. James sang about geese in flight and dogs that bite.

"Hey, Ray," said Billy, "this radio seems to be playing the same song over and over again, on every station."

"Must be broken," replied Ray.

"Must be."

So they rode along listening to "Carolina in My Mind," over and over again at eighty miles an hour.

Guess I'll be going to Carolina, thought Billy.

Finally at the beach, Billy offered Ray a couple of bucks but was refused.

"It was my pleasure, Billy," said Ray, as he blasted off into a shimmering wall of sparks.

And just like that, Billy was back.

Perusing the familiar streets of his past, Billy wondered how Ray knew his name. He didn't introduce himself. And how did he know which beach to go to? Billy didn't tell him that either, but he was alive so it didn't really matter. Billy suspected the spirits though.

Glowing headlights playfully dotted South Atlantic Avenue as Billy wandered around like the latest fair-weather vagabond. He had no place to stay and didn't really want to pop in on anyone, least of all his mother. That was sure to be an interesting conversation. It was one of the many things that would have to wait, because right now, Billy needed sleep.

With limited options, like his first night in Mexico, Billy headed for the beach. Rita sent instructions on where to pick up the key to his house, so he'd head for the post office at first light.

Smelling the salt and feeling the thick sand between his toes, Billy was happy to be back in Florida. Dorothy was right, there's no place like home, and although something wicked was most certainly lurking, he'd enjoy a calm night on the beach. It would be the last one for a while.

Waking to a warm sunrise, the sky was blue and the ocean a torn dark-green. Blustery whitecaps moved steadily along as Billy quickly did the same. Busybodies from the condominiums were beginning to mill about, so he had to go. He also had to eat. This was going to be the interesting part, trying to get around town unnoticed. Billy was heading back to the scene of the crime; to where they'd kidnapped Steve.

First there was Steve's dad, Jim, an ex-professional wrestler who most likely wanted to kill Billy. Then there was Steve, who probably wanted him dead. There was a sheriff who'd been looking for him, and then his old buddy Van, who was sure to surface, and last but not least there was Keller, the career criminal who'd actually gone to jail for the stunt. He hated Billy more than anyone. Billy had an ace up his sleeve though, a spiritual chaperone so to speak. He'd fear no one.

Feeling somewhat invincible, he headed for the post office. They'd be foolish to try anything stupid. Billy was in the best shape of his life, the case was closed and furthermore, he'd moved on.

Walking into the post office, Billy clicked open box #321-572 only to find a single white envelope harmlessly weighted with a key. Billy thought, *She did it!* It was all true. The key was there, as was the deed to 162 Cedar Ave. She wasn't joking. Along with the relief came a sadness, one that would probably always be there.

Billy had the key, but he didn't have Rita. She was gone, and it would be strange to be in the house without her. If what she'd written was true, Rita Polli was now Rita Flake. She was married, living in New

York, and their relationship was effectively over. Rita was in one place, and Billy was in another.

It had been easier to accept in Mexico, but now that he was home, the old wounds opened back up. As he wallowed in more self-pity, the song "Carolina in My Mind," drifted from a slow-moving vehicle and snapped him back into form. Billy was back on assignment. He could reminisce later.

Dotted with live oaks and battered old orange trees, Billy wound through his beachside neighborhood only to find Mrs. King still on patrol.

"You back, Billy?" she chimed in a familiar voice.

"Yes, ma'am," answered Billy. "At least for a little while."

"Had a bad lightning storm the other night, blew a branch off your tree over there. I stacked it out by the road, but the next day, the branch was right back up in the tree just like it never happened. Been some strange occurrences going on over there, Billy."

"You don't say," answered Billy as strange occurrences had become rather commonplace.

"I'll see what I can do about it."

With the house key in hand, Billy slid the worn teeth into a tarnished lock. Following a perfect click, the door opened to reveal his old living room, still furnished and all. The power was still on, for which Billy was thankful, but the refrigerator was empty. He guessed Rita had paid the utilities, or maybe his mom came by. The same ladies that were tearing him down were saving him as well, but maybe he was the culprit.

Billy sat on the couch as scenes from his last night in the house came sharply into focus. He remembered Rita slashing Van's mouth with a boomerang and then pelting the Young Bum with a paperweight. Steve had been conveniently left behind as Billy pulled him out of the house, wiped up the blood, packed a bag, and then drove off into the night.

Rita did it all. She beat the intruders back, shuffled him out of the house, bought him a flight out of town, and then finished writing his book. It was all crazy, but not as crazy as what was happening now.

Knowing that he had to go, Billy wouldn't be able to put any roots down. A tree had blown up in his front yard and put itself back together—the next time he might not be so lucky. He could try and stay, but the thought of the house blowing up with him in it was a little unnerving. Maybe it wasn't the right place for him anyway. Things were still fresh. He'd only been gone six months and wasn't really sure what had happened. He'd have to call his mom.

Almost everyone used a cell phone, but Billy still had a landline and it still had a dial tone, so he dialed. The phone rang a few times before a strong feminine voice said, "Hello."

"Hey mom, it's Billy."

It was a simple declaration, and he wasn't quite sure how it would be received, especially after his disappearing act.

Neither angry nor relieved, Billy's mother simply asked, "Are you finally back, Billy?"

"Yep," he answered, not so much in a celebratory tone, not as a conqueror, but just as someone who'd survived.

"Well, it's nice to hear from you."

"I'm on Cedar Ave., if you'd like to stop by."

He wanted her to stop by. She probably thought he needed something, and he did. It just wasn't the something she thought. He also wanted to see her. It had been a while.

"I'll be by later, Billy. I've had a few issues with the fleet, something I've got to take care of, but I'll be there around five."

Billy's mother was a force to be reckoned with. Cass is what everyone called her, short for Cassandra. Cassandra Jacobs had inherited a fishing fleet from her dad, and instead of selling it, she'd grown it into one of the largest on the East Coast. That's where she ran into Billy's father.

As a young bookkeeper for the fleet, Cass fell victim to the charms of Billy Winslow Sr., a rugged fisherman with a disdain for authority. After a brief courtship, and to the chagrin of Cass's father, more commonly known as the old man, she became Cassandra Winslow.

Constantly at odds with the old man and with a young family at home, Billy Sr. struck out on his own. He bought a boat on the Outer Banks in hopes of starting another fleet, but it didn't happen. There was an accident at sea. He went out and never came back in, and Billy and Cassandra never saw him alive again.

Billy was young when it happened. Cass was broken up, and the old man felt responsible. Billy Sr. had seemed nearly indestructible, so the news came as quite a shock. But Billy had that same twinkle in his eye, that same unyielding spirit, dangerously irresistible and sometimes deadly.

Cassandra tried to take it out of him. She wanted him to go to college, and he did. Billy completed an obligatory two years, and then promptly quit. He worked on the boats for a while but was never quite comfortable being the boss's son. Billy wanted to make his own way; a somewhat dubious decision as of late, but there was still time.

So, Billy milled cautiously around town, slowly easing his way back into the fold before finally heading home. Checking his watch, it was nearly five when a glistening pearl-white Chevy Tahoe pulled into the yard. Behind the wheel sat a platinum blonde wearing a tight sweater and a shiny pair of sunglasses, and suddenly Billy felt like he was in for a stern tongue lashing.

Cassandra got out of the truck as Billy walked to meet her. With the same sharp features and commanding form, Cassandra and Billy were most definitely mother and son.

"So this is it," said Billy, motioning toward his estate.

"It's cute," replied Cassandra.

She and Billy Sr. had started off in a small house, but she didn't live in a small house anymore.

"Kind of looks the same as it did before."

"Yeah, I didn't want it, but Rita left me the deed, paid in full, taxes and all."

"Sure," answered Cassandra.

It was the same *sure* she'd said over and over again. "Sure, you don't need anything. Sure, you got it. Sure, you'll finish it."

It was the same fierce independence his father had shown. Cass couldn't help but feel a little proud that her son shared the same tenacity.

"Are you mad?" asked Billy. It was a question he'd found himself asking far too often.

"Mad, disappointed, sad, happy, I'm kind of all over the place, same as usual."

Billy had that effect; that mercurial, changeable character that pushed and pulled until something finally broke.

"I wasn't sure I'd see you again," said Cass, which was the case whenever he left—remnants of Billy's father, she guessed, and his last fateful voyage.

It pained Billy to add to his mother's distress, but he had a responsibility to the force; to take an idea or a concept or maybe even a thought and follow it through to the end. He was an investigator, not of facts but of feelings and of moments. He was searching for the truth, to see if there was any and if there was, did it answer any questions? Did it change anything? Did it make anything better? Did it make him better?

"I might stay gone for a while, but I'll always come back," replied Billy as they shared a deep hug. It was a hug between a mother and son who'd been set adrift, a hug that spoke of a son waiting for his father to come home. It was the kind of hug that only they understood.

Light sniffles broke the silence as Cass said in a more severe tone, "Don't you ever do anything like that again, Billy."

Like everyone else, she'd been left with only questions, the main one being, "Where's your son?" She couldn't answer. She didn't know. All she knew was that he was alive and well. It's all that Rita could say.

"I didn't do it," said Billy.

"It was supposed to be a joke, or a gag. I just wanted to see what those guys would do, and I guess I found out."

"I'll say," snapped Cass. "We've got a name to protect, Billy. You need to start being a little more respectful of that. If you don't want to help, you damn sure don't need to hurt."

So there was the anger Billy expected.

"Might I remind you that a book was written, and that I ended up with a house."

"You lost the best girl you'll ever have and got run out of town."

"We weren't doing all that well regardless," admitted Billy.

"I wonder why?"

And then to lighten the mood, Billy said, "I've been playing basketball again."

"Great. Playing games. Congratulations."

"I'm playing pretty good."

"They play soccer in Mexico. You've got it backwards, no hands!"

Billy had to snicker, "I'm sorry mom. I've learned a lot, and I won't ever do anything like that again. I mean, I'll do something else, but I won't do that."

She'd hoped to hear something different—a little resignation, but there was none. Something was brewing and she knew it.

"Well, you look nice with a haircut and it's great to have you back, even if it's only for a while."

"How do you know I'm leaving?"

"I'm your mother, Billy, I know things. I know you're searching, and I hope you find what you're looking for."

"It found me. I'm being called to the Carolinas. Don't ask me why. I'm supposed to save someone's son or something."

Cass wondered whether to have him committed now or later. But a light still shone in his eyes, a majestic glint. Just like his father.

"So let me get this straight: Rather than work for me, you're going north to starve?"

"The spirits spoke," answered Billy.

"Same old Billy," sighed Cass. "When are you leaving?"

"Not sure. Pretty soon though. I was also wondering about Aunt Celia. She lives up there, doesn't she?"

"Yeah, she's an egghead at one of those universities. You two would make a perfect pair. She doesn't want anything to do with the business either," added Cass, "too refined, I guess."

"Maybe she just doesn't like fishing."

"Who doesn't like fishing?"

Billy didn't answer. It wouldn't make any sense. He simply told his mother that he loved her and that they'd work together one day. She said she knew they would, sooner rather than later, as a matter of fact.

"Just stay alive and stay out of jail," she said.

"I will."

So it was decided that Cass would rent out Billy's house and in lieu of property management fees, Billy would work for her for a couple of weeks. It was really just a way to keep him around for a while. Relieved to have made his first and most important apology, as Cass pulled out of the yard, the phone rang.

It reminded him of another call at dusk, the one Rita had answered. He'd warned her not to, but she did and now she was gone. So, would he take his own advice?

The phone continued to ring as Billy finally snatched it up and said, "Hello."

"Hey, Billy. It's Van."

Billy knew the drill. "Van who?

"It's Van Dalton man, what's your problem?"

"At the moment it's you," snapped Billy.

And through the booming laughter that ensued, Van chortled, "I knew you'd get it, Billy," referring to the call where he first suggested kidnapping Steve.

"Yeah, I got it, Van."

"You remember? That's how our conversation got started before."

"Before you double crossed me, caused me to lose my one true love and then get run out of town," snarled Billy. "Yeah, I remember."

"Well, when you put it like that."

"How else should I put it, I mean, I shouldn't have talked to you then. I don't even know why I'm talking to you now."

"I can't argue about that," replied Van. "But I called to bury the hatchet, Billy."

I'd like to bury the hatchet in your head, thought Billy. Instead, he said, "What's done is done."

"Heard you got a house out of the deal, though."

"Word gets around."

"Yeah," agreed Van. "Just wanted to warn you that Keller's out and about. He's talked some talk, but I wouldn't worry about anything. They're keeping a pretty close eye on him."

"I'm not worried about Keller. Keller needs to worry about me. I've had enough of that guy."

"He stays in his corner for the most part."

"That'll be fine then. I'm not looking for any trouble, but if I find it, you better believe I'll take care of it."

"Sounds like the old Billy," said Van.

"The new Billy," corrected Billy.

"Yeah well, me and the new Billy need to have a beer one of these days, talk about old times."

"Maybe."

"That's good enough," replied Van. "Adiós, Billy."

"See ya," said Billy, although he hoped he wouldn't. He already needed a change of scenery.

Sleep came lonely in Billy's old bed. It was a lot bigger without Rita in it. There were no serious dreams, no storms or car crashes, so Billy thought he might be in the clear. It was nice to be put back together without any urgency. He needed to come full circle, to walk through the town he'd once called home and feel the familiarity of his past. Billy took it all in and forgave the night. He forgave the darkness that swallowed his father and drove a wedge between him and his mother and then stole Rita.

He'd almost done it. Billy had almost made it so he couldn't come home, so that he had to stay gone, so that he had to come to a different conclusion. One where something was left undone, in his heart, a hole that wouldn't heal, people he'd never see and places he couldn't go. Billy wasn't there yet, and he pledged never to get there. He'd walk with his head held high, like the champion he'd once wanted to be rather than a shamed son being run out of town.

Things were going well so far. No sign of the sheriff or any other agents, which was good. There were no calls, no business cards or anything else, so Billy thought that maybe he was in the clear. He started thinking he could possibly start over. Steve's father, Jim, was back on the professional wrestling circuit, and Steve was gone too. Van called to make amends, and Keller was probably busy being a criminal, so all seemed well. It was encouraging. He even thought he might be able to stay; that the dreams had gone away. Maybe this is where he was supposed to be, with his mom, working in the family business.

All seemed well until the next strange dream.

Working on the docks was refreshing. Billy had worked with the guys before, but he was bigger now and shared more of a likeness with his dad, so he commanded more respect. No one spoke of his time out of town, they knew better. Cass had a keen eye and an even better ear, so they stayed quiet.

Billy had almost forgotten that he was somewhat of a transient. Sleep came easy, and he was settling in quite well until the spirits returned. And after an unusually hard day, they reemerged with a vengeance. He came home smelling like bait and diesel fuel and instantly hit the shower. Then, after a quick dinner and a drink, he fell heavily asleep only to enter a different dimension. The colors came back, and the chanting—*To save a son, to save a son*—echoed eerily through the night. A car careened off the road, and Billy stood at a basketball court while a one-armed black man bounced a basketball. It was a loud, echoing bounce. And then the alarm sounded.

"In my mind I'm gone to Carolina," came lightly through Billy's clock radio.

It was the call he'd been waiting for. Sadly he'd have to tell Cass he was leaving. No more mending nets and scrubbing decks for Billy. He was gone to Carolina.

So Billy said his good-byes and told his aunt Celia he'd be there soon. She said she was looking forward to it and that he could stay as long as he'd like. Cass wasn't too happy, but Cass was never happy.

"How you getting there?" she asked.

"I'm going to walk," answered Billy.

Perfect, thought Cass. *Don't know why I even try.*

What she said was, "You know they have planes, cars, trucks, busses, oh, and they even have bicycles these days?"

Why he was so damn eccentric, she hadn't a clue. He was always writing in his stupid notebook, just like her crazy sister Celia. So maybe now he could write his own book. He was off to a good enough start.

"That wouldn't be any fun."

"I guess not," she conceded.

There was more to say, but all that came out was, "Well, bye, Billy. I love you."

"I love you too, Mom. And I'll be in touch."

"At least I know where to find you, as long as you get there in one piece."

"I'll get there," said Billy, and he already knew how.

Following an early night, dawn came quickly, and Billy was ready. As he left the house and headed north, the morning air was heavy and hot. At a near run, with his backpack bursting at the seams, Billy was already starting to sweat.

Moving swiftly along, heat rose dangerously from the blacktop and singed his reddened skin. Beneath the midday sun, the road suddenly dissolved into a thick molten fog as he slowed to a stop. Somewhat disoriented, Billy rubbed the sweat from his eyes, but still, nothing looked familiar.

He thought about turning back, or maybe just dying, but as the vultures circled, that same black sedan pulled to the side of the road and waited. Suspended in an electrified mist, the door mysteriously swung open as Billy gratefully said, "Wasn't sure you'd make it, Ray."

"It's a long walk," replied Ray.

He had the same slick black hair, black suit, and red carnation on his lapel. He had the same pale complexion, except now, a thick stream of blood showed in the corner of his mouth. How did Ray know it was a long walk? He didn't even know where they were going. Or did he?

"Where we going, then?" asked Billy.

"We're going to Carolina," answered Ray.

So with a bloodied chauffeur in an electrified car, Billy headed north, of course, going to Carolina. When he turned on the radio, surprisingly enough, it wasn't playing "Carolina in My Mind." It didn't need to.

BLUE SKIES

With Ray at the wheel, they made good time. The shiny black car darted through traffic like a remote-control racer, almost like there weren't any other cars around. There *were* other cars around, but Ray didn't seem to notice.

Past the speed traps and over traffic jams, the sky shined a bright Carolina blue when they finally reached their destination. Now that they were out of the tropics, there was a nip to the air, so Billy grabbed a sweatshirt.

"You'll have to get some winter clothes," sounded Ray in a robotic monotone.

"It looks that way."

Wondering if he knew, Billy asked, "Where we going, Ray?"

"We're going to Celia's."

"What does Celia look like?" continued Billy, wondering just how much the spirits had divulged.

"Tall, attractive, with longish brown hair, nice legs."

"That's enough, Ray," said Billy. It seemed like the spirits had been pretty thorough.

Pulling into a wooded subdivision, they were now officially off the grid. Towering pines and hefty oaks graciously clogged the dense landscape as Ray's car moved deliberately along. With dogwoods in bloom and deer scattering frantically about, there wasn't a palm tree in sight, but the bright-green canopy was comforting.

"You been here before, Ray?" asked Billy.

"Grew up right down the road."

"Do you still live here?"

Then, with his pale face and bloody mouth on full display, Ray finally turned to Billy and said, "I don't live anywhere."

Billy knew better than to ask the next question. The answer might not be so subtle. He didn't want to cause a stir anyway. Ray had been a fine chauffeur, and as a large house and a lady appeared in the distance, his mission, for now, was accomplished.

While a barred owl mysteriously tracked the shadowy car through dusk, Ray eased to a stop. Seeing his aunt Celia for the first time in years, Billy gave a friendly wave as Celia excitedly waved back.

"Billy, you look great!" exclaimed Celia. "Can't say as much for your driver, though."

"He's been through a lot, I guess," replied Billy as Ray's head fell sharply down.

Celia looked great as well. Tall and athletic with straight brown hair and sharp features, she looked more like a fitness model than a professor. Attractive to the point of being a distraction, when she was studying literature, most of her teachers were studying her. When she went for her master's, they told her to get into advertising and when she went for a doctorate, they said she'd never make it. She almost didn't. In addition to what Cass contributed, Celia spent the bulk of her inheritance on tuition. It would have been impossible if not for Cass. But there was a reason for the benevolence: when Billy's father passed, Celia came back home to watch Billy. Writing while Billy ran around the house like a madman, Celia finished her first book while Cass resumed her duties with the fleet. With a second and third on the way, she was finally afforded a faculty position, but the acceptance came at a cost.

There were men, but most preferred a more conventional lady to one who'd get up at all hours of the night to write and then sleep for most of the day. She'd stutter and stammer and write everything down in a beat-up old notepad. She was manic and electric, and Billy loved it. Celia actually started him writing. He remembered her always having a pen in hand, scrawling on basically anything she could find. He thought it was cool, so he started doing it.

So there they were, together again beneath the longleaf pines while the owl hooted an excited welcome. Celia had helped Billy before, and she was about to help him again.

Reaching into Ray's car for his backpack, Billy asked, "You need any gas money?"

"No Billy. I do have a favor to ask though."

"Anything, Ray."

"When you get there, tell him that Kurt is still looking out for him."

Billy didn't bother to ask. He knew it would have to unfold.

"I sure will."

"Bye, Billy."

"See ya, Ray."

"Does he need anything to drink, maybe a quick snack or something?" asked Celia.

"Probably not, I think it's time for him to go."

Then, as Ray's sparkling car rose neatly into the air and launched forcefully through a swirling electric field, Celia was concerned.

"We need to talk, Billy."

"We sure do, but let's have a drink first."

"Good idea," agreed Celia. After all, she'd seen a lot of strange things and written a lot of strange things, but this was the first time a stiff with an electrified car had flown out of her front yard. *Things are about to get weird*, she thought.

Celia was impressive, as was her comfortable house in the country. Scattered with colors and textures and songbirds of all kinds, it could have jumped straight off of an artist's canvas.

She was an artist. She had an artist's brain. She thought in flashes and sections, making something out of nothing—an artist's job. It was the perfect place for Billy.

After dropping his things in the spare bedroom, Celia opened a couple of cold craft beers and, delaying the obvious, asked, "So how is Cass?"

"Same as always," answered Billy, "strong, decisive, and still a little angry."

"Can you blame her?"

"No, I guess not."

But that was it. Billy was just going to have to take it for a while, the recurring theme of disappointment. Hopefully Celia didn't think that he was a disappointment, because he sure didn't. He knew something was brewing. That's why he'd cut his hair and embraced the unknown.

There were any number of questions Celia could have asked, like, "What in the hell was that flying car?" or "Why did that guy have blood on his face?" But rather than go into hysterics, Celia simply asked, "So what's going on, Billy?"

"Well that's quite an interesting question."

He started with the peyote and the voices and the dreams and the fact that he probably would have stayed in Mexico if not for the signs.

"I woke up naked and drenched at the foot of a Mayan temple, chanting, 'To save a son,'" said Billy with a disturbed look. "I've had visions of crushed cars and dreams of car accidents, and the other night I was on a basketball court with a one-armed black man. I flew into Orlando and started walking home to see if anything was out there, and guess what?"

"What?"

"There was something out there. A dead guy driving a black car with a radio station that only played one song. Can you guess what song it was?"

"It couldn't have been Enya, could it?"

"No, it was James Taylor, 'Carolina in My Mind.'"

"Hmm, makes sense I guess."

"I guess," continued Billy. "So I get home to discover a tree had blown up in my front yard and put itself back together. I get a strong tongue lashing from Cass, work for her for a couple of weeks, and then, lo and behold, following a vivid dream about a one-armed basketball player, my alarm clock radio sounds."

"Wow," said Celia.

"Yeah. Wow," echoed Billy, "but after one of the freakiest dreams I've ever had, can you guess what song was playing?"

Getting a better handle on things, she answered, "'Carolina in My Mind'?"

"Yeah, 'Carolina in My Mind,' I mean, I like James Taylor but . . ."

"But what?"

"But there's more," stammered Billy. "I got a ride up here from the same dead guy in the same black car, except this time he had blood running out of his mouth, the car was electrified and could also fly, so it seems."

"So it seems," repeated Celia. She'd seen it with her own eyes.

This was strange, but she was no stranger to strange. It was something she'd grown accustomed to. It was something she'd searched for. She wanted this, evidence of the afterworld. That her nephew from Florida was delivering it was an added bonus.

"You don't think I should be committed, do you?"

It was a valid question. Every now and then people need a rest, a retreat from the world. She'd had one. Billy had been under a lot of stress, but he didn't look stressed out. Celia had seen the car, though. But then she caught herself wondering if she'd actually seen it. Maybe it just drove off really fast. That's what happened. It was sunset and the colors blurred. The driver had ketchup on the side of his mouth. It wasn't blood.

But she believed in the spirits. That's why she lived in the woods, among the birds, listening to their calls, hoping they were for her. That's why she watched the trees, to see if she could catch a glimpse of something, of anything unusual. That's why she stood in the wind and dove into the water and stayed still in the darkness. Because she believed. So how could she tell Billy it wasn't real? It was real. It was as real as she was.

"Look, Billy," started Celia in a more serious tone. "It sounds like you've tapped into something."

"You don't say," replied Billy. "But why me?"

It was a good question.

Celia remembered a time when everything was new. Her sister Cass had a kid. She was newly admitted into grad school and had a new beau, but then disaster struck. Billy's father was lost at sea, and Cass needed her.

Without question, she ditched the guy, left school, and headed home. It was an easy decision. It was also a time when Celia began to ponder permanence—what it actually was and what it meant. She wondered if she were permanent, and if everything else was permanent; or was it just one giant slide show connected to other shows at other times in other worlds. So she started writing. She wrote about interconnectedness in her first novel, appropriately named *Other Worlds*.

She wrote while Billy played. Sure, Celia stepped on her fair share of toys, made her fair share of meals, and bopped around making funny faces, but she also wrote. Something else also happened; there was another scare and she didn't realize the significance until now. Early on, after the boating accident, Cass and her father had business in the Outer Banks, to identify the body of Billy's father. For obvious reasons, Celia stayed home with Billy, where he was safe and secure.

He asked about his dad, but he was only five years old, and it hadn't become an issue yet.

So with Cass gone, it was just Billy and Celia. Everything was fine until Billy started crying. It happened in the middle of the night. Billy's temperature rose to 104 degrees, and he was melting.

With an ambulance on the way, Celia hurriedly prepared a lukewarm bath; it was all she could do. Immersed in the warm liquid, Billy began having a febrile seizure. Convulsing violently, he suddenly lost consciousness, and Celia prayed. By the time an ambulance arrived, Billy was awake, but they were rushed to the emergency room anyway.

Celia considered the question of "why me?" certain that Billy hadn't been the first to ask it. She didn't really believe in coincidence, but why had he ended up here and why now? And why was she with him then and now with him again?

Celia didn't believe life was simply a cosmic mistake. She wanted to see the wonder and feel the energy. She liked to find the symbolism and the synchronicity. Cass called it hogwash, but here it was, right at her doorstep. The angels had arrived.

It was a lot to take in. Celia hadn't seen Billy in years, and now he shows up in some kind of a celestial swirl? She'd thought about it. She'd wondered about it. But now she was living it, so she'd choose her words carefully.

"There's not a lot I can be sure of," answered Celia, "but maybe it's not the time to be sure."

Billy listened. He'd had the same thought, and it was nice to hear it from someone else.

"When you were young, there was a scare," she went on to say.

Billy knew she'd watched him for a time when he was young. He remembered them playing. He remembered her scrawling into a notebook—and also some highly questionable meals, but he kept that to himself. He also remembered a disturbance, strangers in uniform taking him from the house, and then white sheets and a hospital gown.

"You had a really bad fever, and your mother was out of town. She was burying your father, Billy."

"I remember it was a bad time, but that's about it."

"You had a seizure. You stopped breathing, and I thought you were dead. I thought you'd both be gone, and I felt responsible."

Billy caught her before a total collapse as she sank into his chest. Celia was crying and Billy was sniffling too. On the couch together, there was closure. Celia obviously felt guilty and Billy just felt strange. Like a child sucked into a vacuum and then spit out a young man with no real direction.

"It wasn't your fault, Celia, it's just my life. It's been strange, but I'm lucky to have had you in it."

"I don't know what got into me," heaved Celia. "I guess after not seeing you for so long and then having you show up under such strange circumstances, it just kind of hit me hard."

"I'm sorry, but I had to come."

"I'm glad you did."

Together in the spacious room with wood floors, thick Persian rugs, and a glowing fireplace, they looked spectacular. Both tall and angular with deep blue eyes and tan skin, Celia and Billy looked more like models than mystics, but sitting in the living room discussing the supernatural, they were definitely out of this world.

Finally collecting herself, Celia said, "But there's something else, Billy. Something I've never told anyone. I didn't think it meant any-thing until now."

Billy wasn't sure he wanted to know, but he was about to find out.

"Cass wasn't home yet, so you were released into my care. I remem-ber your rosy cheeks and blond hair. You looked like an angel, and then said you'd been visited by one. That he held you in his arms, high above the empty hospital bed. Then, from Psalm 91 you recited, 'For He shall give His angels charge over you, to keep you in all your ways. In their hands they shall bear you up.'"

"I did?"

"You did. It sounded biblical, so I checked. Truth be told, I was just so happy you were alive, you could have said anything and it would have been amazing. In other words," Celia tearfully admitted, "it must have gotten lost in the shuffle. But it now seems relevant."

"But how?"

"I'm not certain, but all things considered, you seem to have been visited before, and now it seems like you were visited again."

"But I didn't see angels this time, just loud booming voices, car crashes, dead guys, and one-armed basketball players."

"It's changed, I guess. Different angels for different occasions," said Celia. "Anyway, the ceremony must have opened something up, and when something opens, it also needs to close. You're a special person with a special job to do, so you better rest up."

Billy listened to the crackling of the fireplace and felt its heat. In the spacious room, everything seemed to echo. Celia's mood was elevated as well as they wondered what would come next. Billy never thought of himself as enlightened, unorthodox maybe, but this was way beyond that.

"You should journal it," added Celia.

"Obviously," answered Billy, "but I need to live through it as well."

He wasn't sure how hospitable the spirits were, or if there even were any more spirits. Maybe they were done, but it was wishful thinking at best as Billy drifted into an unusually deep sleep.

Surprised to be alive, Billy woke to a chorus of songbirds unlike any he'd ever heard. It was the most brilliant symphony on earth, and it was right outside his window. The guest bedroom seemed more like a primary bedroom, large and roomy with a king sized bed. Celia had taken the room on the other side of the house, away from the towering pine that seemed poised for a strike. She'd been meaning to cut it down, but now that Billy was here, he could do it. Unbeknownst to Billy, Celia had been compiling quite a list for the strapping young man. He'd have to earn his keep somehow.

Walking into the kitchen, Billy thought about living with his aunt. He was used to living alone, or with women he was sleeping with, but Celia was nice and also interesting and Billy wanted to get to know her again. Delving deeper into his concerns, he surmised that Celia might also be part of the plan—an added spiritual element. He just had to remember that it wasn't forever and that he was lucky to have a place to go. Not everyone had that. He also had to remind himself that he was in North Carolina, so things were sure to be different.

Billy once traveled to the Carolinas for a junior basketball tournament, but that was before the surfing and the fishing and the staying out too late. Somewhere along the line, he'd decided to go with the flow, and the flow led him to Mexico on the wrong side of the law.

In Mexico, at an all-time low and with nothing but a few bucks in his pocket, Billy had returned to something familiar. Feeling the sting of being on the run, he started playing basketball again—under the lights, in the Garden, finishing off the Lakers in seven, the usual delusion. Remembering an age when he was hungry to compete, Billy had rediscovered that hunger. He'd accomplished something, but he'd also left everything in tatters and that wasn't how it was supposed to be. If redemption were to be found, it was going to have to be on a basketball court in Mexico. So Billy went back to the court and he worked. He did drills. He ran suicides. He shot from the outside for hours. He got his step back. He got his jump back. His shirt was off, and he was back hanging on the rim, and it felt good. He shot with only his left hand, and he dribbled that way too. The local kids even ditched their soccer balls to shoot a few hoops with the loco gringo. Billy had even put a halfway decent team together. They played other guys from the states, and they never lost. Billy played like a man possessed. He hit three-pointers at the buzzer as the crowd went wild. He played all the ghosts of basketball's past on an empty court, just like when he was a kid.

Something was driving him. It compelled him to go. It told him that he wasn't done yet. Maybe something was saving his life as well. It was a lot to ponder over coffee in his aunt's house. Celia had yet to rise as Billy scanned the front yard, perhaps looking for a black car. It wasn't there, so he figured he was in the right place.

It wasn't long before Celia strolled into the kitchen for a hot cup of coffee. She knew that Billy was once an aspiring chef and a live-in cook would surely be a thing of value.

"I expected some eggs Benedict or French toast at least," said Celia.

"I haven't cooked in a while," replied Billy. "They don't really need gringo cooks in Mexico."

"It's kind of like riding a bike, though, isn't it?"

"Sure, if the bike is in a hot kitchen full of people running around and yelling."

"So what's next, then?" chuckled Celia.

"I'm gonna have to get out of the house, I guess. I'm gonna have to attract the spirits."

"Like bait?" asked Celia.

"Yeah, like bait," agreed Billy.

COLLEGE INC.

Billy had wanted to be a basketball player, and so it was that he'd ended up on Tobacco Road in the shadow of legends like Dean Smith and Michael Jordan.

Celia gave Billy a map, told him to take care, and then left for the day. He rather enjoyed her house in the woods, watching the birds flutter about through a quaint kitchen window. In the majesty of a new morning, the rolling hills and thick green foliage seemed like emerald clouds floating through a bright-blue sky.

Down a long dirt road is how he got to Celia's, so he guessed that's how he'd leave. She said there was a bus stop at the end of the street, but Billy decided to walk. It's when he was at his best. He also wanted to see if a certain car would show up, and while cars steadily passed, none were scary and black, and none stopped.

Roughly five miles out of town, it was a mere jaunt compared to what Billy was used to. As he forged on, he thought about dying and being held in the arms of angels. Was he still in their arms? And if so, would they ever let him go? He wondered if they'd ever abandon him, or if they already had. He also wondered where he'd see the next signs, or if there even would be any more signs. Billy scanned the horizon for a flying wheel or maybe even a burning bush. It was mysterious and scary and also a little exhilarating. Something was bound to happen; he just didn't know what. Walking down the road, Billy finally came to terms with the fact that he'd been chosen. He also thought he might be disposable but quickly dismissed the notion.

Getting stronger with each stride, he knew he needed to put things together. Rita had been with him for a reason. She saw his potential, but it wasn't the right time. She'd obviously had to go, and so did he.

He wanted to call her, just to tell her he was OK and to ask how she was, but he didn't want to intrude. It seemed like she was doing well, anyway, with a husband and a publishing company. He wondered if they'd stay together and if there'd be kids and if he'd ever see her again. He hoped he would, when he was better. It was just strange, starting a new journey without her. Billy thought Rita would appreciate something like this.

With the sun overhead, signs for town showed in the distance, and Billy was almost there. In a pair of high tops, shorts, and a sweatshirt, he was ready for pretty much anything. Tall and muscular, with his hair still short, Billy didn't feel out of place. It was exhilarating to be somewhere else. He could be someone else—or maybe just a better version of himself.

Moving from the beach to a college town was an immediate culture shock. In contrast to the quiet streets of his past, with their sandspurs and palm trees, there was nothing tropical in sight. Billy had somehow landed in college central, the place where the Wolf Pack, the Blue Devils, and the Tar Heels regularly fight for titles.

It turned out that Billy had come to the right place. Rather than a wolf or a devil, he'd be a Tar Heel. The logo showed a huge blue foot with a tar-stained heel, kind of like the tar stuck on Billy's foot after a day at the beach. But it wasn't meant that way. This tar was a source of pride, a sign that the boys stood and fought while the others ran. Billy thought it the perfect place for him because he wasn't going to run anymore either.

Finally on Franklin Street, bikes sped in between the slow-moving cars as Billy just took it all in. Without an agenda or any real direction, his only job was to observe. In small and large groups, girls and guys jostled amongst the more reserved residents. Some moved with the true confidence of independence, while others would soon find their footing, or maybe return home.

Lined with restaurants, gift shops, and plenty of light-blue apparel, the main street bustled with activity. Everyone carried something. From purses to bags to backpacks, there was an urgency in their energy. Where would they go? What would they do? Who would they be and when would they be it? Answers overshadowed the questions of when and where, with the only true wisdom being the here and now.

Billy walked along, energized by the enthusiasm. He knew now why Celia had left the beach. While the sea offered untold beauty and gifts, there was more to do here on a Friday night. With all the offerings of a big city stored in a bubble of intellectual bliss, there seemed to be something for everyone. There was no shortage of places to get a drink either as blue busses carted students up a long, steep hill.

Various shops and restaurants dotted one side of the street, while the college dominated the other. Seemingly sprung from an old-growth forest, the red brick buildings spread innocuously through town. Like friends from a different age, the large square buildings stood as a gateway into the past. The college had history, and Billy felt like he was walking through a museum with each carefree step on hallowed ground.

An ever-vigilant tourist, Billy discovered a charming arboretum and then went on to an open-air theater, where he bowed to an invisible audience as they feverishly applauded.

"Thank you all!" he exclaimed as the applause faded into the trees.

Moving on, Billy was still searching for clues. The campus was expansive, and everyone was walking or working or scurrying off to class. Billy needed to get back to it as well, but his was a different kind of work, scouring for spiritual remains. Seeing the unseen, sifting through the unknown to restore a certain something to a certain someone. What could that job title be? And how would he explain it? He didn't even understand it himself, which was probably good, because if he did, he'd most likely be terrified.

With a spring in his step, Billy went from the historic to the economic as he walked into a football stadium and gazed down at the field. It reminded Billy of childhood trips to the University of Florida, where they excitedly entered the "Swamp." He felt now like he did then, in wonder of all things communal. Enamored by the colors, the activity, and the enthusiasm for something sacred; it meant something then—an us against them, a rite of passage for those who could go.

Then there was Billy, a spirit hunter walking courageously through it all. Or maybe not so courageously, but moving all the same, past the brick and mortar and down another steep hill to finally see the Dean Dome. In the midday sun it radiated a brilliant-silver glow and seemed to say, "Here, Billy, look over here."

He didn't know why. He wasn't of college caliber and wasn't even enrolled, nor could he get enrolled. Billy had long forsaken any scholastic pursuits, yet here he was on a campus being drawn to a basketball court, and there wasn't a thing he could do about it.

Not an avid Tar Heel fan, Billy sensed that the stars had mysteriously aligned to make North Carolina the center of the college-basketball universe. And then along came Billy Winslow to gaze in amazement as the Dean Dome seemed to be crashing down on his head.

Circling the building like a recruit, Billy heard the bounce of a basketball and wanted in. He seemed to be in the right place. Tall guys in tracksuits walked in and out of the building, while shorter, more businesslike gentlemen buzzed quickly around discussing last night's game. Pretty women strode by with prospective students who looked on in amazement at the place where so many great things had happened. Wins and losses seemed irrelevant as they gazed toward the shrine of Carolina basketball. They could be there as well, with a little hard work and dedication, they could call themselves Tar Heels. They could fall in love in the midst of a chanting crowd. They could rush Franklin Street after a hard-fought win. They could faithfully call Carolina their alma mater. But not Billy; he'd have allegiance to none but himself, and to the spirits, of course. He'd somehow been cast in the role of a pariah, and it was a good place for him. It's where he could operate.

Slowly moving away, Billy distinctly noticed someone limping up a long hill, unassuming and with a full head of gray hair. A couple other guys followed as he gestured in a back-and-forth motion. Every now and then a student would stop for a picture or two, and then he'd continue talking while the others nodded. He was decked out in the newest light-blue-and-white sportswear, and there wasn't a wrinkle in sight.

Billy knew right away who he was. He was the coach, the highest of all high; the brightest star among all the prospective stars. He was more than just a coach. He was a celebrity coach. He could make or break careers. He could shatter dreams, but he could also make dreams come true. He could make a school relevant. With a winning program would come television contracts and big money deals and better recruits, but viewing the man from afar, Billy surmised that it hadn't started out that way. It began under a basket somewhere, with a whistle and a loud voice telling the kids to get back up the court. He'd taken a journey as well, of that Billy was quite certain. It hadn't been easy, and there was more to come but at the moment, Billy wondered why he was here and not on a beach somewhere. A few weeks ago, Chapel Hill, North Carolina, had been the last thing on his mind, but now here he was, at College Inc, staring at a basketball arena.

Heading back into town, Billy needed something to eat. There were restaurants on top of restaurants, and most of them good, so he ducked in for a falafel and then headed back out to the street.

With the young and old equally engaged, everything was lively and colorful, and the pita was good. Then, as he finished his last bite, a bearded man in ragged clothes shuffled up and asked, "Do you have any spare change, sir?"

"Sure thing, my friend," answered Billy, holding out a fresh twenty.

"Ah," sounded the guy in delight, "You saved me, son."

To save a son, to save a son, to save a son. The chant rang through Billy's senses as he feverishly asked, "What did you say?"

"What do you mean?" replied the guy.

"What was that that you said," stuttered Billy, "about saving a son?"

"I didn't say that."

"Yeah you did, you said that I saved you."

"I just said thanks, pal," said the guy, beginning to get agitated.

"No, you said something else!"

"You're not getting the twenty back," growled the drifter as he began a hasty retreat.

"I don't want the money. I'll give you more if you just tell me what you meant!" yelled Billy as the guy ran off.

Falling back, Billy simply watched him fade into the distance like another visiting angel.

Once again calm, he knew what he'd heard, and it was most definitely a sign. Billy was still in the game. He just wondered what the game was.

As the day edged further along, more and more students were on the move.

Stopping a girl on the street Billy asked, "Hey, ah, what's going on? Why does everyone seem to be going to a party?"

"Are you serious?" she asked.

"Yeah, I'm serious."

"It's LDOC, dude."

"LDOC?"

"Yeah," she said more slowly, "last day of class."

"Ah," murmured Billy.

"Yeah, ah," she repeated. "You going out?"

"Maybe."

"Well maybe I'll see you then," she said, already out of sight.

Billy was amazed at how quickly people moved in this town, but to be fair, he was just getting acclimated, and she was cute. Following the herd, Billy wondered if he'd run into her later. He actually wondered if there would even be a later. With so much still undecided, Billy remembered that he was in flux or in limbo, perhaps. He was in search of, so he'd search.

Large, palatial homes flanked busy sidewalks as Billy made his way down fraternity row. The yards, sensibly lined in black plastic barriers, were mostly hidden from the public—and from the police officers as well. As the sun was beginning to set, Billy cruised along, taking whatever would come.

As far as he could tell, the parties were good. Bands played on stage and some places even had water slides. It was early, but Billy noticed some of the partygoers already stumbling. *Careful*, thought Billy, remembering a few of his first parties.

"Careful!" then rang clearly out as a speeding Frisbee hit Billy square in the head.

"Little help, buddy," yelled a red-faced reveler.

I might need help, thought Billy as he felt a growing welt.

But instead of throwing the Frisbee back, and against his better judgment, Billy walked in. With a commanding presence, and of course some spiritual help, he didn't face much resistance.

"Hey, hey, where you going, guy?"

"Gotta return this Frisbee," said Billy, inching his way through the crowd.

The place was packed, and the drinks flowed freely. Watching a band launch excitedly into another cover, Billy heard a loud voice exclaim, "Hey, it's the Frisbee dude!"

Among the vibrant sights and sounds, Billy had all but forgotten the Frisbee until a couple more guys chanted, "Frisbee dude! Frisbee dude! Frisbee dude!"

"Oh yeah, here's the Frisbee," said Billy, holding up the large, black disk. "And don't worry about the concussion."

"Yeah, nice catch, bro," someone replied, "Next time try the hands though, works better."

"He's not a bro, he's the Frisbee dude," announced one of the others.

"Oh, yeah. Yeah! Frisbee dude."

Billy wasn't worried. It was his first day in town, and he was already at a slamming party. Life was good.

"What kind of a party is this anyway?" yelled Billy. He knew where he was. He just wanted to hear one of the guys say it.

"You're at a frat party, guy, and you're the Frisbee dude!"

Wow, thought Billy, *it took me twenty-five years to get into my first frat party, and now I'm the Frisbee dude.*

"Well, as the Frisbee dude, do I get a drink?"

"There's no doubt, Frisbee, follow me," chortled Billy's new-found friend as they wedged through the crowd.

"Move it, move it, move it! We've got a distinguished guest here!"

The others didn't know what to think. Tall with close-cropped hair, searing blue eyes, and square shoulders—they wondered if Billy was on the basketball team.

There were a few whispers as some of the girls edged forward. "Is he on the team? I think I've seen him around the gym. Yeah, he's the cute one from out west."

"I've never seen him anywhere," slurred one of guys. "Looks like an idiot to me."

There were kegs of beer. There was a huge funnel attached to a clear plastic hose that looked dangerous. There were cheap bottles of booze, clear or brown, but Billy got neither. One of the brothers simply handed him a concoction and said, "Here, it's good."

Billy gazed into the cup. It was steaming. He smelled it and winced.

"Ladies and gentlemen, can I have your attention?" yelled the guy as the noise momentarily eased. "This large lumbering fool is neither on the basketball team nor is he an idiot. So, without further ado, I give you the all-encompassing, all-important, all-powerful Frisbee dude!"

The crowd then went wild as the brothers prompted Billy to drink. As the caustic liquid slid dangerously down Billy's throat, his thoughts regressed to Javier and to the dreaded hallucinations at Chichen Itza, but it was too late to turn back now. The cup was empty and the night was just beginning, so Billy buckled up for another wild ride.

"Frisbee! Frisbee! Frisbee!" chanted the crowd, as Billy asked, "What the hell are we drinking?"

"It's a creation from the cabinet, reserved for only the most distinguished guests," stammered the reveler. "Here, drink some more."

Billy took another long swig from the red party cup, and this time it tasted good.

"So what now?" asked Billy.

"Now it's time for the pool."

Billy was then prompted to strip down while he followed the guys up to the rooftop.

"What's your name?"

"The name's Tex."

Thinking it might be short for something, Billy asked, "Why Tex."

"What, are you writing a book, Frisbee?" snapped Tex. "Anyway, I'm Tex, he's Rex, and my other brother's name is Jex. We're the Lex brothers. Lex marks the spot."

Billy knew better than to ask any more questions. He'd simply have to accept the insanity.

So, now on the rooftop, Tex pointed to a little blue dot on the lawn and said, "There it is."

"There is what?"

"There's the pool."

Billy looked down, but instead of a pool, he saw only a round, blue thing that seemed to be holding water.

"It looks like a big blue trash can full of water."

"It's an above-ground pool, Frisbee."

Being from Florida—from the beach, more specifically—he'd never seen such a contraption. All the pools there were in the ground and made of concrete. This thing looked plastic, and dangerous.

Tex then looked to Billy with a wild stare and said, "It's there for you, Frisbee. For your glory. You've come all this way. You've waited.

You've dreamed. You've drank. You've trained." Tex then topped off Billy's cup and added, "Take more of the liquid, Frisbee, and then fulfill your destiny!"

Billy wasn't sure it was his destiny, but he hoped the angels were still awake as he yelled, "Geronimo!" and then like a poor diving horse, leapt spastically into a distant pool full of lukewarm water.

Victoriously surfacing to feverish chants of "Frisbee! Frisbee! Frisbee!" Billy felt suspiciously weightless.

Tex, Rex, and Jex were there with a waiting drink as Billy jumped out of the pool and said, "Man, I can't believe you guys do that. That's dangerous."

"Oh, we don't do that, Frisbee," replied Tex.

"No way, Fris," confirmed Rex.

"No, we've been waiting for someone else to do it," added Jex.

Big, shirtless, and wet, Billy looked a little cross, until Tex said, "But you know what?"

"What?"

Tex summoned Rex and Jex to his side and said, "That was no ordinary feat. It was a stunt designed to discover the chosen one, and to complete an unbroken chain of brotherhood."

"So all I had to do was to get drunk and dive into a pool?"

"That's it, Frisbee. You're now an honorary Chi Phi, you're in, buddy. What's ours is yours."

Billy didn't know what to say, but it seemed to be something of an honor. So, he finally said, "Well, thanks."

"You're welcome, Sir Frisbee. Now it's time to mingle," added Tex with a parting salute.

The drinks were really kicking in as Billy stumbled into the kitchen. While he made his way through the crowd, a high-pitched voice exclaimed, "Hey, it's you!"

"It is?"

At the moment, Billy wasn't sure who he was. He'd been christened Frisbee, the newest Chi Phi, but he hadn't seen Billy in a while.

"Yeah, from the street earlier. You asked me where everyone was going, looking for a party or something."

"Ohh yeah," said Billy.

Noting his missing shirt and shoes, she said, "Well, I guess you found the party."

"I guess," repeated Billy, "but I lost my clothes."

"Where did you last see them?"

"On the roof."

"On the roof?"

"Yeah, I jumped into a pool."

"From the roof?"

So the mild-mannered guy on the street had turned into a party animal. A sexy party animal at that. She was intrigued.

"So what's your name, party animal?"

He thought about saying Frisbee, but instead answered, "I'm Billy. How about you?"

"I'm Gwen."

"How sensational, Gwen."

"It is?"

"Of course. You're cute as a button," he slurred on their way upstairs.

"So what's your major?" asked Gwen, as was the usual question, although Billy was anything but usual.

"I guess you could say its theology."

"You're going to be a priest?"

"Ahh, not in the near future, but I may need to be saved. I don't feel so good."

"You don't look so good."

On his back in a strange bedroom, the room started to spin as Gwen rolled Billy onto his stomach and thought, *Another one bites the dust.*

As Billy painfully woke, Gwen was still there, and he was worried. She yawned and he stalled. Not wanting to seem too frantic, he muttered, "Good morning, Gwen."

"Oh, you remember my name. That's a good start."

"Do you remember mine?

"Of course. It's Billy, the theology student."

"Is that what I said?"

"That's what you said all right, among other things," she replied. "And you said that I was beautiful and that you loved me."

"I did?"

"You did. You also said that you'd never leave me and that we'd be together forever."

"Ha," chimed Billy. "But seriously, did anything happen last night?"

"By anything, what do you mean?"

"You know, anything."

Sensing Billy's concern, she said, "No, you got sick though."

"Whew," sounded Billy.

"What do you mean, whew? You'd rather get sick than kiss a pretty girl?"

"I wouldn't have minded kissing you. I just wanted to make sure it wasn't anything else."

"Would that have been so horrible?"

It was an interesting question. His last one-night stand turned into a few years or more, maybe a lifetime. Maybe it would last forever. Maybe he'd never get over Rita. But lying next to him on the bed was a pretty green-eyed girl. Gwen didn't have the searing looks, but she had a kind, honest face, and Billy was already in her debt.

"No, it wouldn't have been so horrible. It's just not the way I would have wanted it. I'm actually new in town and found myself here by way of an errant Frisbee toss. Now I'm an honorary member of the Chi Phi fraternity and my new name is Frisbee. And I also really need to get home."

Billy had been out all night and feared the worst.

"I hate to ask, but would you perhaps have a car?"

Deflated to have met another car-less bum, Gwen moaned, "Yeah, I've got a car. Let's go."

As they stepped over Billy's new brothers on the way out, Billy said, "See ya, Tex."

"See ya, Frisbee," muttered Tex, "and stay between the ditches."

After last night, it seemed an appropriate farewell as Billy replied, "OK."

With his shoes finally on and wearing a wrinkled, booze-stained shirt, Billy began his first walk of shame. With a headache from hell, he slowly recalled the shining dome that attracted him, then the vagrant who said Billy saved him, then the party, then the drink, then the jump, and then the girl. And that was all on his first day. He shuddered to think what might happen next.

"You're kind of quiet this morning," said Gwen as they walked slowly along.

"My head hurts. I haven't had this bad a hangover since high school," replied Billy before asking, "What were you doing at the party anyway?"

"I was there with a girlfriend, moral support."

"Were you able to give any support, or did you have to spend the whole night with me?"

"I joined the party a time or two, just to make sure she was all right, but somehow you turned into more of a priority. A stray dog. A sick stray dog, I guess."

Great, thought Billy, *now in addition to being an exile and a spiritual hack, I can add sick stray dog to my resume.*

"Well I guess my charm is working."

"Kind of," replied Gwen. "Where are we going anyway?"

"I was about to ask you the same thing."

There was supposed to be a car, but on they walked, beneath the towering trees while cars streamed by and people stared.

"We're almost there. There's not a lot of parking in town, so you have to be creative."

Finally at a little yellow coupe, Gwen popped the lock and again asked, "So where are we going, Billy?"

He wasn't sure. It was all rolling hills and thick, tall trees, quite a change from the sand dunes of his past. He hadn't planned on staying out all night, but this was a different task, so he'd need a different approach. He'd have to go where the wind blew.

"It's about a mile down 54 on the right, named after a church or something."

"Ephesus Church?" she asked.

"Sounds right."

Billy last arrived in a black flying car with a dead guy at the wheel, so now in a yellow car with a pretty girl, things were looking up. As they neared a drive that looked like Celia's, Billy quickly said, "Here, turn here."

"Aye, aye, captain," muttered Gwen.

"I'm sorry. I just don't know the area that well."

Pulling up the driveway Gwen asked, "What are you doing here then?"

Before Billy could answer, a charming country house came into view, and then a lady with a pair of pruning shears. Billy's stomach dropped as he imagined a confrontation. He hoped Celia wasn't mad, because if she was, he could very easily be looking for a place to stay. Gwen had no idea. She was just the driver, but she was delivering some disheveled cargo, so she imagined possible guilt by association.

Surprisingly enough, there was none as Billy got out of the passenger seat only to hear Celia's jovial voice say, "Well, look what the cat dragged in."

"What does that even mean?" strained Billy.

"Cats, they drag things in."

"I've never had a cat."

"Never mind then. So, what happened to you? I was worried," said Celia.

With Gwen waiting by the car, Billy replied, "I'm sorry. This is Gwen. She saved me last night."

There was something about the morning and the way things were moving that made Gwen feel simple. It could have been the novelty of it all, but this tall, handsome guy with the elegant aunt was something of an enigma.

"Thanks for getting him home, Gwen," said Celia, like he was precious cargo, or really something special. He seemed different. She just wondered if it was in a good or a bad way.

"It's no problem. He would have done the same for me."

"Would you like to come in for a drink or maybe a tour? I'm sure Billy wouldn't mind."

"Sure," said Gwen.

With exposed beams, hardwood floors, and plenty of windows, the place was beautiful. A thin ray of light bathed the dining room table as they sat for tea. Celia knew things were going to get strange. She knew Billy would come and go, and then maybe be gone for good. Celia hoped he'd survive, but there were other forces at work, and she wasn't sure how the energy would act. He needed someone to look out for him.

Sitting at the table, Gwen and Bill seemed to make a good pair. Not as flashy as Rita, Gwen seemed to be the right girl for the occasion. Celia hoped she was.

Following the tea and pastries, Gwen said, "Well, it was a lovely morning, but unfortunately, I have to go." She was in the process of moving, so there was a lot to do.

"Please stay," said Celia. "Billy could use the company."

"Billy can help me move if he wants."

"Ugh," groaned Billy, "Billy can't help you move, at least not today. I'll walk you to the car though."

"It's a deal. Lovely to meet you, Celia, and hopefully I'll see you again."

"Likewise," replied Celia, "hopefully sooner than later."

So Celia watched from the window as Billy and Gwen walked out.

It was strange for Billy to be back in the states and involved with another girl. In Mexico it hadn't seemed so odd. It was a different place and he was a different person, but now that he was here, the dysfunction of his past was something he'd have to face.

"Thanks again for last night. I think I bit off a bit more than I could chew."

"You bit off a lot more than you could chew. As a matter of fact, there wasn't much chewing going on at all."

Billy chuckled. Gwen had a nice sense of humor, and she wasn't bad to look at either. Her car was yellow and the sky a bright Carolina blue. Her hair was a darker shade of red and her lips soft and supple. The morning sun illuminated Gwen's green eyes as Billy leaned in and said, "Chewing is overrated anyway, now how about that kiss."

Moving together, lips met and sparks flew as they fell against the car, entangled, aroused, and then separated. Gwen gave her hair a quick shake and sounded a pleasantly surprised "Whew."

"I'm sorry. Was it too strong?"

"No, but I guess it's a good thing we didn't kiss last night."

"Definitely," agreed Billy, "especially since I was getting sick."

"Ha, very true," she said.

They stood against the car and wondered what would come next. Billy had mixed feelings. He wasn't sure he should get involved. Even under the best conditions he had a questionable track record, but now with the supernatural involved, things could get even more complicated.

"So am I ever going to see you again, Billy whoever?"

"It's Billy Winslow, and I think I'd like that," answered Billy, deciding to give it a chance. He'd need a friend anyway. The Lex brothers were his only pals so far, and who knew if he'd ever see them again. He kind of hoped not.

"Pick me up tomorrow, and I'll help you move."

It was one of his specialties, no brain power involved, just brute force.

"Sounds good," said Gwen as she gave him another quick peck. "Dinner will be on me."

"You bet."

"Bye, Billy."

"Bye, Gwen."

Pulling away, Gwen couldn't believe her good fortune, a cute guy who could help her move. But he was strange, or it was strange, someone like that not tied down, drifting around with no real direction. She wondered what was up, but she was intrigued and he seemed like a nice guy, so she'd return. If he turned out to be a jerk, she'd drop him right back off where she found him, in the front yard of someone else's house.

But that kiss was something divine, otherworldly almost, like a quick trip to the outer limits. She wondered about that as well.

Billy watched as Gwen's car moved out of sight. Questions and uncertainties would surely come, but he resolved to take it slow.

"So what happened to you last night?" asked Celia.

"I'm sorry, Celia, but things are going to be a tad strange for a while. I'm not really sure what to expect. I met a bum in town who said, 'You saved me, son,' which sounded like 'To save a son' from that dreaded night in Mexico. Then I got hit in the head with a Frisbee, went into a frat party, met the Lex brothers, got plastered on some mystery drink, dove into an above-ground pool from the roof, became an honorary Chi Phi, met Gwen, and then got sick."

"Sounds like you covered a lot of ground. Did you happen to write anything?"

"Yeah, before all the commotion I toured the town and walked through campus. It's nice."

"That's why I've stayed," replied Celia as Billy handed over his notebook.

On a crinkled sheet of paper, he'd written:

Like old friends or comforting acquaintances, red brick reminders of a different age crept quietly through town. I walked slowly around and wondered about the tortured souls and the car crashes from my sleep.

How could anything have happened here? And why was the grass so green, and the sky so blue, and energy so infectious? Why were the girls so enthusiastic and the guys so eager, and the day so spectacularly speeding along in grandeur and in greatness?

I found an answer in the sky. In the great nothingness I found everything. In the dirt I saw myself, trampled and trodden waiting for the next footsteps, and for the next sign, and for the next clue to the never-ending question of "Who was I?"

Billy waited patiently while Celia read. He hoped she liked it. He wasn't expecting to be graded, but she seemed serious. Then, without a sound, she took the pen from her mouth, scrawled something on the paper, and then handed it back to Billy.

"D minus," read the comment, "Dig deeper."

BILLY'S GOT A GIRLFRIEND

After finally getting a good night's sleep, Billy woke with a bad taste in his mouth. It was difficult enough being in North Carolina on a mystical errand, but now he was getting near-failing grades. Heck, he wasn't even in school. He couldn't even get grades. And the fact that it was from his aunt made it even worse. He was going to have to nip this thing in the bud.

Billy spent most of the previous day nursing a hangover, but now that he was rested, he was ready to take on the world, or maybe just Celia. Walking into the kitchen, the smell of fresh coffee almost made Billy forget his gripe and grab a cup, but he had a score to settle.

With Celia already at the table Billy said, "Wow, eggs and toast, that's a rather common breakfast for such a distinguished professor."

"I'm sensing a little displeasure with your first assignment," replied Celia.

"You're sensing a lot of displeasure with my first assignment, I mean, what kind of sabotage is that? You ask to see what I'm writing and then give me a D minus?"

"Did you expect to start at the top?"

"I'd settle for starting in the middle, or not starting at all. Need I remind you that I'm a published author?"

"I'm a published author," stated Celia. "You've dabbled in the profession. You've scratched the surface, but you need to take a deeper cut."

"Ahh, well, I guess a prophet's not known in his own home."

"It's my home, and if you want a better grade, you need to write a better paper."

"Thanks, professor," said Billy.

"You're welcome," replied Celia, "and don't feel bad, most people have to pay for that kind of advice."

"What do I owe you then?"

"Nothing, just take care of yourself. Get the story, but don't go too far."

Celia knew something about stories, about how they begin and end. For a moment, Billy thought he might be living her story, that this was something she cooked up, that it was her creation.

"So what do I do next?"

"See the girl, I guess. She's coming up the driveway right now," said Celia, pointing out of the window.

Billy then remembered what he was actually supposed to do today. He was supposed to help a pretty girl move.

Gwen got out of the car somewhat hesitantly. There hadn't been a call, but there wasn't a phone or a phone number, so she simply showed up and hoped for the best. What was the worst that could happen—Billy would say that he was mistaken or that he'd had a change of heart? But he didn't say that.

"Hi, Gwen," is what he said. "Glad you came back."

"Why wouldn't I?" replied Gwen, admiring Billy's light eyes and broad shoulders.

"I can think of a few reasons, but maybe we could start over if that's all right with you."

"Or maybe we should just start."

"What should we start doing?"

"Let's say hello to Celia," answered Gwen.

Gently attractive in a pair of high tops, loose-fitting shorts, and a snug shirt, Gwen headed into the house as Billy scrambled to keep up.

"Did you come over to see me or her?"

"I came over to see both of you. This house is a lot nicer than mine. Maybe I should move in here."

"After one kiss?"

"How many kisses do you need?"

"More than one, I suppose," guessed Billy as Celia came to the door.

"Nice to see you again, Celia," said Gwen. "Billy wants me to move in, so we'll just get the small stuff today."

"How marvelous," replied Celia. "Waste no more time. Billy yearns for another live-in lover."

Gwen Reynolds grew up in the old north state, which was another name for North Carolina, Billy quickly learned. As a high school soccer star, she found Chapel Hill by way of a scholarship, which was no small feat considering the intense competition involved.

Meeting, and in some ways exceeding, the rigorous demands of a student athlete, she completed her undergrad, and was then accepted into a nursing program. That's where Gwen's life was now, in flux. Her friends were moving on, and so was she, into another small apartment where she'd dream of a larger apartment or maybe a house, one with enough room for a dog or a cat or maybe a child one day. *Maybe with Billy*, she thought, as Billy stared vacantly out the passenger side window.

It was a new beginning for the both of them, although hers was far more sensible than his. She'd been through some tough times though, like her mother picking her up from soccer practice drunk, and then getting locked up for writing bad checks; but this was different. If Gwen thought life with Billy was going to be easy, she was in for a surprise. But maybe she wasn't looking for easy. Maybe that's why she found Billy.

Billy was full of surprises, but looking at him in her passenger seat, he seemed rather harmless. Maybe he'd be the one to drive her home after a late night out or wait by the phone while she did one last shot. Or maybe not. She'd have to get to know him.

Following Gwen up to the second floor, Billy already didn't like the layout. He liked it even less when he saw the apartment.

"How do you expect to get all these big boxes into that little car?"

"That's where you come in, I guess."

Billy enjoyed the back and forth, and at first blush, they seemed to have a good bit of chemistry. They were still on their best behavior, and Billy wondered if it would stay that way, especially with everything else that was going on.

With the last of the boxes out of her old apartment, Gwen asked, "So what do you do, Mr. Billy Winslow?"

"I don't know."

"You don't know?"

"I'm not sure."

"You're not sure," repeated Gwen. "Well you can't just wander the earth anymore, that's called a bum, not a functioning human being. You need a place to go these days."

In an attempt to explain himself, Billy said, "I guess you could say that I'm slightly unconventional then."

"So you came to North Carolina to unconventionally wander through town, get into a party, meet a cute girl, and then end up at her house?"

"Something like that. But what about you? What do you do?"

It was a good question. The obvious answer was that she'd wake up, and then eat, and then study, and then sleep. But was that really something? And what was it in relation to the world, or in relation to stomping out hunger or curing diseases or solving the climate crisis? She'd found herself framed in some kind of a beauty pageant, ready to give a generic answer about world peace or finding a cure for cancer.

Suddenly unsure, with soft auburn hair drifting into the bright green of her eyes, Gwen answered, "I guess I don't really know either.

I mean, I know what I've been doing, but I don't know if it's what I'm going to do."

"I know what you're going to do. You're going to unpack some boxes."

"That's no fun."

"It could be," continued Billy, playfully swatting her with a big pink pillow.

"Oh, now you've done it," roared Gwen, quickly returning fire. Moving in for another strike, Billy quickly corralled her in a soft embrace and said, "I'd like to get to know you better too, but there's no pressure. I like you already, regardless of what you do."

"I like you too, Billy," replied Gwen as their lips met again.

Then, amid the pillows and boxes and all of the other uncertainties, Gwen took control and unclothed Billy in her sparse, colorless apartment. In an instant, there was no world and no tomorrow, just the two of them moving together, searching for something, searching each other, moving toward a climax, and hoping it's not all they had. There had to be more. They hoped there was, as they collapsed into an exhausted heap.

"So, do you still want to know what I do?" asked Billy.

"Yes," replied Gwen, "but it's not all that important."

As they lay on the floor, mentally and physically spent, they both wondered if it had happened too soon. But Billy didn't seem to be the type to leave. She'd seen him at his worst, or what she thought was his worst, and he had been a complete gentleman. Although there were still some unanswered questions about him, maybe there were some unanswered questions about her as well. There were definitely questions about what they'd just done, which they tried to answer by doing it again.

Still unclothed in the early evening hours, Gwen looked more attractive than ever. She had an athletic build with strong legs, a slender waist, and ample curves. Somewhat conservative, at the very least, she was provocative and, at most, downright gorgeous. Gwen and Billy were a good match. They looked good together.

Billy wondered what she would have thought of him a year ago, with his long blond hair and arrogant attitude. Rita had put up with it for a while, but it didn't last. She moved on, and he changed, but Rita would never know that. It was an odd punishment, that every girl would somehow have to measure up to Rita. Lying on the floor, Billy wasn't sure, but maybe Gwen had.

Satisfied but still cautious, Billy said, "Well, I'd be lying if I said that I wasn't wondering if we'd do it."

"Well, we did it," replied Gwen, "and now it's done."

"What do you mean it's done?"

"It's done, there's nothing else to do, there's nothing else to look forward to."

"We could look forward to doing it again," said Billy as Gwen gave a quick laugh.

"I suppose. But seriously, you've got no obligation to stay."

"Do you want me to?"

"Sure, but I can't make you."

Billy understood. He breezes into town and sweeps a girl off her feet—or knocks her off her feet. Then she asks what he does. He gives some kind of noncommittal answer, and then they sleep together. It wasn't the strongest of foundations.

"Tell you what," said Billy, "why don't we get a bottle of wine and some takeout and then we can talk."

With two cups of wine and a candle, they ate and drank and then slowly eased into the conversation.

"So," started Gwen, "now that we've had the food, the wine, and the sex, are you going to tell me anything about yourself?"

"What do you want to know?"

"Oh, just the little stuff, you know, like what's your favorite color and your favorite food? What's your sign, or where were you born?"

"My favorite color is blue, my favorite food is anything from the sea, and I'm a Pisces born in Florida to Cass and William Winslow Sr.," answered Billy.

"So you're a junior."

"Yeah, my dad passed away though. I never really knew him, but I sure missed him."

"My dad didn't die. He just split. He left my mom and I to fend for ourselves. My mom kind of went off the deep end for a while, but she's better now. My dad has a new family in Raleigh, but I don't see him that often. It's just not the same."

"You seem to have come out all right."

"Thanks, but I don't always feel like it. Sometimes I'm still the lonely little girl waiting for my mom while all of the other kids are running off to their perfect parents and perfect lives. Maybe I've overachieved because of it, but there's still something missing, a piece of my heart on the playground waiting to be picked up and put back together."

"But that's what makes us, our faults and imperfections. Eventually one of our broken pieces fits someone else's broken piece, and then they're not broken anymore, they're fixed."

"Maybe," said Gwen. "Hopefully."

"Surely," said Billy. "That's why we're here, to heal and to be made whole and to make others whole. It's the only thing that really makes any sense."

Gwen couldn't argue, she was too deep in thought. It usually took more time for her to confide in someone, but for some reason, this Billy character brought it all out. There was a glow in the room and a twinkle in his eye. It was a small apartment, but with Billy in it, it seemed like the Taj Mahal.

"Well, who are you, Billy?"

Not such a compelling question before, it suddenly felt more significant because they'd done things and she'd shared her innermost thoughts and feelings. It was still complicated, though, and Billy wondered how much to divulge. He didn't want to scare her off just yet.

"Well since you asked so nicely," smiled Billy, "I'm Billy Winslow from Florida, and I guess you could say that I'm a journalist on assignment somewhere in North Carolina."

"Well, let's see your credentials then, Mr. sexy journalist."

"I don't have any, but I can show you something else."

"Maybe later," yawned Gwen. "I'm more interested in this assignment. What is it? Social justice, child poverty, polluted water, holes in the ozone?"

"It's nothing like that. It's different. I'm not even sure what it is."

"Ah," sounded Gwen. "Investigative journalism."

"That sounds about right," replied Billy.

"That's exciting. Hand me the notebook then," demanded Gwen.

Hmm, thought Billy. He rarely let people read his unfinished work, mainly because most people didn't want to read his unfinished work. Most people didn't want to read his finished work, so maybe it was time for a change. Perhaps Gwen could undo some of the damage Celia had done. Maybe she could paint it with a different brush, a more kind and compassionate stroke.

"OK," said Billy as he handed her the page.

Gwen's eyes bulged at the first few lines of the great Billy Winslow's text.

"Hmm, introspective," she said.

"It's a start," replied Billy.

It was a good day that turned into a good night. Billy didn't check all of the boxes, but he checked a few, and he wasn't completely crazy, so that was a bonus. There was still an air of mystery surrounding the handsome stranger though. Gwen didn't know how close they'd get, but she hoped to see him again, and maybe get closer. At this point, she'd just have to wait and see.

With the night sky gently lightening, Gwen and Billy slept somewhat comfortably on the floor. Stretching into consciousness, Billy groaned, "Are these the four-star accommodations you promised?"

"Nothing but the best for you, Mr. Winslow," replied Gwen in an early morning rasp.

"I expected some hospitality in the South."

"Didn't you get it?" asked Gwen.

"I sure did," answered Billy, moving in for another kiss.

There it was, validation and hope for the days ahead.

"I'd like to see you again, Gwen. I'm not really on my feet yet. Well, I am on my feet, but I haven't really found my bearings. I'm going to be here for a while. I don't know how long, but I'm going to need your help, and your support, and your phone number, I guess."

Billy was adorable, and even if they never did anything again, she wouldn't think of it as a waste. It had been a lovely couple of days, so she'd give it time. Anyway, she thought that's what he was saying.

Leaving the apartment, Gwen and Billy squeezed into Gwen's little yellow car and took off. With Gwen at the wheel and Billy in the passenger seat, it seemed like he was back in the saddle. With a pretty girl on his arm and a dangerous mission ahead, things were shaping up quite well.

There wasn't much else to say as they waited for their brief time together to end, and then to begin. It wasn't lost on Billy that they'd had a special day, and then a special night. He hadn't been completely honest, but he couldn't be, at least not yet. There was still a lot to figure out.

Billy's mind then flashed back to the dreams. Where was the car crash and the son he was supposed to save? And what about the one-armed basketball player? And what about Ray? Would he ever see him again?

Did Celia need him? Was she in trouble? Did she need a steady hand? Or maybe an unsteady hand? Or maybe just some company? And what about Rita, would she come around again? Did they have any unfinished business, or was it all washed away in the champagne toasts and happiness ever after?

Then he looked toward Gwen, with her soft hair sparkling in the noonday sun. Had he made things better for her, or just more complicated? Would he run back to Rita if she'd have him? Or would he stay gone, away from the powerful woman he'd spent so much time with? Or was Gwen the same? From his mother to his aunt Celia then on to Rita and now Gwen, Billy sure seemed to attract some strong women. Was that good, or was he just some kind of a tagalong, a foil of sorts, a medium for them to work through, a bad to make them good? He didn't know, but for some reason, Billy felt like a student. He just needed to learn. He needed to be straight with Gwen, and he would be, after he figured some things out.

As they traveled up the wooded drive, there was a degree of sadness—one, because they had to part, and two, because they didn't know what would come next. Gwen was ready to move forward, to see Billy tomorrow and the day after that. Billy was holding back, and that was all right, but it wasn't exactly comfortable.

In front of the house, Gwen playfully said, "Thanks for the help, Billy. And there's more to do if you're still interested."

"I am. Let me get your number so we can stay in touch."

Gwen grabbed Billy's notebook and scrawled her phone number along with the message, "For a good time call."

Looking at the page, Billy chuckled. It was nice have a girl around, one that he could laugh with and trust. Perhaps that's why he'd gone forward, because she was the right girl for the right time. Now all he needed to do was to be the right guy, and after a final kiss, they both tried to speak.

"Ladies first."

"I was going to say good-bye, Billy, for now, hopefully not forever."

Among other things, Billy had her number, but Gwen didn't think it would be the end of it. She'd just have to hope for the best and not pay too much attention to her phone.

Celia was, of course, in the living room when Billy arrived. She just had to be there when he came home to give him the once-over. That was the problem with roommates, through the good, the bad, the happy, and the sad, they were always there.

Celia was a bit like his mother, and Billy hadn't lived with his mom in a while. It was also her house, so Billy had to be on his best behavior, which wasn't always possible. Especially when he entered to chants of "Billy's got a girlfriend, Billy's got a girlfriend."

"What, are you in the fifth grade? I feel like I'm going in reverse."

"Sometimes you need to go backward to go forward."

"Ahh, thank you, swami," said Billy. "So tell me, oh wise one, what's next?"

"What's next is that you need to hand over the notebook so I can see if you've made any progress."

"Goodness," muttered Billy, submitting his latest entry.

With a pen in hand, Celia grabbed the notebook and read:

In a car with a girl on an unknown street in an unnamed town, we drove into nowhere and turned into nothing. We told stories of here and there, and went to places near and far. We searched for the truth in pillows and boxes, on the floor and in the hall, high above it all, hoping we'd never come down.

But if we fell, how far would we go? And if we left, how long would we stay gone? And if we never came back, would we remember being here, and being good, and being together—in this place.

"Hmm," muttered Celia as Billy waited.

It was stupid for him to even buy into the charade. But at this point, he was all about charades. Whether it be the spirits, the grades, or the girl, Billy was being pulled in all different directions, so why resist?

Finished reading, Celia scratched something onto the paper and then handed it back. Staring blankly at the text, he saw a large D floating harassingly in the top center of the page with a message: "Try harder."

GILDED

With the sun gently starting to rise, Billy was first into the kitchen. Pulling some fresh blueberries and bacon from the refrigerator, his plan was to ease Celia into a food coma and then to get some answers about his grades.

Billy hadn't planned on getting into a kitchen again, but she'd left him no choice. With his confidence sinking, he'd have to deploy his secret weapon: cooking.

The smell of crispy bacon wafted through the house as Celia cheerfully walked in and said, "The chef returns."

"The chef never left," replied Billy, carefully watching the thick blueberry pancakes start to bubble. Flipping the pancakes for a final sear and then onto a nice, warm plate, Billy handed it to Celia and said, "Bon appétit."

"Oui, bon," replied Celia as she cracked off a piece of bacon and then dug into the stack of pancakes.

"Now about that last grade," started Billy.

"What about it?" garbled Celia.

"Isn't it nice when someone cooks for you?"

"Yes."

"So it makes you feel good?"

"Yeah," she quizzically replied, "but I'm beginning to think there's an ulterior motive."

"There is an ulterior motive," declared Billy, "to get you to ease up on those grades."

"But if I give you bad grades, are you going to cook me good food?"

It was a good question. Could her rejection keep him enslaved? Could her mistreatment keep him engaged, or would her correction drive him to succeed?

"If you give me good grades, I'll cook you good food."

Finishing her bite, Celia replied, "I told you before, if you want a better grade, write a better paper, and a D is actually a step up from a D minus."

"But it's still a D."

"But you're getting better."

"Getting better, most improved, honorable mention," muttered Billy on his way out of the kitchen. "The dishes are on you."

"Blah, blah, blah," sounded Celia, content to slather the rest of her bacon in warm blueberry syrup. It was all just for fun really. Celia needed some levity, and Billy needed discipline, so it seemed to be working out.

Surrounded by the empty cups and plates, Celia dipped her hands into the hot soapy water and began to scrub. Between the greasy pan, the sticky plates, and the dirty mixing bowl, Celia wondered what she'd gotten herself into. She had planned on making a simple piece of toast, yet here she was, spraying sinks and wiping down counters.

With the cleanup finally complete, Celia found Billy and said, "Look Billy, I don't need to grade your writing, I'm more interested in what this unique set of circumstances might yield."

"Right now it's not yielding anything more than a new relationship in a new town. It started out fast and furious, but it seems to have taken a turn to the domestic side. I thought I'd be streaking through the universe, snatching dragons and demons from the sky, but instead I'm loading boxes into a little yellow car."

Thinking of Gwen, Celia asked, "How much are you going to tell her?"

"I can't tell her anything, not yet, not until I figure it out. She'd have me committed. But I will tell her about Rita and about being on the run. I just have to wait, but I won't wait long."

It wasn't a good answer, but it was all Billy had.

With Celia gone and Billy in the garden, the quiet of the forest caused some introspection. Things were different now. It was almost like the world had grown up and he hadn't. People carried around phones, and the wilderness was shrinking. He thought about what Gwen had said: that there wasn't any more room for wanderers, for those out of step or for people on the fringes.

He hoped she was wrong. Maybe he could show her that she was, but maybe she wasn't. Maybe it was a warning and he hadn't listened. Maybe he'd be ground to dust beneath the wheels of progress, a relic from a different age extinguished by the cold, sinister grip of technology.

Where would he go? What could he do but surrender to the eternal push of excess and wallow in the new reality of greed? But who would save the owls and the gentle deer wandering through the forest? And who would speak for the tiny burrowing creatures and for the trees?

It would be Billy Winslow. He'd rise from the ashes. He'd wade through the plastic. He'd fight through the smog, the sickness, and the decay and return to something real: to the oceans, and to the skies, and to the thundering drums that sounded in the distance.

A steady drumbeat echoed throughout the woods, and Billy wondered whether it was in his ears or in his heart. Growing louder still, the intense rhythmic pounding increased as Billy's pulse suddenly quickened. The crash of a thousand drums became the deafening wail of a runaway train. Grinding steel then screeched to a halt as Billy dove to the patio clutching his ears. Billy screamed in pain through the sustained metallic squeal, then the yard suddenly went quiet.

A gentle breeze blew through the trees as Billy lay listlessly on the ground. Slow to his feet, he managed a few steps before falling heavily into a waiting chair. Then, like a cheap carnival ride, the rickety chair spun fiercely out of control, hurling Billy violently into a jagged rock wall. Now twisted and bruised, he crawled into the house and went for the phone.

The good news was that he was alive, the bad was that the signs were now getting physical, which was something of a concern because he didn't have any protection. All he had was a girl's phone number, so he called, because he wasn't sure he'd ever see her again.

With blurred vision and a splitting headache, Billy dialed, and waited. As the phone painfully rang, he was about to hang up when a sweet "Hello" breezed through the receiver.

"Wow," replied Billy, "is it good to hear you."

"Is it good to hear who?" asked Gwen.

"It's good to hear you," answered Billy before collapsing onto the kitchen floor.

A splash of cold water wet Billy's face as the blurred image of Gwen slowly appeared.

"Billy!" exclaimed Gwen, with a finger on his wrist. "Billy, what happened?"

"I-I don't know," stammered Billy. "All I remember is talking to you, and then hitting the deck."

"I called Celia. She's on the way. I didn't know what else to do."

"Thank you, for the second time now. You bailed me out again. I guess I need to take better care of myself."

"I guess so," replied Gwen, her intuition sensing something more.

With that, Celia rushed through the door and said, "Goodness, Billy, are you all right!"

"I feel so special," Billy meekly replied, "with two lovely ladies doting on me. I need to collapse more often."

Celia noticed a knot on his head and dark rings below his eyes. She knew better than to ask what happened. Billy wouldn't be able to say, not with Gwen there. Not yet, anyway.

"I called Gwen and then collapsed," said Billy, "just nervous around girls, I guess."

"Ha," replied Gwen. "Are you going to be all right though? I have to go to work, but I'll stop by later, maybe to read you a bedtime story."

"I'll be fine. Celia's here."

"OK then," said Gwen with parting hug and a light kiss on the cheek.

Driving off, Gwen was shaken. She'd never experienced anything like that: a grown man passed out on the floor of a dark house. It was spooky, but she was still smitten. Celia, on the other hand, was worried. She knew what was at stake.

The house was still dark, and Billy was slumped in a chair. His bright-blue eyes were tired and vulnerable rather than strong. It had been a while since he was so physically spent—that morning at Chichen Itza after the spirits and the storm.

He'd survived then, and was safe now, but what about the next time? And just what was this sickness? He wanted it to go away, or he wanted to know how to make it go away. Maybe it was supposed to kill him though. Maybe it was a slow descent into insanity, a desolate path into the wilderness, where he'd be lost and slowly forgotten. But he wouldn't go down without a fight. He had to be patient and to stay alive—two things that were going to be increasingly hard to do.

Shuffling in from the kitchen, Celia arrived with a hot cup of tea and asked, "What the hell happened, Billy?"

"I don't really know," answered Billy. "Strange things abound."

Concerned, Celia remembered when Billy was sick and wrestling with the spirits before. He was just a child then.

"Was it a seizure?" asked Celia, wondering if the angels had visited again.

"No, it was different than that. When you left for work, I went into the garden. In the quiet, I started to think. I thought about saving the world and about saving myself, and then I heard the drums. Far away at first, the drumbeat moved closer, and then it got louder, and then it turned into the sinister whine of a runaway train headed straight for me! Lights flashed, steel screeched, and voices screamed as I dove to the ground, and then it just disappeared. After finally getting to my feet, I collapsed into a chair only to have the chair spin out of control and hurl me into that jagged rock wall!" exclaimed Billy. "And then I crawled into the house and called Gwen."

Celia didn't answer. She didn't know what to say. The sight of her nephew beating himself up, slowly going mad at her house was more than she could bear. But she'd seen the car and the ghoulish driver, and she'd heard Billy's account from the temple, where the skies opened up and sent a message. Why would he lie about something like that?

Getting up to give Billy a hug, Celia said, "Let's get something for those cuts, buddy."

And there she was again, with a tear in her eye, taking care of her nephew again. She wondered about deeper connections and mysterious attractions, the general insanity that connected her to Billy. She wanted to protect him from the pain, or from the danger, but she couldn't, so she'd have to let it go.

Quoting Lao Tzu, Celia said, "A snow goose need not bathe to make itself white. Neither need you do anything but be yourself."

"I've been myself. That's the problem," replied Billy.

"Be more of yourself, don't be afraid."

In a dark room with battered elbows and knees, the passage seemed strangely appropriate. Trying to make sense of it would be a waste; he'd just have to put himself out there to fearlessly confront whatever might come.

"OK," submitted Billy. "More Billy, that's what the world needs."

"That's what the world needs," repeated Celia. "Sir William Winslow, the gilded prince."

He laughed. The gilding must have worn off, or maybe it was just put on.

Running a finger over his scarred elbows, Billy suddenly wanted the fight. He wanted the battle. He just needed to know where it was. But maybe that was the fun part, figuring out when to strike. It wouldn't be now, but it would be soon.

Then, as Billy looked out the window, Gwen's little yellow car made its way up the drive. Watching his sexy new friend arrive, Billy felt a certain way. He wasn't sure he'd be able to feel that way about a girl again: wanting to see her, wondering if he would and then what he'd say before the awkward laughter, the soft touch, and then the calm.

The conversation would come easy. With a slight nudge and a sexy smile, she'd make it that way, for just as the sun knows the day and the moon the night, a girl knows how to get a guy. Driving up to the house again, Gwen knew they'd be together, she just didn't know for how long.

She already felt something for him. They'd spent little more than a day together, yet there she was, concerned for his safety—why? It was a familiar feeling, something from her past, worrying about her mother, wondering if she'd make it home, and if she'd be shamelessly drunk. Where had she been? Driving through town and around parking lots full of children and bicycles? Were there more dents on the car? And when would she finally get caught? Gwen promised she'd never willingly put herself in that situation again, yet there she was, worrying about someone again, and after only a few days.

So, with a book in hand for Billy's bedtime story, Gwen knocked and was promptly greeted with a hearty "Door's open!" from Celia.

Inside and somewhat apprehensive, Gwen moved slowly through the house.

When she finally got to the stairs, Celia rushed to her side and said, "Oh great, you're here. You're just what Billy needs right now."

"I hope so," replied Gwen.

"I know so," declared Celia as Gwen traipsed up the stairs.

She wondered if things were creepy now instead of familiar. That she so quickly felt like family was a little suspicious. If they brought her in so easily, they could dump her just the same way. Was she guarded or obsessed? Whatever it was, it all changed as she opened the door to see Billy on his bed. Tall and handsome with sad eyes and scrapes, something else was there—his smile, shimmering through the discomfort.

Focused on Billy's angelic image, Gwen felt her chest tighten, and she was suddenly floating. A new and powerful energy was emanating. Like in images from the Sistine Chapel, a synthesis of heaven and earth was occurring. In the eerily darkened room, scenes clicked swiftly by like a forbidden slide show. A flood of birthdays and celebrations and disappointments and love and loss frantically merged into a chaotic climax as Gwen suddenly fell.

She slowly awoke to panicked voices as one that sounded like Billy's said, "I don't know what happened. She walked in with a book and then passed out."

Celia gently mopped Gwen's forehead with a warm cloth and added, "Man, this is strange."

"What's strange?" asked Gwen as she opened her eyes to see those of Billy and Celia. It felt like she was in an operating room, slowly coming to and ready to be wheeled away.

Although she'd passed out for no apparent reason, Gwen wasn't panicked. In a foreign place with relative strangers, she was more relaxed than anything. She looked to Billy and Celia and felt secure. She could trust them. They were her people.

The sense of euphoria quickly subsided as she recalled the slide show and then the loss of consciousness. Gwen's life, as it seemed, had flashed before her very eyes. Was it a dream or just a far-flung vision of things to come? It was her, and it felt like her, but who and what was everything else? She shed a tear for the baby in the mother's arms and then another for the five birthday candles that she happily blew out, and then Billy softly asked, "Gwen, are you all right?"

"I guess that depends on what you consider all right," answered Gwen. She wasn't sure.

Celia was right, it was strange. Who were these people, witches and warlocks, and how did she fit into it all? Gwen wanted to run, but she instead asked, "What's going on, Billy?

"I'm not sure."

It was true. He wasn't sure, and this was just a new wrinkle in an already strange story. Now people around him were being affected, and he felt responsible. Things were moving in quite a disturbing direction. But maybe it was all just some strange coincidence. Was it possible that both he and Gwen could have had seizures on the same day in the same house? Billy dismissed the thought almost immediately. There was obviously something amiss.

Gwen remembered the energy as she entered the room. She could almost hear it crackling. She could virtually see the sparks. Whether scary or spiritual, Gwen was shaken either way.

She'd asked Billy what was going on and he said he wasn't sure, but that didn't change the fact that he'd randomly talked to her on the street, then showed up at the same frat party as her, then passed out drunk in her arms, then helped her move, then helped his way into her bed, then called her in distress and then put her under some kind of a spell. Gwen had brought a book to read, but now it seemed like they'd be doing something else.

Wondering what to say, Billy couldn't gloss it over and at this point, he really didn't want to. As he studied Gwen's soft eyes and auburn hair, aside from everything else, he was glad she was there. It would be a shame to lose her.

It was always his fault though. Billy had put Rita in danger and then unleashed the law on her, and now he'd unleashed the spirits on Gwen. It was time for him to come clean.

Billy ran a hand through Gwen's soft ginger hair as she pulled slightly away. He understood. He was hiding something and she knew it.

"You asked me what was going on, and I said I wasn't sure. And that's true," said Billy. "So maybe you should ask me what's happening."

Gwen didn't see the great disparity, but she went ahead and asked, "Well, what's happening then?"

"What's happening is that you look absolutely scrumptious today."

It was a trick, and she wasn't about to fall for it, "Did I look scrumptious collapsed on the bed?"

"No," Billy sheepishly answered.

"Tell me what's happening then."

"It's a long story."

"We've got all night."

Gwen was right. Billy looked outside and it was dark. He looked at the clock and it showed a little after nine. He looked at Gwen and she wasn't moving. There was nowhere for him to go. There was nothing else for him to say but, "It started with a bad idea, and a book."

"What started with a bad idea and a book?"

"My spiritual journey, I guess."

Now she was getting somewhere. No more BS about a journalist on some kind of mystery assignment. It seemed like this Billy guy was about to let his freak flag fly, and it was about time.

Billy was still on the bed, as was Gwen. They wanted to get on to bigger and better things, but the strangeness of the day just had to be addressed.

"We could go on like this for hours. We could waste the rest of the night or the rest of our lives, but that wouldn't change the fact that we both passed out today, and that you might know why. So you need to start talking, handsome."

Finally at ease, Billy said, "Well, there was a girl and a book."

With the talk of an ex, as well as a spiritual journey, Gwen was even more intrigued. She needed some popcorn and Coke.

Like he was in a confessional, Billy instantly felt the need to make a declaration. It seemed like a strange approach, but he needed to start over.

"Hi, Gwen. I'm Billy Winslow, and I'd like to get to know you, if I could."

Of course, he just had to be extra charming. Billy was going to make it difficult for her to leave.

"You've already gotten to know me," replied Gwen, "but we're actually here to get to know you, so please proceed."

"Well, as previously mentioned, I'm Billy Winslow from Florida, and now I'm in North Carolina on a vision quest."

"Well, what about the girl and the book?"

The question took Billy back to the last time he was in love—or to the only time he'd been in love. From here, it seemed like a better time, even being run out of town. At least then he knew what was going on.

Billy didn't think about the loss though, he thought about Rita and how much she meant to him and about how he never really told her and about how much he missed her, even now.

"There was a girl named Rita," started Billy. "She'd recently moved to Florida from Chicago. We worked at the same restaurant. She was a waitress, and I was a cook."

"How cliché," remarked Gwen.

"Of course. She moved there because her father was sick. He was dying of cancer. I offered an aspirin, as her migraines were acting up and it just kind of went from there. She was pretty and smart and actually went to Northwestern until her father got sick again. His cancer had gone into remission and then returned, more aggressively I guess. She dropped out of school to spend some more time with him or to help if she could. The doctors didn't know if he'd recover, but the prognosis wasn't good. He ended up passing away and Rita stayed, to see if we could ever be anything. She should have just left, I guess."

Sensing it was a difficult time, Gwen moved closer as Billy said, "You might not want to sit next to me after you hear the rest."

Gwen then backed off and returned the floor to Billy.

"Anyway, she was like you, smart and accomplished, and I wanted to prove that I was too, but instead I proved I wasn't."

"A guy with something to prove, sounds dangerous."

"It was," agreed Billy. "I tried to stay in the game, but she was out of my league. Heck, you're out of my league. These days, I don't even know what league I'm in. But the journalistic part is true," continued Billy. "I wanted to write a book, a hard-hitting journalistic piece about a crime gone wrong. This nitwit called me about a kidnapping, so I inserted myself into the story. I didn't do it, I just wrote about it. It was supposed to be funny."

"Funny?"

"In a darker sense, but it wasn't supposed to happen. A criminal named Keller got involved and made it happen. He also made me a suspect. I mean, no one got hurt, but it got me separated from Rita and run out of town."

"How so?"

"Rita and I were sleeping when it all went down. After kidnapping a guy named Steve, Keller's gang of thugs tried to lock him up in my house. Rita beat them back, but they still left Steve bound and gagged on my doorstep. Assuming the cops were on the way, Rita drove me to the airport and then bought me a one-way ticket to Mexico. It just so happened that I left the notes for my book in Rita's car, so she took the notes, finished the novel, got it published, and then married the publisher. They bought me a house on the beach for my troubles though."

Gwen didn't react right away; there was a lot to digest. What first stood out, besides the actual kidnapping, was the fact that it was Rita who beat the intruders back and then bought the plane ticket. This guy Billy was quickly turning into a bust.

Of everything she could have asked, her first question was, "Why did she get up before you?" followed by "and why did she have to buy the plane ticket?"

"I guess I'm a heavy sleeper, and I was short on cash that week," were Billy's two best answers.

"Hmm," sounded Gwen. But unbeknownst to her, it was a sound Billy had heard all too often.

Wondering whether to believe him or not she asked, "So what's the name of the book?"

"She named it *Kidnapping Steve*."

"Can I buy it at a bookstore?"

"You sure can, just keep it away from me. I'm not ready to read it yet."

"She didn't share the credits with you?"

"I didn't want her to. She fell in love with the publisher and married him. Corbin Flake is the guy's name. He's some kind of an under-twenty-five millionaire, so she's probably a millionaire too. I wouldn't accept anything, so they bought me the house. I suppose for a place to go when things get tough. It was Rita looking out for me I guess."

So Billy had bounced around and finally landed on Gwen, but in a greater sense, what happened wasn't all bad. Rita got married and Billy got a house. It didn't explain the most recent events though.

Dismissing the other disturbing aspects, the more pressing question seemed to be, "Are you wanted?"

"No. I'm cleared. Rita's mother actually married the local sheriff. I got it on good authority that the case was closed."

"So what are you doing here?"

"That's where things get interesting."

To Gwen things had already been interesting, too interesting, actually. She wanted to ride on the back of a motorcycle or take an expedition to an exotic destination, not have a psychic episode in an old country house.

"What do you mean by interesting?

Following a deep breath, Billy finally admitted, "I've been experiencing some paranormal activity."

"In some places they call that crazy."

"Believe me, I've given it a lot of thought, especially when it started. It all happened when I was on the lam. In a way it coincided with me being on the run because that led me to Mexico, which then led me to Chichen Itza, which in turn led me here. I mistakenly ingested some peyote at the Mayan ruins on the outskirts of Cancun, and then without any shelter, a massive storm hit. It seemed like there were gods and goddesses in the sky, angry, fighting over something, or trying to save it. I laid beneath the thunder and lightning all night long and when the clouds parted, I was left with the phrase 'To save a son.'"

"To save a son?" repeated Gwen.

"Yeah," answered Billy, "but when I finally returned home, a stiff gust of wind plastered a map of Florida to my face, basically telling me to leave Mexico and go back to Florida. Well, I certainly hadn't planned on going back there, but I had to listen. The phrase kept ringing in my ears—*to save a son, to save a son*—so I took the first plane out."

It sounded like a bunch of rubbish to Gwen, but she wondered who could make something like that up, and also if any of it could be verified.

"So if I ask Celia, she'd tell me it's true, right?"

Answering her question with a question, Billy asked, "We did pass out on the same day, didn't we?"

"Yes."

"Do you want to listen, then?"

"Continue."

"So while still in Mexico, I dreamt of a car crash and then on the plane back to Florida, I saw a car on the ocean floor tumbling end over end before evaporating into thin air. I mean, it was there, clear as day, and then it was gone. To test it all out, I decided to walk home from the airport, forty miles of interstate, one way. So there I was, walking along, and sure enough, a creepy car pulls to the side of the road, so what do you think I did?"

Gwen wanted to say "Run" but instead answered, "You got in."

"That's right, I got in, and the car was being driven by a hulking dead guy with a radio that was stuck on the song 'Carolina in My Mind.'"

"Ooh, I love that song."

"I like it too, but not over and over at night in the creepiest car you've ever seen. Anyway, the driver's name was Ray, and he took me exactly where I needed to go. He didn't even ask. When I got back to my house, a neighbor said that a big branch had blown off of my tree and then reattached itself. Then I had another bad dream about a one-armed basketball player, and then woke to my alarm clock playing what song?" asked Billy.

"'Carolina in My Mind'?"

"That's right," said Billy, "you're catching on. And it just so happens that I have an aunt in North Carolina, whom I think you've met."

"Celia?"

"Correctamundo, give that girl a prize," announced Billy as Gwen beamed. "So now I know where I have to go, and I also know how I'm going to get there."

"Ray?" guessed Gwen.

"My goodness, you're a quick study, Ms. Gwen, that's right, Ray. So Ray shows up again, only this time, he's pale as ash with a streak of blood running down his mouth, but at least his radio works. And guess what?"

"What?"

"He knows exactly where I need to go again, to North Carolina. To Celia's house to be exact."

"No way."

"Way. So Celia's in the driveway when Ray and I show up, except when we get there the car is levitating. Celia poked her head into the car and saw Ray and the blood, and then the car disappeared into a cloud of sparks, or a force field of some kind."

"That's creepy," said Gwen.

"It is," replied Billy, "but there's more."

Then, as a faint knock sounded, Celia let herself in to see Billy, red faced and fanatical.

"Today, in the garden, before I called you, I narrowly escaped being plowed over by an imaginary freight train. Then, when I went to collect myself in a chair, the chair spun out of control and threw me into a jagged rock wall, hence the scrapes, the phone call, and the collapse. Oh yeah, and then you came over and passed out as well, caught up in some kind of a strange energy cycle or something."

Billy then turned to Celia and asked, "Did I miss anything?"

"Unfortunately no," answered Celia. "It sounds pretty accurate."

"Well, if I leave, will it go away?" asked Gwen.

"It might."

"If I stay, will it continue?"

"I don't know. That's how I met you in town, looking for clues. I'm really glad I met you though, and I really don't think it's a coincidence, but if you need to leave, I understand."

Maybe she should have, but there had been some romance and now a hell of a lot of intrigue. Gwen was still interested, but she needed to know if this Billy guy had any backbone.

"So you're just going to let me go without a fight?"

"I'll fight. I just don't want anyone to get hurt. I barely survived my last episode, and now here I am, back at it again, except this time, it's a lot more serious."

"Well, is there anything else you're hiding?"

"No," answered Billy, "but I've never had to say anything like this before. That's why I stalled. I waited too long, and you were involved, and I want it to be the last time."

"So you saw the driver of the car, Celia?" asked Gwen.

"Yes," answered Celia, "and I agonized over it too, imagining a pale driver with ketchup streaming down his face. But try as I might, I just couldn't reconcile the flying car, which subsequently disappeared into a field of sparks. But it's real, as real as anything is. For some reason, an unearthly energy is on the move, and it seems to have chosen

Billy to move through, and now you as well. The main problem is that the energy seems to have become physical, and neither of you are protected."

"Well if you know so much about it, then what's next?" asked Billy.

"My guess is that there'll be another sign."

Great, more signs, thought Billy. He was already exhausted, and things hadn't even started.

With Celia gone and Billy and Gwen still on the bed, there was a softness between the two, an end-of-the-day kind of satisfaction. For Gwen, it was a time unlike any other, and she didn't know what to do. A train seemed to be leaving, and she could either jump on and enjoy the ride or wait for the next. But maybe there wouldn't be another, and she'd forever wonder about the train and where it went and what happened. She couldn't be completely sure about anything, but there was one reassurance that could be helpful.

"I didn't know how to tell you, Gwen. I wasn't looking to meet anyone, it just kind of happened, but I'm glad it did. I want you to stay, and I'll do everything in my power to protect you."

Billy had some power, so his claim of protection was obviously reassuring, but rather than wonder about the ghosts and ghouls Gwen asked, "Well, what about Rita?"

"What about her?"

"Do you still love her?"

Billy would have rather talked about the spirits, but it was a fair question. Rita seemed to be one of the main spirits, hovering far above everything else, just waiting to make an entrance.

"Yes," said Billy, "but I wouldn't get back together with her. Even if she returned, it wouldn't be like me to try, and it wouldn't be like her to want to. We were just two ships that passed in the night—or that smashed into one another and then limped into port to somehow get fixed. I think she got fixed better than me though."

Lucky for Billy, it was the right answer. Had he replied any differently, she would have most certainly left, because from here on out, Billy needed to be completely honest.

"Well, there's one more thing," added Gwen.

"What?"

He'd already confessed to some of the most bizarre events imaginable, and then been forced to proclaim his love for an ex-girlfriend. What else could there be?

"I trust you wrote an entry after our night together."

Billy had almost forgotten about his notepad, but Gwen jogged his memory. She was slowly peeling his layers back, and he was slowly remembering what it was like to be hitched.

"Yes, I did."

"So, let's see it."

He could have said no or that it was personal, but he liked Gwen. Her tight curves and pretty eyes already had a hold on him and furthermore, he probably owed her as much.

Grabbing his notepad, with a slight grin he said, "I went from a D minus to a D. Celia said it was a pretty good improvement."

"We'll see," said Gwen.

So she read about driving into nowhere and turning into nothing and searching for the truth in what they'd done, and then maybe finding some happiness in it all. It sounded good to her. Or good enough as she leaned into Billy and asked, "So, what's next?"

GUIDED

Unmistakably naked, Billy and Gwen were officially an item. Billy had shared perhaps the strangest scenario he could have imagined, and Gwen had stayed. But there was still time for her to flee.

Awake in a strange room, Gwen quickly had to sort it out. She wasn't in her apartment; she was with Billy. They'd slept together again, but now she had to clear Celia. And what did it mean? Did it mean they were together or just that they'd mistakenly come together again, and what about the other stuff? It was a rude awakening at best, but not for Billy. He snored away without a care in the world.

As she lay wondering, Gwen gave Billy a stern shove and hissed, "Wake up."

"Wha," groaned Billy.

"Wake up, Billy, its eight o'clock, and I have to go."

"So go."

"That's all you have to say, after luring me over here with a fake seizure and then hypnotizing me and then telling me a cockamamie story about imaginary trains and flying cars?"

Half asleep, Billy drearily asked, "What happened to the mild-mannered ginger with the pretty green eyes? What did you do with her?"

"She's still here," answered Gwen, "but she has to go, and she needs you to walk her downstairs."

"That's right," remembered Billy. "We're at Celia's."

Now traipsing around in the nude, Billy kicked the book she'd brought over and exclaimed, "Holy shit!"

"What happened?" asked Gwen.

"I've got a clue."

She snickered as Billy asked, "What's so funny?"

"You, the naked professor."

"Well take a look at this," beamed Billy as he showed her a picture of Pilot Mountain.

"Looks like a big rock to me."

"But read the caption."

Quickly scanning the text, the description of Pilot Mountain read: "The rounded, rocky summit resembles a massive stone observatory like El Caracol, the renowned Mayan ruin at Chichen Itza in Mexico."

In yesterday's rambling admission, Gwen remembered the mention of Chichen Itza and a storm of some sort, but it was hard to keep it all straight.

"So what does it mean?" asked Gwen.

"I don't know, but I guess I'm going to have to find out," answered Billy.

"How?"

"I'll have to go there."

The statement only furthered her consternation as Gwen asked, "Well, are you coming back?"

"I'll be back. I have a feeling this is just the beginning."

"It better just be the beginning," said Gwen, stretching into her shorts. "Because if you left now, that would probably be the ultimate letdown."

"I might be doing you a favor."

"Don't say that, Billy I'd miss you, and I'd never get to see how this ends. I'm riveted. You've got a heck of a story going."

"It's your story too, I guess."

"You guess?" repeated Gwen. "The spectacular new guy who makes me late, weak in the knees, and worried better know I'm part of the story."

"You might just be the story, Gwen. You and me down a long country road with a melon patch, tomato plants, and a couple of goats to boot."

With a twinkle in her eye, Gwen pictured Billy in a straw hat, shirtless, of course, spreading out chicken feed and chasing the cattle back inside the fence. That was it for the farm fantasy though as she checked her watch. This new job would quickly be an old job if she continued to be tardy. But Gwen had Billy, and he was actually becoming a full-time job.

"Come on, handsome, walk me out. I really do have to go."

As Gwen sped off, Billy was back in the game. He was still amazed at the way things were working out, or maybe just stunned because he hadn't been able to make any sense out of it. The scars on his elbows and knees were painful reminders of his brush with the netherworld, and the thoughts of Gwen unconscious were chilling, but some good had also come. The fact that Billy came clean seemed to have brought them closer. When he finally did tell Gwen the truth, he knew she'd either go or stay, but he hadn't wanted her to come under fire.

Whether it was all just a crazy dream, Billy didn't know. He hadn't woken up yet, but the spirits sure had. If he didn't believe it before, he most certainly believed it now so it was time to get going.

He walked back into the house only to see Celia puttering around, watering plants and such.

"Good morning, Ms. Celia. You look especially radiant this morning, if I do say so myself."

Celia was suspicious. "With a greeting like that, you've either done something, or you need something, so which is it?"

"Can't I just be cheerful for a change?"

"Yes," she said, "but the main question is why?"

"The main answer is that I got a clue."

"Really?" chimed Celia.

"Really," replied Billy.

Unbeknownst to Billy, Celia had taken a short sabbatical to look after him. He wasn't going to end up on the pavers again under her watch. It now seemed to have been a good choice, because something was obviously brewing.

"Well, let's have it."

"Gwen brought a book over yesterday, to brighten my spirits, you know," started Billy. "So this morning, on my way back from the bathroom, I kicked the stupid book and it opened to a most interesting page."

"What kind of book was it?" asked Celia. "Fiction, nonfiction, biography, autobiography, reference, medical, linguistic, educational, religious?"

"OK, OK, professor," stammered Billy, "it was—or is—a reference book on North Carolina's Piedmont, and I kicked it open to a page comparing Pilot Mountain to the sacred Mayan religious site Chichen Itza."

"So?"

"So, Chichen Itza is where I first encountered the spirits."

"Oh," murmured Celia. "So what are you going to do?"

"I'm going to Pilot Mountain."

"How are you going to get there?"

In true Billy fashion, he simply answered, "I'm going to walk."

There was more testing to do. If his calculations were correct, Billy guessed that a certain car would most definitely be at a certain spot.

Expecting an interesting trip, Billy first read up on Pilot Mountain. It seemed that the ancient Saura Indians had first named the mountain Jomeokee, which loosely translated to "Great Guide." Later, European settlers similarly called it "pilot," for its navigational value.

It also said that the Saura were later driven out by the Cherokee, who formed their own mythology around the mountain, one of the Nunne hi, meaning either "malevolent tricksters" or "benevolent guardians." Billy also read that the summit was off limits and sacred to the Cherokee as the home of the Nunne hi. Reading on, Billy found that the Nunne hi were credited with protecting the Cherokee during the time of the Indian Removal Act of 1838 and with defeating a team of Union soldiers during the Civil War.

Protection—that's what Billy needed, and now he knew where he could find it. When he called Gwen to let her know what he'd discovered, she said, "As strange as it seems, it sounds like you're on the right track. Just take care of yourself."

She was sick of saying it, and he was probably tired of hearing it, but what else could she say? If this were the beginning of any normal relationship, it would have been over before it even started, and while they seemed to be together now, Gwen wasn't sure for how long.

"I'll call you when I get back," he said.

Leaving town on a crisp spring day, Billy felt strangely at ease. Things at the house had gotten more complicated, but that was to be expected. In Mexico, it was a relief to be alone, but he was dragged out of there and thrown into here and forced back into the cauldron to take more heat.

As Billy continued west, he shed his old skin. He wasn't the whole universe, only part of it, a small fiber in the mesh that encircles galaxies, ensnares planets, and weaves stories throughout space and time. Billy didn't invent it, and he sure hadn't perfected it, so he just walked valiantly along like a cosmic traveler in search of a new star.

Keeping a quickened pace, Billy was heating up. Wondering where Ray was, his stride mysteriously slowed as a black car drifted to the side of the road and stopped.

"Man, what the hell took you so long, Ray?" asked Billy as he jumped in and shut the door.

With a bloodstained mouth and a red rose pinned securely to his lapel, Ray's suit was perfectly pressed. The hulking mass of a man then faced Billy only to reveal a new, grotesque lesion: a raggedly empty eye socket.

"I had other business," replied Ray in a gothic drone.

"Well, it's good to see you, no pun intended," said Billy to no audible reply. None was expected as Ray sped back onto the road.

Billy was glad to see Ray, first, because it meant he was doing the right thing, and second, because it was really cool to be driven around by a dead guy in a spaceship on wheels.

"Where we going, Ray?"

"We're going to Pilot Mountain."

And just to see what other information he could glean, Billy asked, "What are we going to do there?"

"I'm not doing anything there."

"I'm sorry, Ray," corrected Billy. "What am I going to do there?"

"You're going to meet somebody."

Now that actually gave Billy chills as he then asked, "Who?"

With his new deformity on full display, Ray again looked to Billy and answered, "You're going to meet a Cherokee Indian medicine man."

After what he'd seen and read, it made sense that he was going to a place of power. He was in need of wisdom and protection, but maybe he'd get neither. Maybe he was finally being driven to his death. Or to the place where the final nail would be hammered into his shoddy, dilapidated coffin.

Billy was cautious. On the previous rides, he had been going somewhere familiar, but now that he was facing the unknown, he needed some answers.

"Am I going to die, Ray?"

"Eventually."

"Am I going to die here is what I meant," snapped Billy.

"I can't answer that," moaned Ray.

"But do you know?"

There was no reply, only hills, trees, tiny wooden shacks, and, in the distance, a giant stone monolith rising from the forest floor, showing, or piloting, the way.

Nearing dusk, the park was empty and Billy wasn't surprised. He couldn't very well search out an ancient medicine man with the trails full of red-faced tourists.

Coasting through the parking lot, Ray slowed as Billy prepared to exit.

"What am I supposed to do?" asked Billy.

"I don't know."

But Ray stopped anyway, and Billy hopped out. The car then turned an eerie shade of purple and shot dramatically through an electric field, leaving him stranded in the middle of nowhere. As the smoke cleared, Billy wondered what would happen if nothing happened. *It'll be a hell of a walk home*, he thought.

In an empty parking lot, staring at a big round rock, Billy felt compelled to walk. So he did. As he poked around the base of the mountain, the trail he was on suddenly closed in, and he was stuck. Pushing feverishly through the dense, thorny brush, Billy guessed he was supposed to get lost. Hopefully he'd be found as well, because he didn't want to live like this, at the whim of the spirits with his loved ones under fire. It was sheer insanity, and Billy needed to keep moving.

Forging on, Billy heard a faint drumbeat as he finally reached a stunning vista. In awe of the sheer rock faces and giant trees, he imagined a creator, a benevolent protector, and then a destroyer, a malicious trickster, much like the Nunne hi, who were known to exist in the same woods.

Then, in the shimmering glow of sunset, Billy saw a crouched figure bounding vigorously through the undergrowth. First at a distance, a final powerful leap brought the shadowy specter dangerously close. Showing a creased, earthen face, his eyes gleamed with visions of birds in flight and great migrations pulsing through the plains. His expressionless gaze then revealed birth, death, and decay and oceans grinding against craggy cliffs turning into huge snowcapped peaks racing through silver skies. As the images sped into a blur, his blank stare became a searing red light with a menacing, hypnotic blink.

Captured in the shaman's ominous eyes, Billy soared high above the mountains and over small peaceful villages. Huge, bustling cities clouded with smog fell into oil-covered oceans as warring armies marched through smoldering fields. Seeds grew into towering forests as storms moved dangerously across the land. A lone car then tumbled fatefully through the trees as a faint chant reverberated against the hard stone walls of an ancient cave.

In the heart of a raging fire, a cloaked Indian circled the flames before dissolving into a caustic mist. Billy was then thrust into the fire, but he didn't burn. He watched the flames tear at his flesh, but it didn't hurt. And as the chants grew louder and more intense, the wail of a train became the crash of a car as he rose high into the sky. Weightless in a calm oasis, the air was clear and the water clean and people gathered in joy rather than in violence. Peacefully floating, Billy was suddenly trapped in a padded white room with the same medicine man.

"This is the room you've made for yourself, a place with no escape," said the shaman.

"I didn't make it. They made it for me."

"You grew the walls and sheltered in the shelter. You tried to hide away from all that is."

"Nothing is," said Billy.

The shaman then waved his cane, and the scene shifted into deep red canyons and dry desert cactus.

"Is this a different room?" asked the shaman.

"No," answered Billy.

"Why?"

"Because I'm still me."

"And why are you still you and the room still the same and things still unchanged?"

"Because I'm human, and I can't be as strong as I need to be and I have to fail and I need to learn."

"But you also need to help."

"And I also need to survive."

"In the fire you were given protection, in flight you were given vision and in your travels you were given time, so you must use it wisely."

As the ceremony closed, the shaman then gave an affirmation. With his ancient eyes trained on Billy, in a hearty rhythmic voice he said, "Look forward and not away. Move onward to live another day."

Raising his cane and pushing it firmly into Billy's forehead, the shaman spoke in an ancient, unknown dialect and then disappeared.

Curiously absent before, the sightseers had arrived in force as Billy felt the pitter patter of tiny stones against his tender face.

"Evan, Julie, leave the poor guy alone," said a spectacled dad holding a canteen and a camera.

Shirtless with a bandana tied tightly around his head, Billy slowly opened his eyes to the barrage. Perched precariously on yesterday's vista, he was dangerously close to the edge.

While Evan found a suitable stick to poke his sister Julie with, the father offered a hand.

"I remember my younger days. I'd be lying if I said I'd never passed out before."

Billy then rose unusually tall and said, "Thanks, sir. Hopefully this will be the last time."

"Oh, you'll be chasing a couple of these around in no time," replied the dad, running off to corral his kids.

As he walked down the trail, Billy ran a finger over his forehead and felt the slight bump from the knotty cane. The scars on his arms and legs had healed though.

Look forward and not away, move onward to live another day, thought Billy, remembering the words of the shaman. He also recalled soaring through the sky and dancing in the fire , and then the white room.

Following his previous two encounters, first at Chichen Itza and then in Celia's backyard, Billy was drained, beat up, even, but now he felt energized. Hungry and dehydrated, he skipped past the park rangers for a long swig of water and then continued on.

Minus his shirt, Billy wondered where the tight, colorful bandana came from. It was red and yellow, so it may have signified fire, but he wasn't sure. He didn't need to be sure though; it didn't matter. He had protection.

Trudging down a narrow shoulder of road, Billy wondered if the power was weakening. Maybe the faucet had turned off and the water dried up. After all, he couldn't expect a creepy car to show up every time he left his house. Regular people didn't get that kind of treatment. Celebrities maybe, but not guys down to their last dime.

The sun was getting hotter and the day later as Billy started to lose his bearings. Nothing looked familiar. Not like the Atlantic Ocean with its meandering currents and gentle tides. Billy missed it, especially walking through the heat of another strange day.

Dreaming about tiki bars and flip flops, in a slow, suspicious fashion, Ray finally appeared.

"I was beginning to wonder, Ray," started Billy, of course to no reply.

Ray just stared ahead and drove. His appearance was, of course, impeccable, except for his open wound and missing eye.

"You're looking good today, Ray," offered Billy.

"You didn't die," replied Ray.

"What was your first clue?"

There was no answer, and of course, none was expected. Billy knew how to get him talking though as he asked, "Where we going, Ray?"

"We're going to Celia's."

"What are we going to do there?"

"I'm not doing anything there," answered Ray as Billy grinned.

Heading home, Billy hoped Celia was there to see the car again. She was, and this time she had a camera. Keeping her distance so as not to spook the driver, Celia couldn't help but notice an empty eye socket through the windshield.

As the car slowed to a stop, Billy wondered if this might be their last meeting, but Ray wouldn't say.

"Am I going to see you again, Ray?"

"I don't know," answered Ray, this time showing his whole gruesome face.

"Well, thanks then."

Billy wondered what happened to Ray. Since they were in a car, Billy wondered if maybe that's where he'd met his end. And what had held him up? Why was he in limbo? Was he incapable of passing or was it sheer will, a resolve not to leave until something was done? Or was he just a heavenly messenger called into duty by something greater? Maybe they were both in the same boat, doomed to a life of servitude until something was finished. If that was the case, Billy needed to hurry up and finish it.

And sure enough, with his landing gear up, Ray's car turned a shiny purple before speeding into a cloud of sparks, unfortunately sucking Celia's camera into the force field as well.

"Hey," she bellowed as her camera sailed off and landed in a far-away field.

"Curiosity killed the cat," said Billy.

"Yeah, but it didn't break the cat's camera."

He didn't bother to say that cats don't have cameras as Celia walked to retrieve the damaged hardware.

Billy had thanked Ray again, but he wasn't sure for what—for giving him a ride or maybe for putting this whole charade in motion. Maybe he and his spirit buddies were conspiring to drive Billy crazy, which was impossible because Billy was already crazy. Maybe that's why he was chosen, because any normal person would have already thrown in the towel.

But Billy had already quit. He'd already been stripped, so now he could build it back up, piece by piece, brick by brick. He could make it better. He could make it stronger. If he survived, that is.

He needed to talk to Gwen, but that could wait. In search of his notebook, he wanted to get something down.

With a full head of steam, Billy launched into his latest entry. Putting pen to paper in the most fanatical way, after twenty minutes of quick-fire text, Billy was done. Drenched in the evening's mysterious events, he tried to summarize things as eloquently as possible. After all, it wasn't really for the public—it was for him.

With Celia calling from the bottom of the stairs, Billy grabbed a shirt and headed down. He'd been shirtless for quite a while, so it felt good to have something on.

"How's the camera?" asked Billy. "Did it survive?"

"Would you survive if you dropped a hundred feet out of the sky?"

Maybe, thought Billy. He wasn't sure.

"Well at least there's something to grade."

"Great," said Celia, waving her little red pen.

Opening the page, Celia read:

There was something in the air.

There was trouble in the night.

From a different darkness came a different light.

From other places came other people, ageless, faceless, and wise.

And like the sun they'd rise, and like the light they'd shine, and like the rivers they'd run, and like the time they'd pass, and like the message they'd speak of death and rebirth and harmony and energy and unity.

From the edge of the earth, looking over the ledge, there was a fear that changed into being that turned into me and moved into you and remembered a time when all was well in the world.

Alone in a white, sterile room wondering how it would end, the medicine man waved his magic wand, and I awoke on a round, floating rock, vulnerable, immeasurable, and alive.

With a pen clasped in her mouth, Celia wanted to strike, but she didn't want to hit too hard. Billy was still learning about life and about other things as well. She also enjoyed the words. She didn't really understand, but maybe she would someday as she lowered her pen and wrote, "C+, getting better."

FLIGHT

Billy called Gwen, and she was on the way. Eager to hear about the latest adventure, she was also worried.

Concerned for her safety as well, Gwen wanted to know if Billy had secured any protection. What kind of protection could be guaranteed anyway; which led to the eternal question of how does one go about contacting the ever present for a possible truce. It was hard enough to navigate this world, never mind crossing into another. What if he'd only garnered safety for himself and she was destined to go through life unprotected, terrified by the sights and sounds of another dimension? It wasn't a pleasant thought, so she decided to just drive. After all, she felt better today, hopeful that her collapse was just an isolated incident, or a reaction to her own special powers.

As she again approached the house in the woods, it was sure to be an eventful afternoon. Gwen remembered when she'd first dropped Billy off, half-drunk and exhausted. In a way, she wished things had started differently, that they'd been more predictable. That's what she wanted. She really did like him though.

Walking up to the house, Gwen wasn't sure what to expect. She'd found Billy on the ground the first time, the next in his room, seriously injured, then she passed out.

"Knock, knock," she cheerfully announced.

Billy, just as cheerfully, opened the door to see a beautiful red-haired girl waiting for her guy, or at least that's what he thought. Maybe Gwen wasn't waiting for him at all, maybe she was leaving him.

But she wasn't. She gave him a deep kiss on the lips, forgetting, for the moment, her other concerns. Seeing him standing in front of her, tall and handsome, wearing a strange and colorful bandana, Gwen couldn't help it.

"What's with the buff, hot stuff?" she said to a tired-looking Billy.

She'd never seen him at his best, which was kind of a shame, but maybe he'd never been at his best. *Maybe his best is yet to come,* thought Gwen.

Right away she noticed his knees and elbows had miraculously healed. That was strange, as was the fact that he was even here. Gwen had expected him to be gone for a couple of days, yet here he was, blue eyes sparkling and smiling that same gorgeous smile.

Billy gave her a big hug and replied, "Man, is it great to see you."

"It's great to see you too, lover. Where have you been all of my life?"

"Oh, here and there, riding in flying cars and visiting ancient Indians and soaring through the sky. You know, the usual."

It seemed more fantastical than factual, but with Billy it was somehow believable as Gwen settled in for what was sure to be an interesting story.

Celia made some afternoon tea while Gwen and Billy walked quietly into the kitchen. If Gwen wasn't mistaken, they seemed to be turning into quite a team. Celia could be command and control, and she and Billy the infantry. After all, if the other side had a squad, they'd need one too.

As their meeting commenced, there was a more strategic feel to the gathering. It was evident that Celia had adopted a different stance. No longer the familial type, she seemed to have taken a more serious tone; perhaps sensing the gravity, or maybe feeling like it wasn't just going to go away. It wasn't going to fix itself; it was going to have to be fixed.

"Greetings, Gwen," said Celia with an endearing smile, "before we get into anything else, could I interest you in some tea and crumpets?"

she playfully asked, because there were no crumpets, only pleasant little tea sandwiches neatly arranged on a ceramic platter.

"Lovely," replied Billy.

"Of course," added Gwen, even though she wasn't really hungry. She couldn't be. She was more unnerved at the prospect of sitting for their first battle-plan.

"So, how was work, Gwen. Did you make it on time?"

"Sure," answered Gwen, "with no real help from Billy boy over there."

"I've been a handful lately, I guess," said Billy. "I really am sorry to keep messing things up though."

"It's not important. There's more interesting things going on, I guess."

"You guess?" asked Celia with a raised eyebrow.

Celia really was different today, or at least Gwen saw her differently. She saw a more strong and protective side. But she wasn't protecting Billy from Gwen; she seemed to be protecting him from the unknown, which was a much bigger job.

"I know," corrected Gwen, "but there's still a life to live," she continued, just to establish that things connected to her mattered as well.

"Yes," agreed Celia, "we all have to continue, even through the strangeness of the times."

"That's easy for you to say. I'm the one getting beat up," offered Billy.

"And I just started fainting for some unknown reason, so I guess we've all got some skin in the game," countered Gwen. "And by the way, Billy, what happened to the scars?"

"On my knees and elbows?"

"Yes," said Gwen, lightly tracing the places where the cuts used to be.

"Disappeared miraculously, so it seems. I need to bottle it up and sell it."

With things a bit more relaxed, Celia said, "Billy's my nephew, and I love him. We've been through a lot together."

Billy slowly nodded as Gwen listened.

"I took care of Billy for a while after his father passed away in a fishing accident. Billy died the same week, but he came back to life, visited, or saved, by angels. He had a dangerously high fever, which led to a febrile seizure, and I thought we'd lost him. We were rushed to the emergency room, and by some strange miracle, he recovered. Following the sickness, Billy recited a passage from the bible. I didn't know it then, but it was from Proverbs: 'For he shall give his angels charge over you, to keep you in all your ways,' I believe. He was only four years old. He hadn't even seen a bible yet."

"So she says," added Billy, just to minimize the event.

"Well, he doesn't remember, but I do. And it was terrifying, but we got through it. And after everything stabilized, I came back to North Carolina to finish my degree, and Billy stayed at the beach. When I heard he was coming to live with me, I was thrilled, but then when I saw how he arrived, I was mortified."

"That's when she first met Ray."

"That's right," agreed Celia, with a raised finger, "that's when I first met Ray, and guess what?"

"I met Ray again, earlier today. Only this time, instead of just blood streaming down his mouth, he had an empty eye socket."

"An empty eye socket?" repeated Gwen.

"He was missing an eye."

"But he could still drive," added Billy.

"Precisely," agreed Celia. "It's paramount that the dead guy driving a flying car has adequate vision. But the things that are happening right now are downright freaky, and while I can't say that I'm not enjoying it, I'm also concerned. When Billy first arrived, I was somewhat skeptical. Even after seeing the flying car and the deceased driver, I tried to explain it away. But this afternoon when the car and the driver again blasted off into a cloud of sparks, my camera blasted off as well."

"Was the camera OK?" asked Gwen, as it seemed to be the most logical question.

"No, the camera was not OK," answered Celia. "But I digress. A unique situation has come to be, and the sooner we make peace with it, the better. So from now on, Billy's not the only spirit hunter—we're all spirit hunters!"

"Oo-rah," shouted Billy.

"Sweet!" exclaimed Gwen. After all, she hadn't had a problem with the spirits before, but it seems like she did now. Or maybe they had a problem with her.

"Anyway, I seem to be immune to the reaches of the unknown, so the best that I can do is offer support."

That's quite a step back, thought Gwen as she asked, "What does that mean for us?"

"It means that from here on out, you're going to have to put aside your former truths. You're going to have to forget what you thought made sense and embrace the senseless."

Gwen listened but didn't quite understand. It seemed like she was joining a cult or that she'd already joined one. But it was Billy, and she trusted him. Even at the frat party when he was inebriated, he was the perfect gentleman. She knew Billy hadn't been looking for anyone, and as much as it pained her to think it, she had. She wasn't looking for a high priest of the bizarre, but things don't always go as planned. And she was a little weird herself.

"She's right," said Billy. "The life you thought you knew—well, it's not gone, but it has most definitely changed."

That much was obvious, especially after she'd passed out the other day, but she needed to change. She carried around too much baggage and too much blame. Instead of smooth sailing, she'd been smashing through the whitecaps, and it was tiring. It was also time for something new as Gwen asked, "So what happened?"

"Well, my first episode occurred at Chichen Itza, some forty miles outside of Cancun. As I mentioned before, I mistakenly ingested a rather powerful hallucinogen, and in a manner of speaking, the skies opened up."

"It started to storm?"

"Yes, it started to storm, but for some reason I stayed, imagining the thunder and lightning as gods and goddesses debating on whether to save something or not. And then I woke, tattered and torn with the phrase *to save a son* emblazoned on my soul."

Celia was more proud of Billy than she'd ever been. That he could pit himself against the elements to discover something mystical was impressive. It suddenly struck her that he was very important, and that this was very important.

"Anyway, when the book you brought over compared Pilot Mountain to the stone observatory, El Caracol at Chichen Itza, I was drawn there to learn more of the mystery. And what's been consistent throughout this whole exercise is that the signs keep coming and I keep investigating. I'm putting myself out there to see what happens. I first ran into Ray walking home from Orlando International Airport. He pulled over in a creepy black car and knew exactly where I needed to go. So the next time I needed to be somewhere, Ray again picked me up and brought me here, to you."

"Thanks, Ray," chimed Celia and Gwen.

"And the other day, when I needed to go to Pilot Mountain, I started out on foot, and sure enough, Ray appeared. Only this time, in addition to blood streaming down his mouth, he was missing an eye. But do you know what was most intriguing?"

"What?" they both asked.

"He knew that I was going to Pilot Mountain and also that I'd meet a medicine man. So, at the base of the mountain, at dusk, I started to explore. Finding a well-traveled trail, the path suddenly collapsed into a twisted wall of shrubbery with no way out. Fighting through the undergrowth, I came to a steep cliff only to hear that same familiar drumbeat. The shaman first appeared at a distance, and then in an instant, we stood face to face. He looked old, like the earth parched by an angry sun, and as we faced one another, his eyes showed visions of birth, death, and decay turning into the pulse of a hypnotic red light. Then I took flight. High above the earth, I saw villages and cities, polluted and sickened, before landing in a cave where the medicine man danced through a tremendous inferno. Thrust suddenly into the flames, I too weaved through the fire, but I wasn't burned. And through the blaze came scenes of a smashed car, as the medicine man and I then sat peacefully in a white room."

"What did he say?" asked Celia

"He said I had created the room for myself, and then I said that they'd created it for me. He then said that I'd reinforced it and tried to hide from all that is. I said that nothing is. Then the room turned into a desert, where he told me that the fire had given me protection, the flight had given me vision, and the travel had given me time so I needed to use it wisely."

"That's good," said Gwen.

"It is, but he also gave me an affirmation. It simply said to, 'Look forward and not away. Move onward to live another day.'"

"Look forward and not away," repeated Gwen.

"Move onward to live another day," finished Celia.

As Billy slowly unspooled the bandana he'd received at the ceremony, it revealed a second long scarf hidden inside. Was it for Gwen? It made sense that she would be included, because he'd gone there for her as well.

Then, as the scarf fell away, a cloud of silver dust encircled Gwen in wisps of translucent fiber, clinging to her and then releasing into a shower of light. Billy and Celia watched in amazement as it spoke in an inaudible whisper and then drifted through an open window into the waiting sky.

Staring in awe, they looked to one another and again into the emptiness, before they suddenly joined hands. There was a new focus in the room. A new energy moved through the house. It was clean and clear and spoke only to the good that exists in the midst of all else.

Gwen hoped they weren't spooked. She'd wanted to keep some things hidden as she asked, "Did you guys see that?"

"Yes" and "Yeah" were the two astonished answers.

"What did it say?" asked Billy.

"It told me to look forward and not away, and then it sang something I couldn't understand. It was a slight voice, and it spoke to something powerful, because I'm happy for a change. I hope it lasts."

"That was the most beautiful thing I've ever seen," remarked Celia. "The flowing silver strands were majestic. I feel like I'm in an enchanted forest covered in fairy dust. It's kind of hard to understand."

"It's not meant to be understood, only believed. Without belief it doesn't work. Without faith it doesn't appear, and without trust it doesn't exist. No one tells flowers to bloom or birds to fly south; they do it on their own, just like we can do this. Believe," implored Billy.

There was more to discuss. Things were evolving, but they still lacked direction. Gwen had her armor, but did Billy have his? He had half the bandana, but maybe his wasn't the important half. It also seemed that Gwen knew more about strange occurrences than she'd initially let on.

"Well, how are you Billy? You must be exhausted. I've never known a mere mortal to take a journey like that. How are you holding up?"

"I'm tired and amazed and enlightened and scared. Everything you might imagine following a trip to eternity and back in the blink of an eye."

"Do you feel lucky?" asked Celia.

"Lucky and cursed; same as always, although I must be gaining a little strength, I just hope it's enough."

"You'll know when the time comes."

"I need to know now. The medicine man said I was protected, but he didn't say for how long."

"As long as it takes," guessed Gwen. "It seems like everything's falling into place, perfect in nature, open for you to become the hero you've always wanted to be."

"How do you know so much about me? Maybe I enjoy being the underdog, the mangy mutt that just might bite if you get too close."

"Because it shows in your eyes, in your desire to win and to be useful. There's nothing wrong with it, as long as it helps rather than hurts."

"Well it hurts, but I like the pain. It's something I've always had and maybe something I always will have."

"You'll find happiness, Billy. Tonight, under the stars. So let's go!" exclaimed Gwen with a twinkle in her eye.

Perhaps due to the pixie dust or possibly because of the scarf wrapped tightly around her wrist, all Gwen wanted was to gallop wildly through the countryside. She wanted to grow with the flowers and buzz with the bees. She wanted to shine with the sun and fall with the rain and breathe in the cool Carolina air. She wouldn't be alive forever, but she was now and she wanted to feel like it, not like some sad sack moping around town.

Billy shouldn't feel too bad, anyway. Sure, things were strange, but he could handle it. He was chosen for it. And some people just function better as outcasts. Billy was the consummate antihero, the lovable rogue who was playing the part perfectly.

"You'll survive, Billy," she said.

"How do you know?" he answered.

"Because you don't have a choice."

"I could give up."

"You wouldn't."

"I could quit."

"You couldn't."

"I could leave and never return."

"But where would you go, Billy? Back to Florida or maybe to Mexico? And what about us?" asked Gwen, fluttering her pretty eyes.

Full of beauty and life, she was nature speaking directly to him, and Billy needed to listen. Gwen was new to the game though. He'd have to see how she felt after being run out of town, besmirched, ripped off, and beaten. But that wouldn't happen to her, it was only for him as he followed her out into the night.

"I wouldn't leave," said Billy. "I just get a little unsure at times."

"All heroes do, until they learn how to use their powers. Then there's no stopping them."

"The unstoppable Billy Winslow. It's got a nice ring to it."

"It does, doesn't it?"

So they fluttered down the road, looking for Ray, the medicine man, and whoever else wanted to show up.

"No fainting tonight. Tonight we party, for we know not what tomorrow brings."

"A headache probably," replied Billy.

"Maybe for you, pretty boy," she announced as they entered her favorite bar for a shot and a beer.

"To the great Billy Winslow!" she exclaimed.

"Here, here," replied one with a raised glass.

"Who the hell is Billy Winslow?" offered another, as yet another said, "Don't know, but she's cute."

Billy had to laugh. He was a leader with no followers, a shepherd with no sheep, a general with no army, but that was OK because he had what he needed: a pretty girl and a bar tab.

As they moved to an outdoor patio for burgers and more beer, Billy guessed he could grow to enjoy college life.

"Is it always like this?"

"Pretty much, except it's usually more crowded. School's out now, so most of the students are home, but when they get back, watch out."

"It's chaotic."

"Controlled chaos," answered Gwen, "but there's always something going on, not to mention the basketball team."

"Basketball, eh?" echoed Billy.

"Yeah, basketball," repeated Gwen. "You got something against that?"

"No, no. I'm just kind of wondering why you haven't asked if I play. I mean, I'm pretty tall."

"Well, do you play?"

"I used to."

"Were you any good?"

"I used to be."

She then queried, "Where did you play?"

"I played in high school."

"Well, this ain't high school, pal," muttered Gwen.

"No, this isn't high school," agreed Billy.

"No, it's not high school," she repeated, "and that ship's probably sailed. You can obviously do a lot of things, but if you think you're good enough to get on that court, you need to think again."

"You think?"

"Yeah, I think," barked Gwen. "What's with you, anyway, Billy?"

He paused, perhaps to choose his words more wisely.

"I have a feeling this whole thing is somehow tied into basketball. When I was in Mexico, for some strange reason, I started playing again."

"Don't they play soccer in Mexico?" asked Gwen as kind of a rhetorical question.

"Yes, they play soccer in Mexico, but they also play basketball, especially at the resorts. They have outdoor courts, and they're hot."

"Sounds fun."

"It was fun, but it wasn't. It felt more like a compulsion, but at the wrong time. Like you said, that ship sailed. I had aspirations, but I started doing other things. Or maybe I just knew I wasn't good enough."

"I didn't mean it that way."

"No, no, that's fine. It wasn't meant to be, but in Mexico, I was a new player. I was stronger and faster, and for some reason, more motivated. I even put a team together, and we played a couple of nights a week. Some of the local kids even got involved. They didn't want to pick up the ball at first, but they got the hang of it."

Gwen understood. In soccer a handball is quite a serious infraction. But more concerned with his time on the basketball court she asked, "So why do you think that has any connection to this?"

"Because in my dreams, I've seen a one-armed black man bouncing a basketball. It's loud and piercing, and it last occurred the night before

I came here, to one of the most storied places in basketball history. I toured campus and ended up in front of the Dean Dome watching the coach make his rounds. It was strange."

Gwen gave it some thought. What Billy said was right; they were in a hotbed for college basketball. If one wanted to play or to be seen playing, this was the place to be. But there were still more questions than answers.

"We'll just have to wait and see," she said, "but even if nothing else happens, I'm glad you came up here, Billy Winslow, and that you met me, or that I met you, because it's been like nothing else, ever."

"I'm glad to be here and to be with you too, especially tonight, when we can feel normal for a change."

It wasn't the response she'd expected, but Billy was obviously on a mission, and maybe she was too. Gazing into one another's eyes, she knew the normalcy would soon end. It just wasn't a normal kind of night.

As the town began to clear out, Billy and Gwen brushed gently against one another, stumbling toward Gwen's house. They didn't have a car—Gwen's coupe was at Celia's—but they didn't need one. While they marveled at the day's earlier events, someone else's car took a wide corner and careened dangerously toward them. Accelerating before impact, Billy quickly brushed Gwen aside as the car smashed brutally into his legs. Flying spastically through the air before crashing back to earth, Billy miraculously stuck a perfect landing and then rushed quickly over to Gwen.

"Are you OK?" he frantically exclaimed.

"I should be asking you the same thing," answered Gwen, surrounded by shattered glass and radiator coolant.

Billy then looked at his legs and they were unscathed. The car hadn't hit anything else, yet there it sat, smashed up and hemorrhaging fluids. The airbags had deployed. The driver wasn't leaving and as usual, Billy and Gwen really needed to talk.

Running quickly through the streets, Gwen exclaimed, "Oh, my goodness, what in the hell happened!"

"I just got killed, I guess."

"Wait a second, you weren't dead already, were you?"

"I don't think so."

It wasn't the answer she'd expected, but the question concerning Billy's protection had most certainly been answered. After what she'd just witnessed, he seemed to be ready for pretty much anything. They both were.

Like superheroes waiting for their next assignment, they poked in and out of the darkness, hidden in plain sight. Like freaks from another planet, they couldn't tell anyone. It was the only way they could cope, knowing that it was for good instead of evil. Still reeling from the night's events, they wondered if anyone could identify them. Would they be hunted down and put behind bars where they belonged?

Billy was beginning to have some serious doubts about his sanity, but at the moment, he really wanted to know if he could fly. Wild eyed and alive, he jumped valiantly into the air and then fell to the ground, laughing hysterically with Gwen quick to join in.

Singing songs, they skipped along with a newfound energy until they finally reached Gwen's cluttered little apartment. In the relative safety, Billy was still coming to terms with the most recent revelations as Gwen plotted her next move. She felt better with Billy. She was more at ease. With the things he'd been going through, Gwen wanted to show some of her own uniqueness.

The place was littered with densely packed boxes of all shapes and size, a perfect canvas for Gwen's most intimate art. Slowly lifting her hand, the contents of the boxes gently rose and began finding their way into the closets, the cabinets, and finally into the drawers. Billy watched in amazement as the boxes then folded and stacked themselves neatly in an empty corner. Gwen probably could have floated them out to recycling, but she didn't want anyone to see.

"Wow," said Billy, "You're right, this has been like nothing else, ever."

"I told you, lover," replied Gwen as she grabbed Billy by the collar and led him into her room.

Then, like cosmic voyagers, they sailed fearlessly through the heavens, testing each other's strength before landing safely in a cocoon, waiting to hatch.

Wrapped tightly in a plain white sheet with a dry mouth and a headache, Billy woke first and asked, "Where are we?"

Gwen wearily turned to the side and answered, "We're at my house, remember? We took a bus into town."

"Whose bright idea was that? Mrs. fairy dust, I presume?"

"Yes, it was my idea, and thank you so much for tagging along, Mr. fairy dust."

Billy couldn't help but laugh. It had been fun, and after all, he didn't have to go to work because he didn't have a job, but Gwen, on the other hand, always seemed to have to speed off.

"Are you working today?" asked Billy.

"Superheroes don't work."

"Are we superheroes or just faithful servants making the world a better place?"

"Well, you can be the servant if you want, but I'm going to rule the world," she said, jumping naked out of bed and raising her hand to the sky as her bedside table crashed clumsily into the ceiling.

"Oops," remarked Gwen, "guess I'm going to have to work on that."

"I guess so," said Billy, "but I don't want this to change anything."

"It won't, because I've always had this."

"What!"

"It's true. I just haven't been able to show anyone. I kept it hidden, but when I met you, I sensed something different. When I passed out at your house, I knew there was an opposing energy involved, but I still couldn't say anything. But after last night, when you destroyed the car—"

"The car hit me."

"Excuse me, when the car hit you, I knew that I could finally trust you."

Billy thought back to when they first met, when she'd shown up at the party, how she was so suspect of his motivations, and how she didn't flat out run when he told her what that was happening. And then how she didn't finally leave when something happened to her.

"No wonder you didn't leave."

"Well let's just say there were things you couldn't tell me and also things I couldn't tell you. But it's all in the open now."

"But I wasn't born with this."

"I don't think that matters. Whether you want it or not, you got it. Now you need to learn how to use it."

If this was a test, Billy didn't know if he was passing, but he wouldn't quit. He couldn't quit now, not with his newfound powers and his newfound girlfriend's powers. He seemed to have some kind of a responsibility, but to what he wasn't sure.

"How else does your power work?" asked Billy. "Did you know I was coming?"

"I didn't know, but I went through a power shift."

"A power shift?"

"Yeah, things were off kilter, polarities changed. It's happened before, but only in times of struggle or arrival. I can't tell the future or even read minds. I can just move things."

"But when we met, you must have felt something."

"I did. It was strong and it pulled me to you, I just hope it doesn't push me away as well."

"I won't let it, at least not without a fight."

"You promise?" replied Gwen.

"I promise," said Billy.

GWEN'S DILEMMA

Morning light shone softly through the towering oaks that encircled Gwen's horseshoe-shaped apartment complex. Songbirds chirped comfortably in the canopy as the world slowly started to wake. Spring had definitely sprung as the sprawling Southern landscape showed azalea in full bloom and delicately flowering irises. It was a charming town with narrow, sleepy streets alongside bustling city centers. Civil War markers commemorated forgotten events in quiet neighborhoods as people started to move about.

With Gwen beside him breathing a soothing cadence, there was a lot to think about, and Billy was thinking about it all. In the big picture, it should end equitably, but what if it didn't? What if it never ended? What if it kept going on and on in a random display of unearthly events? Billy wasn't sure he could handle that; he'd have to join a circus or just kick cars in for a living. And what would come next, his aunt Celia flying through the sky or maybe his mom would teleport into town? Billy hoped it didn't come to that, because he needed to maintain at least some sense of normalcy. The weirder the better, Billy had always thought, but that was in theory; this was real.

Putting it quickly into perspective, he'd been run out of town, with his strength at an all-time low, and now here he was, flying through the sky, jumping over cars, and sleeping with beautiful superheroes. Things had most certainly changed.

Billy also wondered about the changes. He wondered if they'd help or if it was all for naught. Something told him that it wasn't all for nothing and that he still had a job to do. Billy thought about his new-found importance, and it reminded him that with great power comes great responsibility.

He then thought about Gwen and his responsibility to her. She'd shared something special with him, and he'd have to act accordingly. If he didn't, she may never share anything again. He wasn't the same either. Even if his powers ceased and the visions faded, he'd be forever changed. He needed to stay centered, because in spite of all that didn't make sense, a lot did: the immense energy of the universe and the idea that it's there for all to see. In the majesty of nature, all questions are asked and answered. In the relevance of time, all things begin and end. But energy survives and spirits endure, and Billy believed. There was an ebb and flow to everything, and he sensed a precarious halfway point. He'd gotten his weapons and had his vision. Now it was time for some new revelations.

Billy felt different today, more complete and not quite so vulnerable. He also felt dazed from the night before. It was the morning, and oddly enough, Billy was no longer the strangest game in town. He needed to reassess. Things had happened, things that he'd never thought possible, yet there he was in the midst of it all, waiting for the next shoe to fall. He'd listened to gods and goddesses fight in the sky. He'd asked where to go and was then plastered by a map of Florida. He'd had dreams and visions of car crashes. He'd driven with a ghostly chauffeur listening to a song about Carolina. He'd had dreams of one-armed basketball players. He'd been run over by an imaginary train and spun out of a chair. He'd taken a vision quest with a medicine man, destroyed a car with his legs, and then went to his girlfriend's house only to witness her levitate and unload boxes with the flick of a wrist. To say that things were abnormal would be an understatement.

Still, he was in bed with an attractive woman who seemed to like him, so it couldn't be all bad. He did have some questions though, things that only she could answer. He gave her a light shake and asked, "Hey, honey, where's the coffee?"

"Ah, I don't know where it went."

It was just an innocent question, but an important one all the same. If Billy didn't have some coffee soon, he might really go crazy.

"Can't you just summon it to the counter or something?" asked Billy.

"Is that what I do, Billy, summon things?"

"What I meant to say was good morning, sunshine."

"Oh, so sweet, honey. Good morning to you as well," replied Gwen. "But if you ever wake me up on my day off again, it might not be such a good morning."

What, would I be thrown through a window? thought Billy as Gwen quickly said, "I heard that. I told you I couldn't read minds, but what I meant to say is that I can't usually read minds."

"Figures," replied Billy. "But I asked about work last night, and you didn't give a straight answer."

"Maybe it's because I wasn't straight."

"I guess neither of us were. We were kings and queens, gods and goddesses, mystic travelers in distant galaxies chasing dreams and fantasies."

"I thought we were just boyfriend and girlfriend on a date, two normal people out for a night on the town."

It was a sobering comment for such a revealing night, but Billy understood. He was new to the paranormal, but Gwen obviously wasn't. He was eager to test his strengths and abilities, but he could also imagine being born with a condition, trying to understand it, and then having to hide it.

"We were," agreed Billy, "more than anything else."

Gwen smiled and then tugged Billy beneath the sheets for a little more discovery. After all, they had plenty of time to talk, but not enough time to explore. And who knew what the future held, and if it would even be her and him. But they were together now, so they made the best of it in her small, charming apartment.

This time Gwen was up first, and Billy finally smelled some coffee. Discombobulated as usual, he wasn't even sure what day it was. Truth be told, he didn't care what day it was, only that he was alive and in love.

Gwen moved through the kitchen like a dancer, with each choreographed step perfectly placed. Her hair had a delicate sheen that sparkled in the noonday sun. Smaller than Billy but by no means short, Gwen seemed to have more secrets than he did. Things had only heated up for him in the last few months; she'd had a whole lifetime of it.

Gwen was no ordinary girl, and Billy didn't know if she was his or just part of the story. Was she meant for him, or was she just another variable, one of the planets caught in his orbit? Whatever the case, Billy resolved to enjoy it while it lasted, because truth be told, he didn't know what his expiration date might be. He wasn't sure how long he'd be hanging around. Maybe he was on a suicide mission, and everyone would live but him—or in spite of him.

And what about what Gwen had done? That was perhaps more interesting than how he'd smashed a car; and then how she didn't really want to talk about it. He understood, although at some point, they'd need to talk about it. He also wondered if maybe he'd need her powers, or if she offered some kind of protection. It was all really confusing, but also interesting.

As Gwen poured a couple cups of coffee, Billy slowly wandered out to the porch. She had a nice patio where they could sit and see how the neighborhood worked. There were couples with dogs, families with baby strollers, single joggers working up a sweat, and walkers out for an afternoon stroll. Then there was Gwen and Billy on a second-floor patio, drinking coffee and wondering what to say.

Attractive and athletic, Gwen and Billy blended right into the college scene. They looked the part, and Gwen actually was the part, but with an added twist. Billy playfully wondered if he should enroll. He had a few credits under his belt, but he was obviously on a different track. He needed to stay malleable and available and open to the next spiritual transaction. Billy didn't want to punch in and say, "Hi, how was your weekend?" He didn't want to take lunch at a certain time and then have to clock out and go home. Billy wanted his life to be his work.

"Not bad for a barista," said Billy as they gently sipped the hot coffee.

"That's my job," replied Gwen, "not who I am."

"I wasn't saying that's who you are; I was merely complimenting your many talents."

She could have corrected him by saying it was easy and that anyone could do it, but he was trying to be nice, so she merely replied, "Thanks."

"In a past life I was actually a cook."

"In which past life?" she asked. "Don't we all go through a series of permutations, moving from one form into the next until we're finally sitting on a patio drinking coffee and exchanging pleasantries?"

"That's a debate for another time, but what I was trying to say is that I used to be a line cook. I was the guy in the kitchen slinging out greasy fried food to little brats like you."

Gwen finally snickered. Billy had done it. He'd broken through her defenses, and with minimal damage.

"Well, I don't just make coffee; I make all kinds of drinks along with sandwiches and some other lunch items."

"Can you make me lunch?"

"You can make yourself lunch. I think they're hiring."

That shut Billy up. He wasn't looking to get back into a kitchen, at least not yet. But he would cook for a pretty girl.

"What if I make you lunch?"

"Suit yourself, if you can find anything."

With the gauntlet laid, Billy sifted through yet another women's refrigerator. Celia's had been stocked to the gills, but all that seemed to be in Gwen's was sprouted wheat bread, cheddar cheese, lettuce, a tomato, and onions.

So, what to do? thought Billy.

The sprouted wheat bread was coarse but not bad for a grilled cheese. So that's what he'd make, a tomato-and-onion grilled cheese with a side of vegetable straws and some sparkling water. Billy knew better than to ask where the pans were as he rummaged through the kitchen only to find a single, solitary frying pan.

With the sandwiches golden brown and ready to serve, Billy plated his creations and searched out his waiting clientele.

Meeting Gwen back on the porch, Billy slid the plates onto the table and, of course, said, "Enjoy."

"Ah," sounded Gwen, "grilled cheese. My favorite."

She examined the browned edges and the perfectly portioned tomato and onion and instantly recognized the work of a professional. Then, like a chef carefully eyeing a food critic's every move, Billy waited while Gwen ate. As steam rose from the tomato and a string of cheese dangled deliciously from the crispy bread, Billy was satisfied. Now he could eat.

With the both of them now chomping mercilessly away, it was evident that Gwen had also been famished. As they took their last bites along with a swig of cool carbonated water, Billy changed into the ever attentive waiter.

Looking at Gwen's empty plate he said, "I trust that everything was satisfactory?"

"Maybe," replied Gwen, sucking noisily on her teeth. "But I might have to try another just to make sure."

"The kitchen's closed."

"For the day. But what about tomorrow, and the next day, and the day after that?"

Gwen promptly recognized the value in having a man who could cook. It excused his numerous shortcomings.

"Ah, did I say I used to be a cook?"

The cat was out of the bag, and Billy couldn't put it back in. Of the things he'd learned, knowing how to cook was one of the most important. If done right, it was always a treat. From the simplest plates to the most complicated menus, food formed a connection unlike any other, a unique bond between who we are, who we want to be, and who we want to be with. For Billy, the skill had paid dividends. He'd used it throughout the years to make a living and to entertain, and it may have even led him here to do battle with the spirits. Looking at Gwen, Billy saw that it had worked for him again, because there she was, smiling and hopefully ready to talk.

"I'll cook more if you're nice, just ask Celia. I made her blueberry pancakes and bacon the other morning, and lo and behold, my grade went from a D to a C."

"You seem to be the kind of guy that gets your way no matter what," remarked Gwen, not quite ready to capitulate to Billy's charms.

"While it's true that I've had some good fortune, I don't give up, and I've had my share of failure and thoughts that I'd never amount to anything. Talented but blighted, they'd say."

"Well how about being called a circus freak at five and listening to your parents fight over which new school to move you to and what new town to move to."

There it was, she'd broken the ice. Now they could get somewhere.

"It must have been hard," said Billy.

"It was excruciating. I had no one. There was no one like me. No one understood, and it made people scared, not only of me, but of my family as well."

"When my father passed away I felt strange too," replied Billy. "All the other kids had their families at games and at parent-teacher conferences. I know it's not the same, but it still hurt."

Gwen ran a hand through Billy's soft, blond hair as he leaned into her.

"I don't think you get through life without a few bumps and bruises. It's just not how it works."

"I guess not," agreed Gwen, "but it would have been nice to not have a bomb dropped on me."

Billy didn't want it to end there. He wanted her to talk. He wanted Gwen to accept her gift and herself.

"I think it's special."

"Come to think of it, that's how they labeled me—special. That's what the first doctor said. It started early. When I wanted a toy, all I had to do was point and then it would instantly be in my hand. I loved it. Eventually, I could raise a few toys at once."

"A few?"

"Well, I could raise all my toys at once. That's when my mom first saw, and consequently, when she started to drink."

"Are you sure about that?"

"I'm sure about the toys. I can't be completely sure about the drink, but it would make sense."

"I suppose," agreed Billy.

"But anyway, I saw from my parents' reaction that it wasn't considered normal. I tried to suppress it, but couldn't. I was young, and it was just like learning to walk or talk or anything else. How about bringing a plate to the sink, but instead of going in the sink, it ends up smashing through the window and landing on the front lawn? I got paddled for that one. And that wasn't the worst of it. At birthday parties. That was fun. The cake suddenly goes everywhere, and that's Gwen's last invitation to the Andersons' house. And how about going to the principal's office for dumping the teacher's desk after a bad test score? Oh, and what about showing a friend something cool only to be ostracized the next day. Goony Gwen, they called me."

"No!"

"Oh, yeah, and it gets worse. That's only the social stuff. Having to hear the low-frequency fights of my parents after another episode at the psychiatrist, another busted plaque, and then more restraints. Finally, I guess, my father couldn't handle it anymore, because he left. He didn't even say good-bye," added Gwen, her pretty green eyes flooded with emotion.

"It wasn't you," replied Billy, "they had their own problems."

"Well if they did, they only got worse, cause that's when my mom really hit the bottle. I used to shut all of the doors and windows, but she cut her arms breaking out, so I had to stop."

"And, oh!" exclaimed Gwen. "Don't let the high school quarterback see you throw a football sixty yards down the field. That's not going to do much for your popularity."

"Sixty yards?" repeated Billy.

"That's a moderate estimate," smirked Gwen. "Anyway, as time went by, our moves became less frequent, and I learned to control it. I actually started to play sports and that helped dull the powers. It lessened my energy I guess."

"But doesn't it help you on the field?"

"It can, but I don't let it. That would be like cheating, and I'm not a cheat."

Billy's thoughts were in overdrive and oddly enough, they weren't about him. Addressing what Gwen had done with the boxes, Billy asked, "Why didn't you just unpack the boxes without anyone around?"

"Because I don't use it. Not using it gets me out of the habit, and I'm less likely to make a mistake."

It was always Gwen's dilemma, whether to use her powers or not.

Billy then understood the gravity of her situation. That it required discipline, and that it was damaging, and she'd have to deal with it for the rest of her life. Billy further surmised that Gwen might be part of his task as well, part of the reason he'd taken the trip here and to the outer limits, to let the world see her light.

"You want to see someone's expression change, try levitating a coffee cup or getting a gallon of milk from the refrigerator without lifting a finger."

"I have to admit," replied Billy, "there was a time when I would've thought something like that was strange as well. But now, with everything else that's happened, it seems rather commonplace."

"I guess that's why I showed you, but I'm not so sure now," said Gwen with her eyes turned down. "I'm not sure where I would have ended up if not for sports, maybe locked up in a strange room heavily sedated. I wasn't far from it. There were dangerous times, times when it could have gone either way. But to my mother's credit, she protected me. She bought me my first soccer ball. She moved me when things got too tough. She turned everyone away when talk of 'a girl with exceptional powers' and 'strange occurrences' circulated. And more importantly, when the government came to call, that was our quickest move. We actually lived in our car for a couple of months and relied on local churches for food and clothes. It was then and only then when I really learned control. It was out of necessity. It was a matter of life and death."

That was a sobering statement. Having the military complex sniffing around was serious business. It was all serious, and it made what he'd experienced seem trivial.

"I know it's been hard, but there's value in it too. It's a part of you, and it doesn't want to be locked away. It wants to be appreciated and loved and used."

"There's been no value in it. It's been difficult and complicating, and for the most part forgotten, that is, until you came around."

Billy listened. He heard the pain in her voice, and after an extended pause he said, "When I first came here, I was lost. I'd just gone through the most devastating period of my life. I'd put people in danger for personal gain. I lost the only woman I ever loved. I lost my home and my family. I woke up in the rain muttering strange things about strange people, and then strange things started happening. I was being pushed into the path of an oncoming train, and I fully intended to face it alone. I didn't ever want to put anyone else in a compromising position ever again. I'd given up on love until I met you, and even after we met, I still had reservations. But you stayed, and you came back, and I think what I'm trying to say is that I'm so glad to have met you, Gwen. I need you. We're the right people, with the right problems, at the right time. So let's forget about our limitations for a change and just fly."

What an interesting concept, she thought, *feeling good again*. Gwen had held so much in that she'd almost forgotten who she was. She'd forsaken her powers in disgrace.

Gwen had always wanted to meet someone like her, and now, maybe she had. Maybe she'd gone through a shipwreck and washed ashore, and maybe meeting Billy wasn't such a bad thing.

"It's just hard for me to trust. It's so deeply engrained—the pain and the shame. It's hard to readjust."

"Trust the process, it's fun," said Billy as he suddenly vaulted into the courtyard from the second floor, and then jumped back onto the porch to give Gwen a kiss.

Charmed, Gwen coasted the plates into the kitchen where the faucet then sounded and the plates ended up spotless in the dish drainer.

"Now that's what I'm talking about. Work smarter, not harder."

Gwen laughed. She knew she'd never be able to walk around town moving things here and there, but it was nice to use it without feeling weird, and it was also nice to have someone around who could appreciate it.

"A word to the wise, hotshot, don't go jumping around like that in public or you're going to attract some major attention. Trust me."

"I've got to test it though."

"At your own peril," warned Gwen. "I've been dealing with this for a long time. You're new to the game."

"I'm a quick learner though."

"That's what you think."

"That's what I know," said Billy.

"I know that I accidentally threw my last boyfriend through a wall," admitted Gwen. "I told the police he stumbled into it and they bought it, but that's just the kind of thing that can happen."

"He called the cops?"

"He tried to get me arrested, such as my love life has gone."

"My last romance nearly got me arrested too, so I guess we're in the same boat."

They shared a somber laugh before Billy asked, "So is that why the silver strands from the bandana were attracted to you?"

"Yes," answered Gwen, "I attract things. Anything magical, like birds and butterflies and maybe even you, Billy Winslow. Like that evening, on the street, you could have talked to anyone, but you talked to me."

She then thrust out her arm only to have the most brilliant red cardinal land perfectly on her outstretched hand.

"Amazing," said Billy as she summoned yet another bird, a female cardinal this time. Not as bright, she had a pretty orange beak and after a short pause, the two cardinals darted off together.

"Doubly amazing!" exclaimed Billy as Gwen smiled.

It felt good being able to trust someone with who she really was. Truth be told, Gwen didn't know who she really was, but she didn't know who Billy was either, so it seemed to be working out.

"I don't know the full extent of my powers because I couldn't use them."

"Most of us don't," replied Billy. "Maybe you're one of the lucky ones; at least you know you have powers. Most people just look for power in other people, not realizing their own potential."

"Really?" asked Gwen.

"Possibly," answered Billy. "It's just something I've been working on."

"It sounds good."

"Thanks. But were you ever going to tell me about this?"

Gwen thought about when she'd asked Billy a question. She asked him if he still loved Rita, and he'd said that he did.

"No," she answered, "not before last night."

"Not even when you saw what was happening to me, and then when something happened to you?"

"I didn't know how advanced you were. I couldn't risk it."

"So what do you think now?"

"I think I've finally found a guy that I really like and that I can trust and who's maybe more powerful than me. But he's in love with another girl."

"I don't think about her anymore. I only think of you."

Gwen searched his mind, and it was clear, as clear as the blue in his eyes. Billy sat next to her on the porch as she clasped his hand. It was a nice touch, and it reinforced her belief. They both had history, and it was time to start looking forward. It reminded her of the affirmation.

"Look forward and not away."

Then Billy came in to say, "Move onward to live another day. You didn't forget!"

"No. And that's another thing. I've also got a photographic memory. I don't forget anything."

"You really are a superhero, aren't you?"

"No, I'm just a mild-mannered girl from the suburbs," grinned Gwen. It was nice having someone make a fuss over her, especially a handsome guy who could leap off of small porches in a single bound. Of course there were other questions, but Billy didn't need more questions, he needed answers. The only thing he knew right now was that he really didn't know anything. He'd entered a parallel universe, and he was meeting those who'd done the same. It was frightening but fun.

The conversation ceased as Billy and Gwen laid down to rest. Healthy, young, and attractive, their scars were on the inside, but rather than heal, they'd simply be covered by less harmful scars until one day, they'd hopefully disappear.

For Billy, things were starting to make more sense, but for Gwen, it was truly an awakening. Billy had been granted special powers, but why and for how long? The medicine man said he had protection and time but that he had to use them wisely. To Gwen that meant they'd run out. But even the fact that she'd witnessed it was empowering. She felt vindicated in a sense: she wasn't the only freak in town; there was another, and his name was Billy.

Gwen couldn't believe her good fortune. In the brilliance of this new and amazing day, her troubled past seemed less troubling, and even if Billy didn't retain his ability, he was obviously a person of power. He needed to be careful though, because there were larger forces at work.

"So what's going on in that pretty head of yours?" asked Billy.

"I was hoping you'd be careful."

"As careful as I can, I guess."

Not the most reassuring answer; under the circumstances, it would have to do.

"So do you think the power is permanent?" he asked.

"I don't know, but I'm guessing it'll wear off. If you're lucky, it will."

It was a strong statement—that such a thing could be harmful rather than helpful. It was different, and sometimes being different was enough, enough to be hunted down and persecuted, or even worse, exploited for an evil purpose.

"Well on that note, we'd better get going," said Billy.

"No, Billy, let's stay. We'll live here forever, hidden from the world, just me and you. I'll juggle dishes, and you can jump off balconies."

As appealing as it sounded, on their way out of town it was agreed that Gwen wouldn't move anything, Billy wouldn't jump over anything, and together they'd be a nice, boring pair.

After flagging a bus and finding a couple of empty seats, Billy wrote while Gwen stared out the window. Then, as the brakes squealed and the doors of the bus flew open, Billy and Gwen made their exit.

Walking the long dirt road to Celia's, Billy said, "I need to tell Celia what happened to me, but I won't say anything about you, I promise."

"I'll tell her when the time is right," replied Gwen. "I don't really want to keep it a secret, at least not with people who are close."

It sounded nice. That Gwen could share such an explosive detail with someone she barely knew. The revelations had brought them closer, and quickly.

As they neared the house, of course the first thing that came into view was Gwen's yellow car.

"I need to get a different colored car," said Gwen.

"Why?"

"Because it sticks out like a sore thumb. I mean, I don't have anything against canaries, but they are kind of yellow."

"Yes, and the sky is blue and your car is noticeable. But that's what I like about it, because I know it's you."

"Aw, so sweet," replied Gwen as she grabbed Billy for another kiss.

"How nice. The love birds have returned," blurted Celia.

"I was tempted to take a joy ride in a cute little yellow car, but I couldn't find the keys."

Quickly jangling them, Gwen turned to Billy and said, "See."

"See what?" asked Celia.

"The car, it's too yellow."

"But that's how we know it's you."

"So I've heard."

With everyone around the kitchen table again, Celia asked, "So did you crazy kids have fun last night?"

It was an interesting question, but instead of answering—and because he wanted Gwen to see Celia in action—Billy said, "I've got a journal entry."

"Oh, even better," she said, running to get her pen as Billy and Gwen snickered.

Back with a red-ink pen clasped between her teeth, Celia read:

They cut through the night to find some sanity. They drifted through town seeking normalcy. Being on a collision course with destiny wasn't all it was cracked up to be.

But in the ineffable substance of the mind, they were floating instead of struggling, running instead of walking and flying instead of dying. From aging days and ancient skies, they made something new. From pain and disappointment, they finally grew.

They walked a seldom-traveled road to the great beyond.

They laughed, talked, and struggled till dawn.

There was a new power in play that simply said it's not in your head, but in your heart instead.

With a look of concern, Celia marked the page, but the notebook floated miraculously out of her hands and slowly over to Billy. Celia jumped up from the table and then fainted.

GROUNDED

"**O**h my god, I killed Celia! It was a mistake. I looked at the note-book and just thought . . ."

"Calm down. Celia's not dead."

"That's why I don't use this stuff," continued Gwen with tears welling up in her eyes.

Running to the sink, Billy grabbed a damp rag and a glass of water as Celia slowly asked, "What happened?"

"Are you OK?" asked Billy as both he and Gwen looked fearfully down.

"I-I suppose," stammered Celia. "After reading your entry, the pen and paper floated away and when I suddenly stood up, everything went black."

"I caught you before you went down," replied Billy. "Here's some water."

With Gwen now sobbing uncontrollably, Celia took a sip of water and then asked, "What's wrong with her?"

"I'm so sorry, Celia. I didn't mean to do it. It was an accident."

"You didn't mean to do what?"

"I didn't mean to move the pen and paper," sniffled Gwen as Billy gently guided her into a chair.

Her pretty hair was tousled and green eyes swollen and wet as Billy kissed her on the cheek. He knew the danger, but he needed to get Celia up too as he lifted her gently off the floor and guided her back into her chair.

With everyone again seated, Billy said, "Let's all just take a step back."

"That's what I did, and look how that turned out," replied Celia.

"Well, maybe no more steps, but let's just calm down," offered Billy.

"All calm here," added Celia, her sharp features and strong eyes still showing fatigue.

"How about you?" she asked, turning to Gwen and clasping her clenched hand.

As usual, Celia didn't know what was going on, but she sensed it had something to do with Gwen.

"I'm not calm. I'm sad."

Billy then held Gwen's other hand and said, "Celia's all right. She just gets a little weak in the knees sometimes."

"It's Billy's writing. It's just so captivating."

"Can I read it?" asked Gwen.

"Sure, although after that review, I don't know why you'd want to," Billy said.

"Because you wrote it, silly," replied Gwen as Billy slid the entry over to her.

As she read, her thoughts returned to the night she'd learned something about Billy and when Billy had learned something about her and maybe when they'd learned something about each other. Gwen thought she'd taken a step forward, but now at the same place, with the same demons, having to make the same explanations, she wanted to run. She couldn't though, there was nowhere to go.

"I like it," she said. "So what's next?"

"I guess that depends on what happens next," replied Billy. "You'll be the first to know."

Gwen smiled. It was nice to hear, because it sounded like they might still have a future. She wasn't sure. After causing Celia to pass out, Gwen thought this might be their last evening together. If it was, she wouldn't have been surprised; she'd lost a lot already.

With her strength finally back and hoping for some clarity, Celia asked, "Could you hand me that notebook, Gwen?"

Under Billy's watchful eye, Gwen gingerly slid the notebook over to Celia.

"What I meant was, could you hand me that notebook the same way you handed it to me before?"

"Go ahead, it's OK," said Billy.

The notebook then floated slowly up, and with Celia's eyes trained intently on the item, it stopped in front of her, rotated into a straight position, and lowered perfectly into place.

Celia then took a deep breath and said, "I never thought I'd see something so wonderful."

"Well, I can jump over cars," added Billy. "We had a really interesting night."

It was the understatement of the year, if not the century, but things were getting increasingly odd.

They seemed to be moving further and further into the stratosphere as Celia asked, "So what happened then? Something must have happened, because it made something else happen and then I ended up on the floor."

"The medicine man told me I had protection, and time, but that I had to use it wisely. I didn't know what he meant, but on our walk back to Gwen's, a speeding car jumped the curb and ran straight into me!"

Celia looked Billy over and said, "You look fine."

"I am fine. It didn't do anything to me, but it totaled the car."

"Really?" gasped Celia.

"Really," affirmed Gwen.

"He tumbled over the car and landed right back on his feet. The air bags deployed and everything. It was a mess."

"Wow!" exclaimed Celia. It was all she could say. But it made sense: if he was interacting with the supernatural, he'd need special powers as well.

"But what about the levitating notebook?"

"Can I tell her?" asked Billy.

"Sure," answered Gwen.

"OK," started Billy. "So after the incident with the automobile, when we finally made it back to Gwen's, Gwen decided to finish unpacking, although she doesn't unpack in the traditional way. You know how you or I would unpack a box piece by piece, kind of organizing and storing?"

"Yes."

"Well she does it differently; Gwen levitates the boxes, and then the contents miraculously find their way into the drawers, the cabinets, and the closets all on their own."

"Really?" Celia again asked.

"Really," Gwen again answered.

"And it just so happens that she's always had this talent. She was just afraid to tell me, that is, until I got hit by the car, or until I totaled the car."

"That's why I don't use it," added Gwen, "because of what happened to you."

"Oh, that was nothing; I faint in the middle of scary movies," replied Celia.

She didn't want Gwen to feel bad for having such a special skill. She didn't want anyone to feel bad about anything. All she wanted was for things to continue and to grow and to evolve and then to end. Celia didn't want to ruin it with logic and doubt. She wanted to feed it with wonder and amazement. After all, it was really amazing.

"I was shocked that you fainted, and I'm sorry," said Gwen. "That's what happens when I haven't used it in a while. I actually swore never to use it again, but with all the activity, I thought I could bring it out. I thought I could handle it, but I was wrong."

"You have to use it. It's part of you. It's who you are. Lesser things will try and break you down, but don't let it happen. Don't feel ashamed of being yourself. Feel better and feel stronger. Feel powerful and then one day you'll be unstoppable!"

Gwen cried again, but this time tears of joy.

"I feel like I'm on some kind of a seesaw, going up and down, and I don't really know when it's going to end."

"It's not always a straight path," said Billy, "but at least we're taking it."

Strained to the point of exhaustion, Gwen was relieved that she could finally be herself. Her condition had long been a source of anxiety, so it was nice to hear something inspirational and to be around people who understood. Even though it was a lot to take in, they seemed to be in synch and ready for more revelations. The awakened energy was moving into other places, and into other people, and Gwen wondered how it would end. She also wondered how it found her.

Reflecting on the time before Billy, rather than happy, Gwen had been content. She was moving, albeit slowly, but seemingly in the right direction. She had a comfortable apartment and a nice little car. She had a decent job and was starting grad school in the fall, and then—kaboom—there came Billy. It seemed like he'd fallen from the sky and landed straight on top of her. It was a soft landing and she'd been happy to help, but it didn't ease the fact that things were pretty hectic now.

Yes, she liked Billy, or maybe she loved Billy, and yes, Celia was great, but between the blackouts and the visions and the reliving of her checkered past, it was a trying time. It almost seemed like the best and worst of times, or maybe the best and strangest of times.

"Thank you for the kind words, Celia, especially after what happened."

"I'm Billy's aunt and I'm also a teacher, but instead of teaching, I'm learning, and you both have made this a very memorable time," replied Celia.

"Glad we could help," added Billy.

"I'm not saying you helped, I simply meant that out of everything else, there could be a silver lining."

"When you find it let me know," muttered Gwen.

"I'm not going to find it," said Celia, "Billy is."

"How am I going to find it?"

"The same way you found me," answered Gwen. "I was perfectly content being normal and anonymous, and then here comes this big handsome guy who sweeps me off my feet. The next thing you know, I'm passing out and using my powers again."

With Billy it was always a mixed bag, a little good and a little bad—or a little good and a lot of bad—but he was determined to use his powers for good rather than evil.

"I don't know what's going on," declared Billy, "but I can promise you this, when it's all said and done, we'll be in a better place."

"I thought I was in a decent place before," said Gwen.

"Yeah," added Celia, "I was doing all right."

"But don't substitute good for great," stated Billy.

"I don't mind good," continued Gwen.

"Yeah," said Celia, "good is actually pretty good."

"You know what I mean."

"Sure," replied Gwen, "in Billy we trust."

"Yeah, Billy or bust," added Celia.

The girls snickered as Billy stewed. But there was a new levity in the house, and he was glad. After Celia's collapse, he felt responsible, not only for endangering Celia but also for bringing Gwen out of her shell. Shells are for protection. Billy had shattered Gwen's, and he couldn't put it back together.

He was convinced there'd be a silver lining though; he'd just have to find it. Thinking back to when he'd first arrived, Billy remembered getting out on the town. That's when he ran into the guy who said, "You saved me, son," and when he met Gwen at the frat party.

Squinty eyed and inspired, Billy said, "Celia's right, I am going to have to discover it. When I first got here, I walked into town to see what I could find, and I found Gwen."

"Nice," quipped Celia. "Picking up girls right off the bat."

"He didn't waste much time," added Gwen.

"You're not getting it, ladies. I put myself out there before, and I'm going to have to put myself out there again."

"Billy's the bait!" said the girls in unison.

So with the latest calamity resolved, they were once again a tight-knit group ready to take on the world, or at least the town, and Celia was ready to take on a drink. Rather than join Celia, Gwen and Billy took a walk. While they walked, they talked.

"So, how are you doing?" asked Billy.

"I'm OK. It's just a little odd, the way things have happened, I mean. I thought some of this stuff was gone, and now it's rearing its ugly head again."

"I feel responsible. If you want to go, I understand. But I'd like you to stay."

"I thought you'd want me to leave after I made Celia faint."

"It never crossed my mind. I actually thought it was my fault. I felt like I'd found something ancient and unleashed it on an unwitting public."

"It wasn't you, Billy, you've been great. Whatever's happening must be happening for a reason, so maybe it's not all your fault."

"Well that's kind of reassuring."

"I don't want you completely off the hook, pretty boy," added Gwen. "I need to keep you in debt somehow."

"I'm already in debt, Gwen, and probably for a long, long time."

There was a strange resonance in the statement. It was almost like an ending before an actual end. Nothing more was said as they took in the beauty of the evening.

Past the brilliant wild flowers and busy bees, they continued on with a new appreciation for one another. It's all they wanted to do: to enjoy the day without any other concerns. They wanted to be simple, content, and in love.

Still in the dream of blue skies and lazy afternoons, Gwen brushed willingly against Billy as they strolled happily along. She wondered where he'd gone wrong. She wondered how he'd veered from the path.

But maybe he hadn't veered from the path at all; maybe he'd veered into the path.

"So what's your plan?" asked Gwen.

"I'm going to have to get out there again, into the community. Like you said, I'm going to be the bait."

"Do you think it's safe?"

"No, but it's not supposed to be."

Like a soldier in a dangerous place, Billy would have to live in it, he'd have to learn it, and then he'd have to defeat it. It should have been the calm before the storm, but it seemed like they were in a never-ending storm, each day with a new and more powerful squall.

It felt like a time in between times, or a day in between days. They seemed to be in a place where nothing was real or actual and everything was subject to change. Standing still; the world was spinning with oceans overflowing and colors intermingling and days beginning and ending as they watched in wonder.

Wandering through the beautifully deserted field at dusk, they saw only themselves beneath the heavens and wondered if it was enough. They wondered if they were enough to change the world, or if it could even be changed. But maybe that wasn't their job. Maybe they just needed to make a difference. Maybe a small difference now would cause an immense change in the future. Maybe it would make something better for someone. Maybe that's what they were supposed to do—to sacrifice themselves for the greater good and in the fading orange light of sunset. It seemed like a valiant enterprise.

"You are going to be careful, aren't you?"

"I'm done being careful."

"I guess you're done being with me, then."

"Of course I'm going to be careful," corrected Billy, "that goes without saying."

"You didn't say it."

"I meant it though. I've got some power. I don't know for how long, but it should be good for something."

Gwen hoped it would be good for something, because she knew energy doesn't always act like it should. It's unpredictable and sometimes harmful. But he'd find out soon enough.

"That's what you think," said Gwen.

"Being with you has been a lot of fun," started Billy. "You're pretty and smart and you have a great sense of humor, but if you think that levitating a couple of boxes is anything like totaling a car with a single body part, then you are sadly mistaken."

Then, as Billy rose gently into the air and started to float away, Gwen said, "I didn't think you were the too-big-for-his-britches type, but I guess I was wrong."

"Hey, put me down!" shrieked Billy.

"What's the magic word?"

"Please?"

"Please what?"

Goodness, thought Billy. "Pretty please."

"That's better," said Gwen as she lowered Billy back down to earth.

"I guess I had that coming."

"I guess you did. I didn't know your voice went that high though."

As they walked along, Gwen had moved even higher in Billy's esteem. He wondered if he'd moved higher in hers, or maybe lower. If that were the case, he wouldn't have been surprised.

Reflecting on his predicament, Billy felt a certain type of restlessness. He couldn't just hang out with the girls and go on spiritual journeys. That was fine for now, but at some point he'd have to resume a normal life. Being a vagabond was fun, but it was also tiring, and he didn't think it would last.

Billy needed to start doing the things he used to do. He wanted to go fishing, but all his gear was in Florida. He wanted to surf, but the beaches were three hours away. He could play some basketball though.

ONE ON ONE

With Celia on her third glass of wine, Gwen breezed through the door and announced, "What a lovely walk, Celia. Billy got mouthy so I gave him a ride. He's got a charming falsetto though."

"Ha," laughed Celia. "Serves him right. So what are you two doing tonight?"

"Going to bed," replied both Billy and Gwen. It wasn't late, but they were tired, and as usual, there was a lot to discuss.

"So what are you doing tomorrow?" Gwen asked.

"I'm gonna play basketball."

"I wanna go."

It would have been nice for her to join, but Billy needed to sort some things out. He had his power; now he needed to use it.

"I'd love to play in the park with you," replied Billy, "but not tomorrow. Tomorrow's detail is one of intrigue and exploration. After that, it's just me and you, meandering aimlessly through the day, playing like children until dusk."

"Oh, do you promise, sweetie?" Gwen sarcastically asked.

"Yep, pinkie swear."

"You might want to get a basketball, then."

That could be helpful, thought Billy as his eyes slid peacefully shut.

The songbirds sang an unusually lively chorus as Billy lay next to Gwen wondering what they would become. He'd settle down and live a normal life, and she'd finish her studies. He'd write, and she'd work in a hospital. They could use the house in Florida as a vacation home, or maybe even buy another. Domestication seemed pretty good as Gwen woke and said, "Good morning, lover. And why are you staring at me?"

"I was just appreciating your beauty," replied Billy.

"First thing in the morning?"

"Especially first thing in the morning."

"Liar," declared Gwen. She looked at the clock and said, "I gotta go."

"What's the hurry?"

"Work."

Billy remembered it. In a way, he kind of missed feeling useful. He missed the simple satisfaction of completing a menial task. It was him. It was who he was, at his core, before all of the complications. He'd be that again after all of this was behind him, but right now there was a larger purpose.

With Gwen spinning like a low-grade tornado, she asked, "Are you going to walk me out?"

"Of course," answered Billy. "Your chariot waits."

"What, exactly, is a chariot?"

"It's a figure of speech. Your chariot is yellow, if that's any clue."

"I get it. More car jokes, real funny," she said with Billy trailing her down the stairs.

Now out of the house and with her car squarely in sight, she said, "Bye, Billy."

"But aren't you going to buy me a basketball?"

Driving quickly away, she poked her head out the driver side window and replied, "Buy your own basketball, Billy!"

Buy your own basketball, eh? Bet they didn't tell Jimi Hendrix to buy his own guitar or Rembrandt to buy his own paint, thought Billy as he shuffled back into the house to plan his next move. Seeing Celia's strong, elegant form at the sink, Billy asked, "Do you think Rembrandt bought his own paint?"

Perplexed, she answered, "Rembrandt died penniless and was buried in an unmarked grave."

"He painted some great paintings though."

"They're called masterpieces, and that was never in dispute," continued Celia, still working away.

"Oh," replied Billy, now feeling extra useless.

Gwen was at work, Celia was banging away in the sink, and all he could do was desecrate Rembrandt. The day wasn't off to a very good start.

Easing past Celia to get to the refrigerator, Billy was still getting used to having a roommate. But it was good to have someone else around, if only to verify some of the oddities.

"Excuse me," said Celia.

"You're excused," replied Billy as he walked to the toaster with the bread and butter. He added, "You need a bigger kitchen."

"It was the perfect size before you showed up. It's not a soup kitchen either, so we're going to have to discuss some rent."

There it was. She'd done it. Celia pulled rank on him, and not a moment too soon.

"Talk to your big sister Cass, she's supposed to be renting my house for me."

"You talk to Cass," replied Celia. "You probably need to call her anyway."

"Soon."

With Celia's head stuck in a newspaper, Billy asked, "How do you feel this morning? Any soreness after the fall?"

"I'm fine. Still amazed, really," answered Celia. "So what are you up to today?"

"I'd planned to go to the park and play some basketball, except I don't know where the park is and I don't have a basketball."

Billy sure had a strange way about him, but he got results. All she needed to do lately was buckle up and watch the Billy show. It was the most entertaining act in town, and it was completely free.

"I know where the park is, but you're on your own with the basketball. You can check the garage. There might be one in there. A family lived here before, so it's not out of the question."

"If it's there, I'll find it," declared Billy, already on his way.

Easing into the quaint, weathered structure he whispered, "Basketball, basketball, where are you?"

At first glance, the charming garage seemed frozen in time. Hand tools covered in cobwebs rested in cluttered corners, while boxes of unused hardware sat precariously on rickety old shelves. Bird feeders, tarps, and spent paint cans littered the periphery, while boards and misshapen sheets of plywood hung haphazardly in the rafters. There were household supplies and do-it-yourself items but no sporting equipment.

He moved some more stuff and wondered what projects could have been done. Nothing was complete or really made sense; it was all just odds and ends. No conclusions could be drawn other than whoever owned it just disappeared or maybe aged out. A weathered workbench sat defiantly beneath a calcified old window as Billy wrestled the window up to let in some much-needed fresh air.

"Basketball, basketball, where are you?" whispered Billy.

Pulling back some boards, he muttered, "Where are you, basketball?"

Opening a decrepit closet, he chanted, "Basketball, basketball, where are you?"

"Where are you, basketball?" he asked, knowing that if he looked hard enough, he'd find it.

On his knees under the bench, scraping through a pile of old rags, Billy said, "Basketball, basketball, where are you?"

"Where are you, Basketball?" he again asked as an odd little knock came from the loft.

Turning quickly toward the sound, a strong burst of wind blew purposefully through the garage and in an instant, a large, brown ball dropped heavily to the floor and rolled straight over to him.

"Basketball, basketball, there you are!" exclaimed Billy as the ball rested innocuously at his feet.

Billy looked but didn't touch. He didn't know what would happen. Would it blow up in his face or just fly out the window? Would it propel him to greatness or hasten his destruction? Would it make something better or just add more confusion to an already confusing life? All valid questions; they couldn't be answered unless Billy picked up the ball. Stalling for a few more seconds, he had a feeling that when he touched it things would change, that his life could very well be marked by the time before the basketball and the time after.

As it bumped innocently, almost lovingly against his feet, he still waited. Billy continued to examine it, just as a scientist would study a sample, crouching even closer to observe the sphere. Was it alive? Could it talk?

"Hey, what's happening, ball?" asked Billy, as a distant voice answered, "Nothing, Billy. You're talking to a basketball. You've finally lost it."

"This is no ordinary basketball."

"It looks like an ordinary basketball," continued Celia as she went to grab it.

"No, no, no," stammered Billy as the ball again rolled to his feet.

"You're right. It's not an ordinary basketball. Are you going to pick it up?"

"Should I?"

"It seems to like you."

Taking a step back, both Billy and Celia shared a quick laugh. Miracles just kept happening.

With Celia over his shoulder, and just to see if maybe he missed something, Billy gave the basketball another hard look.

"What are the chances that a ball could be in such perfect condition after three or more years in a garage?"

Celia didn't answer but instead said, "Pick it up, Billy."

Billy kind of liked it on the ground, following him around like a little puppy, but something had to be done, so without further ado, he scooped it up.

With the ball finally in hand, he eyed the brilliant brown sphere with the passion of an archeologist in King Tut's tomb. It was perfectly round and worn in, and Billy guessed that if he were to check, he'd find it was properly inflated as well.

"Amazing."

Giving the ball a first few bounces, it popped sharply back into Billy's hand as if it were magnetized. Imagining clicking cameras and excited fans, he palmed the ball and held it out. As he spun it on this finger, the most curious thing happened. The ball traveled up Billy's arm, circled his shoulders, and then rolled down his other arm.

It then dropped to the ground as Billy excitedly asked, "Did you see that?"

"I sure did!"

They stood there dumbfounded and completely stunned as Billy gave the ball a couple more strong bounces and then spun it for all it was worth. Sure enough, the ball again traveled up his arm and around his shoulders, only this time, it ended up spinning away on his other finger.

"What do you think about that?"

"I think you need to find a court, and I'd also suggest not letting anyone else spin that ball."

"You're right," agreed Billy. "So where's the court?"

"Take a right on 54, it's called Anderson Park."

Anderson Park was within walking distance, so Billy started to walk.

As he picked up the pace, Billy wondered where Rita was and if he'd ever see her again. He didn't know what happened to her. He didn't know what was going to happen to him either, but as he ran down the road with a special basketball, the entrance to the park came into view. It reminded him of Mexico, where he'd found a basketball court and forgot everything else.

Billy was excited to play again. Like a kid with a new ball, he was ready to do some damage, but to whom? The court was empty but nice, and he wondered if there'd be any pickup games happening. *Maybe I should just see if I can still hit a basket*, thought Billy as his first shot completely missed the hoop and bounced helplessly into a nearby field.

"Guess the only talent this stupid ball has is for tricks," muttered Billy as he reached for the ball only to watch it gently scoot away.

"I'm sorry," said Billy. "It was me."

Then after the ball rolled gently back into his hands, he galloped back onto the court to take some easier shots, which all sunk perfectly. It was a basketball unlike any other. The leather was dark and soft, and it seemed to spring right back into his hand after every strong bounce. Whether his eyes were on it or not, whether he was using his right or left hand, the ball always returned. He could run with it and stop on a dime. It was amazing on the crossover dribble and soft as silk on an uncontested lay-up—although all his shots were uncontested at this point. *Man, I wish I'd had this ball growing up*, thought Billy. *I would have been unstoppable.*

Remembering his days as a college recruit and then as an expat playing in Mexico, Billy ran end to end, hitting three-pointers, turnaround jump shots, and, with the aid of his newly acquired powers, making the occasional dunk. He felt strong and fast and not even close to being tired.

Tall, with close-cropped blond hair and a chiseled physique, Billy was far removed from his days at the beach, where he'd quit playing basketball in favor of more gratifying pursuits. But now, with a lightning quick fast break and a thunderous dunk, Billy was back.

The park bustled with activity. People rode bikes, walked dogs, and even played tennis. Some paused, but none wanted to play, none were really players. Billy noticed someone in the distance—taller than him and wearing ratty clothes—who seemed interested, but as Billy turned to fetch an errant ball, the guy disappeared.

He was still feeling good and knocking down shots when the temperature suddenly dropped and a stiff gust of wind surged through the trees. Under the darkening skies, Billy's touch faltered as the ball again sent him scurrying.

As he pushed intently through a thick shrub, a heavy, familiar bounce echoed throughout the park and put Billy instantly on guard. It was the sound from his dreams, the hollow sinister repeat of a one-armed black man bouncing a basketball. Hair stood up on the back of Billy's neck as he then turned to see the specter from his sleep.

Shorter than Billy, the man had round, tight muscles, and he bounced the basketball with a special kind of ferocity. His right arm was perfectly formed and functional, but his left arm was gone. As the slow, deliberate bounces turned quicker, Billy walked back onto the court to face the demon from his dreams. Billy was scared, but he couldn't show fear. And he was protected, or so he thought.

The player had thick, tight cornrows and a flat sewn-up nub where his left arm used to be. Shirtless in a pair of army-surplus cutoffs, he wore high tops with no socks and an empty stare like a young Mike Tyson looking for his next knockout. Billy didn't notice the sky or the breeze or whether the park was full or empty. All he saw was the guy in front of him, and the guy in front of him was scary.

Still bouncing the ball, the one-armed man asked, "You lookin for a game?"

"Nah, I'm just about to take off," answered Billy. "Maybe next time."

"There ain't gonna be a next time," said the specter as he hurled the ball toward Billy with the force of a small cannon.

Catching it with a thud, Billy wondered what would have happened had he not visited the medicine man. He would have been laid out in the bushes with his cowardly basketball.

"You need to warm up, slick?" asked Billy.

"I'm already warm."

He'd never played an amputee, but it looked like he was going to now.

"We'll play to twenty-one. Make it take it."

"Fine by me. You got the ball, man."

That's right, I do, thought Billy.

Taking a couple bounces to size the guy up, he then sunk a towering outside shot and mistakenly thought it might be a quick game. Brimming with confidence, Billy took a few more bounces before the player surged powerfully forward and with the speed of a jungle cat, knocked the ball loose and recovered it. So now Billy was on defense.

Moving from side to side, the specter shot suddenly to Billy's left, wedging his nub into Billy's chest while cradling the ball into a perfect right-handed lay-up. It was a thing of beauty, fast and smooth, but not nearly as impressive as his outside attack. Behind the arc, with Billy's arms all the way up, the guy moved quickly to the side and launched a flawless one-handed shot.

Barely clearing Billy's fingertips, he turned to see the ball drop straight through the hoop. He heard the guy say, "Two to one."

"I can count," replied Billy, with the player back at the top of the key bouncing the basketball.

He kept bouncing it. That same eerie pop from Billy's dreams, that same muscle-bound arm moving up and down. But that was a dream. This was real, and Billy was in a game.

Checking the ball to Billy; Billy threw it back and just as quick as the specter caught it, he shot straight toward the basket for another quick hoop.

"Three to one," said the specter with his eye bubbling a gelatinous new lesion.

The bouncing continued and Billy needed to get the ball back, because if he didn't, he might not be able to. Just four points into the game, it was completely evident that this guy could play. Billy didn't know what had happened to him or how he'd ended up in Billy's dreams, but at some point, he must have played at a high level. His mechanics were perfect, his movements fast and deliberate, and he could jump. Billy saw that as the guy flew past Billy for a spectacular one-handed slam.

"Slam dunk," he said.

"I can see that."

And with the ball still bouncing, Billy asked, "What's your name?"

"It's Lewis," he said as he again surged for the basket only to have Billy pin the ball against the backboard and then, luckily, retrieve it. Now with the ball back, Billy summoned his power and shot past Lewis to land a powerful dunk of his own.

"Slam dunk!" exclaimed Billy to an indifferent Lewis.

But as Lewis, again, stole the ball, the real punishment began. He started slamming into Billy's chest with his left shoulder, over and over again. Billy imagined sparks flying as he collided with the place where Lewis's left arm used to be.

From the strength of his legs to the fluidity of his movements, Lewis used everything he had. He laid the ball in and shot effortlessly from the outside. He rebounded and played ferocious defense, continuously knocking the ball out of Billy's hands.

As Lewis and Billy traded outside shots, lay-ups, and dunks, Billy couldn't believe he was in a game like this. He was soaring—they both were—through the heavens on a basketball court.

"You were in my dream," said Billy.

"I know," replied Lewis, as another shot went in.

"Why?"

"Because you need to do something."

Billy was tired and beat up. He might have been dead if not for the Indian, but he guessed it was all connected. But maybe he was supposed to be dead, or in limbo like Lewis and Ray. They could send him out to harass the living in flying cars and blood-sport basketball games, forever in a state of suspended animation. He'd take that over this, because he was about to collapse.

As he blocked another shot, Billy flung the ball far off the court and asked, "So what do I need to do?"

Lewis didn't bat an eye as the ball circled quickly around and popped right back into his outstretched hand.

"You need to put a team together," said Lewis as he hit another shot. "Twenty-one. I win."

Billy eyed the shrub where his ball had been hiding and sure enough, it was out and ready to go. He then saw Lewis slinking off and asked, "What, no handshake?"

"No," answered Lewis, still heavily bouncing his ball.

"Hey, Lewis," yelled Billy, "do you know Ray?"

"Maybe," answered Lewis, moving steadily away before vanishing into a thin flash of light.

Staring into the emptiness, Billy walked back over to his ball and asked, "So where were you when I needed you?"

As it shrank back into the bushes, Billy said, "Come on, champ, it's time to go."

The ball then jumped into his outstretched hand, and they started home.

Slowly making his way back to Celia's, Billy felt like he'd been in a football game. Things were getting more painful, but they were also getting more interesting. The mystery was unraveling, but there were still a lot of questions, the main one being, *How in the hell am I going to start a basketball team?* Forget the fact that he'd just played the game of his life against a one-armed ghoul, now he had to get a team together. But what if he didn't? Would the same guy show up and rip one of Billy's arms off?

Billy scanned his chest, which was covered with thick red welts. Without his powers he would have been ground to dust. He'd never felt that kind of force before. It almost seemed divine, perfect in its brutality. But one thing was certain: it wasn't a basketball game, it was a battle. And who was the big kid that Billy had seen in the distance?

He looked similar to the other beings, stoic, strong, and apparently trapped in a different realm.

Senseless in their inception, the events seemed to be evolving in a practical manner. It was organic and guided, but Billy's mind was now more blown than ever. The day had started off like any other day, except that Billy found a basketball that seemed to be alive and then played and lost against a disfigured spirit. What could possibly happen tomorrow?

Then, as Celia's house came into view, Billy unconsciously started bouncing the basketball. Opening the garage door, he gave the ball a final strong bounce and watched it float neatly back into the loft. Continuing toward the house with a wide, appreciative smile, Billy thought, *Remarkable.*

Celia was nowhere to be found as Billy went for his journal. With his world turning like never before, he recalled the spirits at the temple and then the dreams of car crashes and one-armed basketball players. He remembered Ray, the car driving stiff, and then the deadly runaway train followed by a spinning, psychotic chair. Then there was the flying medicine man, his mystical girlfriend, and then a human basketball. It all made perfect sense as Billy scrawled:

Things that made sense were all senseless.

In the kingdom of shadows there was something lurking, something stalking, something that needed to be fed.

It hadn't descended on a hero, it landed on an outcast. It chose a castaway to stand up and be counted. Things weren't made; they were discovered. Souls weren't saved; they were recovered. Love and loss was never absolute in the land of the unknown.

In dreams there was mayhem. In scenes there was chaos. In the constant barrage of insanity there was a strange kind of grace.

Walking down a cobbled road, a force seemed to say, keep going, keep moving, keep learning, keep trying, start living, and stop dying.

It was powerful and magical and everything that it was supposed to be.

SOMETHING STIRRING

Billy leaned heavily against the bedroom vanity as the front door slammed.

"Billy, I'm home," yelled Celia.

"Be right down," replied Billy, tromping down the stairs.

"Where's Gwe—Ah!" sounded Celia, as she quickly noticed the marks on Billy's chest.

"Did you mean to say, 'Where's Gwen?'" asked Billy, with Celia's gaze still focused on his torso.

"Yes," answered Celia with a slight wince.

"She's on the way. I'll explain when she gets here."

As Billy went back upstairs, he was amazed but also scared. He needed to start a team, and judging from the game he'd just played, Billy guessed it was supposed to be a basketball team. But when did he need to start it? And did it need to be a good team? Where would he find players? And who were they going to play? Before, people just showed up, but now that the pressure was on, would they still come?

Billy also wondered how long things had been in the works. It couldn't have started while he was with Rita. They couldn't have had their eye on him then. He hadn't even gone back to basketball yet. It was only in Mexico that he'd been searching and praying and wondering where his life would lead. He might have been adrift in an angry sea or dashed against a craggy shore if not for the spirits. They had come to his rescue as well.

He wondered where or when it would end. If he didn't succeed, would it be OK? Would it be fine if he at least tried? Or, if he failed, would he have to keep trying? Would he have to relive it, day after day, hour after hour until even the spirits abandoned him? Billy had always taken his redemption for granted, but now he wasn't so sure. Maybe they'd picked the wrong guy?

But there were promising signs, signs that he wouldn't fail, signs that he, like everyone else, was being guided. It was all really big and tremendous and dangerous and unbelievable, and for a moment, Billy pondered reality in the sense of what was real or perceived. What could be made or created from the mystical elements of life? What could be started with a thought or an action or a supposition, and had Billy started this and would he end it? It was all compelling and interesting, but stepping out of the shower, it was also cold as Billy yelled, "Celia, can you get me a towel?"

"No," answered Celia, "but Gwen can."

Great, Gwen's here, thought Billy. *Now I can get this off of my chest.*

For Gwen, it was always an interesting trip up the stairs. She never really knew what to expect. Whether it was a slide show of her life or a fainting act, it was always interesting.

Undressed, with round, red welts across his chest, Billy looked tired. She guessed it would be different tomorrow, after a good night's sleep, but it looked like he'd had a hard day.

"Here's your towel, sweetie."

She wanted to say more but figured he'd talk soon enough. Something had obviously happened—more bruises for a bruiser, she guessed. But it was tough to see someone under siege, always with a different, suspicious injury.

"Thank you so much," replied Billy before drying off and getting dressed. "Let's go downstairs to see Celia. I need a drink, and you probably will too."

Trailing Billy down the stairs Gwen thought, *This should be good.*

With Celia, Gwen, and Billy all exuding their own special kind of charisma, there was a strong presence in the war room. Celia's shiny brown hair rested comfortably on her strong shoulders as she lowered herself into a dining room chair. With sharp, attractive features and searching eyes, she carried an unmistakable aura of intelligence. Gwen's auburn hair drifted into the pretty green of her eyes as Billy's tall frame shone with the strength of a celestial warrior.

"I'll trade you my notebook for a beer," offered Billy.

"A beer," chirped Gwen.

"Make it two," amended Billy.

"Two beers coming up, and it better be worth it."

As Billy exchanged the beers for the notebook, Celia went to work. Muttering all the while with a red pen sticking out of her mouth, she scrawled a bright, red C+ on top of the page along with the message, "Getting better."

"To getting better," said Billy with a raised glass.

"May we all be as brilliant as Billy," added Celia.

"Here, here!" cheered Gwen as they took lengthy swigs and settled in for another one of Billy's epic tales.

Billy then turned to Gwen and said, "So, after you left yesterday, I found a basketball in Celia's garage. I started chanting, 'Basketball, basketball, where are you?' At first there was nothing, but as I kept searching, something led me to an old calcified window, so I opened it. Continuing to chant, a stiff gust of wind surged through the garage and somehow blew a perfectly good basketball out of the loft."

"That's not too strange," replied Gwen.

"Not unto itself, but then the ball rolled straight over to my feet, and as Celia walked into the garage, I moved, and the ball followed."

Gwen then looked to Celia, and Celia nodded.

"And when I spun it on my finger, the ball traveled up my arm, over my shoulders, and down my other arm all on its own!"

"Interesting," said Gwen.

"But that wasn't the most interesting thing," replied Billy. "When I finally made it to the park, it was bustling. People were everywhere, walking dogs and playing tennis, so I started shooting some hoops, you know, running around the court like a kid. But then the wind came up, that same eerie breeze that's been following me around. Anyway, after I missed a shot, the ball bounced off the court and wedged itself into a shrub. So with my head stuck in a bush, I heard the bounce of a basketball, and as I turned to face the sound, I saw the one-armed black man from my dreams heading straight for me."

"No way!" exclaimed both Celia and Gwen. "What did you do?"

"I stood my ground. There was nothing else to do. The guy looked like a one-armed Mike Tyson and when he threw me the basketball, it felt like it had been shot out of a cannon."

"Don't you need two hands to play basketball?" asked Celia.

"Apparently not," answered Billy. "At least this guy didn't. He played like a professional. He said that his name was Lewis, and he was fast as lightning. He hit outside shots. He drove to the basket. He dunked the ball. He rebounded. I mean, I've never seen anything like it."

"So I take it you lost," remarked Gwen.

"Yes, I lost, but it wasn't about winning or losing."

"That's what I'd say if I lost," added Celia.

"I played good too, the best I've ever played. If I hadn't seen the medicine man, I probably wouldn't have survived. There was an unnatural strength in play. That's how I got the welts. Lewis kept slamming me with the shoulder of his missing arm. He was stitched up and also had a cut below his left eye. Whatever happened must have happened to his left side."

Both Celia and Gwen then clutched Billy's hands, and they were again joined in a powerful circle.

"Lewis obviously wasn't of this earth. He was another anomaly, another miracle to behold, I guess."

Further pondering miracles, Billy guessed that Gwen and Celia were miracles as well, and that all life was miraculous, no matter how large or small. Signs and wonder were all around, they just needed to be noticed.

"As we continued to play, Lewis was wearing me down. I also wanted some answers, so I threw the basketball as far off the court as I could."

"What happened then?" asked Gwen.

"He stuck out his hand and sucked the ball right back in. It was amazing. I mean, I hurled that thing."

"Well how did he like that?" asked Celia.

"He didn't seem to mind, because he obviously got the ball back. But when I asked him what he wanted me to do, he said that I needed to start a team."

"What kind of a team?"

"A basketball team, I guess. A few guys on a court, that's the only thing that I could figure. It obviously wouldn't be a professional squad."

"No," mused Celia, "you're attracting someone."

"I attracted him, I guess. I asked him if he knew Ray, the deceased limo driver, and he said maybe. These guys aren't much for conversation."

Looking at Billy, Celia was impressed. As a child, she never would have guessed that he'd be here, in rarefied air, functioning in the heavens, taking this kind of abuse and still staying sane. She wouldn't have been able to, but maybe he couldn't either. Maybe there was a second and third choice already lined up.

Gwen was equally fascinated. She couldn't believe she'd met a real live gladiator, and actually slept with him or became his girlfriend, if that's what she actually was. She'd gone through life thinking she was some kind of a circus freak, and now this. It was the first time she ever felt normal, and it felt good, and it was because of Billy.

"So, what are you going to do?" asked Celia.

"I'm going to bed," answered Billy. "Are you coming, Gwen?"

"Of course."

"Well don't get into any more trouble tomorrow, because I'll be at work," added Celia.

"OK," answered Billy, but tomorrow was a new day, and he couldn't promise anything. And then like a champion, bruised but not beaten, Billy put his arm over Gwen's shoulder, and she hoisted him up the stairs. From now on, there wouldn't be any more wondering. He'd been directed up to North Carolina to start a basketball team, so that's what he was going to do.

Back in the bedroom, Gwen asked, "So what was Lewis like? Was he scary?"

"Man, I was terrified. Imagine a ghoul from your dreams appearing in person and having an issue with you. I wanted to run, but I couldn't. I had to face my fears. The basketball didn't though. It hid in the bushes until after the game. I'll show you the ball tomorrow. It's tricky."

"What do you think happened to him, Billy?"

"There's no telling. He had army-surplus cutoffs, so it could have happened in some kind of a battle somewhere. Ray the driver also wants me to deliver a message to someone. He seems to think I'll run into him, but I guess I'm not there yet. I'm just going to have to connect the dots, but at the moment, I need more dots."

"Interesting," said Gwen as she rubbed Billy's back in slow, deliberate circles.

It felt great. If Billy had ever needed a massage, he needed one now and as his eyes slowly shut; his day was most certainly done.

Waking up beside Gwen was becoming a common occurrence, as was Billy's morning trip down the hall. Twisting awake as well, Gwen wearily eyed Billy's chest and noticed it was clear. There were no marks, not a hint of what had happened the day before. It was indeed spectacular.

"Hey, honey," said Gwen, "your chest is clear."

Billy looked down, and sure enough, gone were yesterday's bruises. Thumbing his chest, he felt no residual pain either. He seemed to be miraculously healed. He just wondered for how long.

Moving around, Billy said, "Let's go to the garage, I've got something to show you."

Down a dark staircase, Billy opened the door to an unusual explosion of color and life. Beneath the angelic glow, Billy felt like he'd been born again. It felt like he was taking his first steps and saying his first words. It seemed like something was gone, a weight, or maybe even a worry that he'd never find his way home.

Billy was in a new place with a new girl, and there was a new energy in the air. Maybe his past was finally behind him. Maybe there was something therapeutic in the game. Maybe the beating and the losing had all led to something—hopefully the final mission.

Opening a creaky door to the musty garage, Billy whispered, "Here we are, and it looks exactly like it did yesterday."

"Why would it look any different?" asked Gwen. "And why are you whispering?"

"I don't know. It just seems like the thing to do."

"OK, I guess we're whispering then."

Scanning the garage, Gwen noticed the odd collection of items as well. Forget the fact that she could move things; she was there to see something else move.

Standing beneath the cluttered rafters, Billy opened the window and said, "Basketball, basketball, where are you?"

Watching Billy summon an inanimate object was laughable, but Gwen didn't doubt his methods. So far, they'd been pretty effective.

"Basketball, basketball, where are you?"

"Basketball, basketball, where are you?" he continued, examining the window, making sure that it was all the way up.

"Basketball, basketball, where are you?"

Now Billy was really starting to think, *Where the hell are you, basketball? I've got an audience, so don't make me look bad.*

Then a breeze suddenly filled the garage, and Billy's eyes lit up.

"Basketball, basketball, where are you?"

At first there was nothing, and then from the loft came a soft rolling sound. The ball moved along like a little round baby, nudging its way to the edge until finally plunging down and bouncing straight over to Billy.

"Basketball, there you are!"

Truth be told, he wasn't sure it would happen, especially not with a guest, but the pull was strong, and something was obviously stirring.

Billy beamed as Gwen showed a wide, unfettered smile. Standing there with the ball, he felt like all was well in the world, like they'd found divinity in an old, unused garage. There was sanctity in the space, a usefulness that, despite the years of neglect, still existed.

"There was happiness here," said Gwen, "but then something happened."

"What?"

"I don't know. Like I said, I'm not psychic, but I attract energy and I feel something here, a sadness, but also hope for the future."

"That sounds psychic to me."

"I'll let you know when I get next week's lottery numbers then," mused Gwen.

As Billy knelt to pick up the ball, it jumped into his outstretched hands, rolled up his arm, over his shoulder and straight into his other hand. Gwen watched in amazement as it then made the same trip in reverse.

"This basketball might have you beat," said Billy.

"He can have it," replied Gwen, "or she or whatever it is can have it."

The ball then dropped out of Billy's hand and rolled into a corner.

"It's sensitive," added Billy.

Gwen then walked over to the ball and said, "I'm sorry, be whatever you want to be, but right now you look like a big, beautiful ball."

Then as the ball popped into her hands, Gwen had to remind herself that she was talking to a basketball. It was warm, almost like a child, but it was also conveying something—loss and a lot of questions.

Gwen suddenly hugged the ball and felt an overwhelming rush of emotion. With tears streaming down her face, she handed it back to Billy and said, "We'll be back soon."

And with that, the ball took a strong bounce out of Billy's hand and shot straight back into the loft.

Billy was dumbfounded, and Gwen was sad so she levitated a little red feather into the attic to keep the ball company. Billy wondered if it would ever come down, and as the feather floated away, he hoped everything would be all right.

Finally leaving the garage Gwen said, "At least now I know what not to say."

"I'm just learning myself," replied Billy. "I blamed it for a bad shot, and it nearly ran away."

"But when I said we'd be back soon, it triggered something. It was also communicating, but I couldn't tell what."

"The plot thickens. I just hope it comes out again, because if it doesn't, you truly owe me a basketball."

"I can't get you one like that," said Gwen. There obviously wasn't another like it. But that didn't change the fact that she'd talked to a basketball, and it had basically answered.

Being immersed in wonder was great, but walking away, they both wondered if it would ever end, and what if it didn't? Or what if they were both dropped back to earth in a big, anticlimactic thud, back to the land of mere mortals, where she was weird and he was mediocre? But if that happened, they'd always have this moment—and maybe each other. And if they didn't, at least they'd have the memories and hopefully a wisdom of things larger than themselves.

Walking back to the house, Billy asked, "So what's for lunch?"

"I'm taking you out, lover."

It sounded good to Billy.

"We'll call it a victory lunch, even though I didn't win," said Billy, referring to his basketball game.

"But you survived. I'd call that a win."

It was true, but Billy wondered if he'd have to survive again or if he could ever actually win. He hoped his life wouldn't amount to only conciliatory victories while everyone else took the real prizes. But he was sitting next to Gwen and living with Celia and his life was full of wonder and intrigue, so maybe he was the real winner.

Being driven around was nice, and Billy didn't ever want to drive again. He didn't need to. There seemed to be two busses at every stop as Gwen muttered about being stuck behind one.

"Let's eat here," said Billy pointing to a restaurant around the corner from the university.

"It looks busy."

"You want it to be busy. That way the food's fresh."

"If we ever get any."

It was a good point, but they'd waited this long so a few more minutes couldn't hurt.

With Gwen now complaining about parking, they pulled in as someone else pulled out and they were good.

"Follow my lead," said Billy.

Gwen followed his lead, and sure enough, it led to the back of the line. So now she grumbled about that as a shiny white BMW with dark tinted windows pulled into the parking lot. With an air of importance, a no-nonsense crew emerged, all wearing the latest light-blue gear emblazoned with a Nike swoosh. They looked slick and important, and they didn't wait at the back of the line. No, to Gwen's dismay they walked straight over to an open table, where their food was promptly delivered.

"Hmmph," sounded Gwen. "What do you think about that?"

Gwen watched the line as Billy watched the table. Among a few younger guys sat a distinguished gentleman who seemed to be the boss. Friendly patrons spoke in passing, and he'd either nod or smile or maybe offer a quip in return. He looked familiar, and Billy suddenly remembered him from the basketball stadium. He'd walked with a limp, and Billy thought that he might be a coach. Under closer examination, Billy thought that he might be the coach of one of the most decorated college basketball teams in history.

"I think he's the coach of the men's basketball team."

"Coaches don't wait in line?" asked Gwen.

"Not that one."

Now at the counter, they ordered a couple of sandwiches and went outside to wait. As the food arrived, Gwen frowned while Billy ate. Forty-five minutes into the ordeal, with the coach finally making his way out, Billy wondered what to do. He couldn't ask the coach any questions, and he wouldn't meet anyone sitting at home. Gwen chomped while Billy thought, and the answer suddenly materialized. He was going to have to get a job.

Billy had noticed an obvious lack of help, and the place was packed. Empty tables sat cluttered with plates, cups, and silverware as patrons milled about. Billy knew the drill. Restaurant work was hard enough with a full staff, but when shorthanded, it was torturous. He felt sorry for whoever was going to have to clean up.

With Gwen finished and finally calm, Billy excused himself to the bathroom. Wedging his way through the dining room, he mistakenly walked into the kitchen as a wide-eyed chef exclaimed, "Finally, you're here!"

"Who's here?"

"You," said the guy as he threw Billy an apron. "You're late."

With an apron in hand, he had a choice. Billy hadn't planned on getting into another kitchen, but an opportunity had presented itself. It reminded him of another assignment, in another hot kitchen. Billy was kidnapping Steve then, but he had no idea what he was doing now.

"Oh, sorry, uh, what do you want me to do?"

"Do me a favor and clean the patio first."

Billy didn't know who he was supposed to be, but he knew his way around a restaurant, so he grabbed a wet rag and a bus pan and headed out. Wondering what was taking Billy so long, Gwen soon found out as he gently lifted her plate and asked, "Are you finished with that, ma'am?"

"Ah, I thought I was, but now I'm not so sure."

"I can always come back."

"If you do, maybe you can bring my date back," muttered Gwen.

"Doubtful," replied Billy, "but short story even shorter, I walked into the kitchen instead of the bathroom and they threw me an apron."

"And you took it?"

"I'll explain later," continued Billy with a quick kiss on the cheek, "on the ride home maybe."

"Maybe," repeated Gwen as she stormed off.

What was supposed to be a lovely afternoon had turned into a long wait for a decent sandwich and a lonely ride home. *How romantic,* thought Gwen.

Billy, on the other hand, didn't have time to think as people kept walking in and the dishes kept piling up. What kind of a place didn't even know what their employees looked like? After an hour, he was already disgruntled. As always, it was sure to be a tumultuous tenure.

Finishing the patio, and then moving inside to pour water and roll silverware, he felt good to be back.

"Hey, new guy, what's your name?" sounded a frantic voice from the kitchen.

"It's Billy," answered Billy, equally frantic.

"OK, Billy, if you're caught up out front, maybe you can give me a hand on the line."

"Sure."

That was a pretty quick promotion, thought Billy as he heard the hot pans crackling and felt the sharpened steel rest heavily in his hands. Billy had sworn off kitchen work, blaming it partly for his demise, but now he was back, and it felt good. Maybe this was part of his redemption, rediscovering something he loved and getting a second chance. Or maybe it was just more misery.

Flipping burgers and dropping chicken tenders into the deep fryer, it wasn't one of the fanciest places Billy had worked, but it was busy. Being right outside of a college didn't hurt either. The other good thing was that it was a breakfast and lunch place, no dinners. He wouldn't be mopping floors at ten thirty at night with a beautiful girl waiting at home. But he didn't know if he'd be mopping floors here either, because he wasn't really sure he worked here. He was an impostor, but that didn't stop him from pushing out plates, one after another, and building the bacon, lettuce, and tomato sandwiches to perfection.

With the kitchen caught up, Billy again left for the patio to do a final cleanup. Working his way around the tables, he saw someone tall, disheveled, and familiar. As the guy drew even closer, Billy noticed he was nearly seven feet tall and also young.

Sunburned and glassy eyed, Billy swung the door open as the guy simply ducked his head and walked in. Peering through the front window as he picked up his order, Billy quickly opened the door again and said, "Didn't I see you at the basketball court the other day?"

"Maybe," the guy answered, and kept walking.

He walked quickly too. He was out of there in no time, but where did he go? Did he live in the woods, or at the park? And what happened to him? These were all good questions, but right now, Billy wanted to know if he had a job.

From what Billy could tell, the kitchen manager's name was Rick. There was a prep guy, a dishwasher, and a few waitresses. Gina, the floor manager, seemed to be off. They had an unexpected rush, and she couldn't get in; the usual stuff.

The waitresses gave Billy a couple of bucks before they left as Rick said, "You said your name was Billy. I thought you'd be Glen. Gina said a new busser named Glen would be coming in today, so I just assumed."

"I don't know what happened to Glen, but I walked into the kitchen instead of the bathroom and you threw me an apron."

"That's a first," chuckled Rick, "but Glen or no Glen, if you want a job, you got it."

Not really sure what the job was Billy, replied, "I'll take it."

But he had a question. What Billy really wanted to know was, "Who was that tall kid who came in for the takeout order?"

"That was Andy Völler," answered Rick as he then told of the Völler family tragedy.

ANDY VÖLLER

Kurt and Ingrid Völler's first and only son was simply named Andy. From a proud farming family in Indiana, Kurt came east by way of Fort Bragg, North Carolina. With both farming and fighting in the Völler family tradition, Kurt did the farming part, then as tensions rose in the Middle East, he went on to do the fighting.

Kurt's grandfather narrowly escaped Nazi Germany, and his father served in Vietnam, so when Kurt came of age, it was his turn. Kurt was one of the first soldiers with a one-way ticket to Operation Desert Storm. Instructed to watch rather than engage, he was on an early reconnaissance mission when disaster struck. His convoy was hit by small-arms fire, and then some larger artillery, which, unfortunately, caused casualties. With one seriously injured and two deceased, it was a dark night in the desert when Kurt had to battle his way back to base.

They called it heroic, but he said it was nothing. Kurt said they would have done the same for him, and they would have, except they didn't get the chance. Two coffins draped solemnly in the stars and stripes arrived quietly home while another soldier hobbled painfully off the battlefield with an honorable discharge. Determined to finish his tour, Kurt spent the rest of the conflict on a computer, tracking the enemy from a safer distance.

Drawn to the rolling hills and soft sand beaches of the Carolinas, in the waning days of the war, Kurt and his lovely wife, Ingrid, decided to make North Carolina their home. It was a homecoming of sorts as he flew into Raleigh-Durham airport to be reacquainted with an old army pal. Taking advantage of the area's burgeoning tech industry, he took a job at IBM in the Research Triangle Park, found a home, and started a family. Ingrid also started a garden, in part for fresh vegetables and also to stay close to her agricultural roots.

With Kurt's job going well and Ingrid's garden growing, Andy was the first to come, and he was followed shortly thereafter by his sister, June. The Triangle seemed to be the perfect place to raise a family: it was affordable and held another one of Kurt's passions sacred—basketball. Being from a farm in Indiana, Kurt had played his fair share of ball. Larry Bird was, of course, his favorite player, and he'd shoot until the sun went down. Kurt showed promise as an amateur, but rather than follow his athletic dreams, he decided to serve, hoping to preserve the opportunity for others. He still sometimes wondered what could have been, but Kurt had a son, and his son was good. His son was really good, better than he'd ever been.

Andy Völler played all the time, almost too much, and his sister, June, troubled him to no end by hiding his basketball, which he always found and then promptly made her pay the price. They were the best of friends. There were two worlds in the Völler household: the authoritarian, hardworking one of their parents, and the innocent, playful one of theirs.

Kurt had worked on the farm all day, and here was his son, playing. But Andy was good, and he was getting tall. At fifteen, he was almost as tall as his father, and his father was six foot six. He had a good outside shot and a lightning fast first step, and he was lethal around the basket. Andy loved to score, but he especially loved to rebound and block shots. He took it as an insult for opposing players to score on him.

Things were lining up for Andy to play professionally. Scouts were showing up for his games and leaving business cards, but he was still young. The Wolfpack of NC State had already come calling, as well as the Duke Blue Devils, but the Tar Heels kept their distance.

It was a new day for collegiate athletics and for people with athletic dreams. The stakes were high, and the competition even higher. If teams weren't getting better, they were getting worse. In other words, the arms race was on, and there were no limits. For basketball, the days of bounce passes and lay-ups were long gone. It was now a game of dunks and three-point shots. It was a game of power and prestige and, in many ways, money. A global search was on for the best players in the world, and one of the world's best just happened to be Andy Völler. He was all first team, All-American, and all everything every year.

The recognition was fun, and in some ways, it brought the family together, but it also caused a rift between Andy and Kurt. There were free shoes and free tickets; there were Völler jerseys, gifts for Andy's sister, and calls to his mother. There were offers for travel and trips to different schools near and far, but Andy couldn't take any of it. He was averaging thirty-five points and fifteen rebounds a game and still had to take out the trash. At seventeen years old and six feet eight inches tall, he didn't even have a car yet.

June, his sister, was always at his side and on his side, but she couldn't visibly go against Kurt. She'd always commiserate with Andy, because after all, her big brother was her hero. He'd always find her after a game and they'd walk to the parking lot to wait for their mother. Andy promised to let June drive his car when he finally got one. He'd already received calls from dealerships and had even decided on a Ford Mustang—a convertible—for his first car.

When he finally borrowed one and gleefully showed it off, Kurt marched him right back into the car and promptly returned it to the dealership. Ingrid then picked them up in front of the shiny new showroom and slowly drove off with Andy steaming and Kurt resolute.

"It's a lesson in humility, son. You need to learn the value of citizenship and community. That's going to serve you better than a pocket full of money."

While true, it didn't make sense to a young star athlete who'd just been admonished at a car dealership in front of the staff and patrons alike.

Instead of fighting or arguing, as a light rain started to fall, Andy simply said, "I hate you. I hope I never see you again."

"I love you, Andy, and it's for your own good," replied Kurt as Andy stormed off to his room.

It was the worst blow up June had seen. Andy wouldn't even open his door this time, and he was making plans to leave. He looked out his window and was relieved as the car again pulled out of the drive. He felt better knowing that his father was gone. Maybe they'd see eye to eye one day, but it wouldn't be today, and it wouldn't be tomorrow either, because Andy wouldn't ever see him again.

What started out as a light rain quickly turned into a deluge as Andy's rage eased. He felt bad for what he'd said, and with his head held low, he was going to have to apologize. What made him mad also made him great, but he was going to have to temper it. His father was right: he didn't need handouts; he just needed to play.

It was getting late, and his family hadn't gotten home yet. Andy wondered if it was because of him. He wondered if they stayed out a little longer because of what he'd said, just to teach him a lesson. He checked his sister's room, to see if maybe she'd stayed, but she hadn't. She was gone too.

Traipsing through the empty house, Andy heard the rain fall heavily on the roof as he finally laid on the couch. It was an odd thing for him to do, but he wanted to be there when the family returned—to say he was sorry and that he loved them.

It was later than usual for the Völler family to be out, and the roads were bad. It was pitch black on a narrow stretch of highway as Kurt vigilantly held the wheel, weaving and dipping through the dense countryside. Water had collected in the low spots, and the car started to get loose. What had begun as a pleasant ride to a friend's house had suddenly turned dangerous.

Large trees flanked the lonely thoroughfare, but rather than pleasant, tonight they were wooden fortresses void of any feeling or sympathy. As the Völler family car reached the top of another hill, a blinding pair of headlights cut straight through their windshield. A big box truck was completely in their lane, and all Kurt could do was yank the wheel so they didn't go head on. But there was still a crash as the vehicles shot like pinballs into the roadside forest.

There was a chance they'd land safely. It was possible they'd skate through unscathed. But they didn't. Kurt had been lucky before, in the desert, when he'd survived and others hadn't; but not this time. The car was smashed, flying through the air weightless, completely out of control before coming to a complete stop against the trunk of a large oak. Folded helplessly around the smooth contour of wood, with the brake lights flashing and a lonely headlight shining, the night went painfully quiet.

Rescue vehicles were quick to the scene, but the extraction was challenging. The car was wrapped neatly around a tree and had to be cut away before the occupants could be released. By the time the wreckage was cleared, Kurt and Ingrid were completely lifeless, but there was a glimmer of hope for June.

The phone at the Völler house rang off of the hook until Andy rose to answer. With the house seemingly empty, it was a blank, hollow call. Andy confusedly shook his head and rushed to get dressed. He'd heard through the line that his family had been in a car accident, but that was it. Then, as the headlights of an approaching car shone through the living room blinds, Andy ran to meet it.

The hospital was relatively calm as Andy reached the third-floor waiting room to meet Kurt's old army pal Gene Shatterly, better known as Coach Gene Shatterly of the North Carolina Tar Heels. The mood was somber, to say the least, as the coach informed Andy that both his mother and father had perished in the accident.

Andy's head fell hard when he heard the news, but there was hope. His sister was fighting to survive. There was life as Andy's world died.

Instead of sight, there was a colorless blur. Rather than sound, there was only a faint heartbeat. He waited for word of his June's survival, but it didn't come.

People came and went, but after a final solemn sunrise, June's light dimmed. Tears welled helplessly up in Andy's eyes as Coach Shatterly delivered the second fateful message. It was a harsh and swift rebuke for the young superstar. But he wasn't a superstar anymore; he wasn't anything anymore. Everything simply stopped. They wouldn't know what happened earlier in the night, what Andy had said earlier. No one would know, because he wouldn't tell them. He wouldn't tell them, because he wouldn't speak. He'd said enough already, and now his whole family was gone. And in a way, he was gone too.

It was supposed to have been a good year. Andy was looking forward to senioritis and then on to university, but not now. Now it was gone, shattered, and worthless, and he was suddenly alone. Coach Gene Shatterly still wanted him at Carolina, but he had shut down. Everyone expected him to come around at some point, and maybe he could have, but he was holding a secret, something so painful he couldn't bear to think it, not to mention say it. So he just didn't speak.

After a while, Andy's appearance changed. He eventually dropped out of school. People talked, but he wouldn't listen. He was in the stratosphere searching for his family, floating through the heavens, seeking sanity. But it wouldn't come.

A once gregarious youngster, Andy now drifted around with empty eyes looking through things instead of at them. People spent time with him, but as the days passed, any kind of breakthrough seemed more and more unlikely. Instead of a rescue mission, it now seemed like mitigation, and there were only a few people left who might be able to help. As his godfather, Coach Shatterly was forced to sell the family home and to check Andy into a halfway house. There was a place in town where he'd be clothed and fed and still be able to get out and about, so that's where he stayed. It seemed like an impenetrable wall had gone up, and it was going to take something out of this world to bring it down.

Billy had noticed him at the basketball court, before his game—a tall, looming figure in the distance. He almost thought Andy was a spirit, but it now seemed like he was the subject of the spirits. It seemed like Billy had found the son he was supposed to save. Now he just needed to save him.

He couldn't tell his new boss that, but maybe all Billy needed to do was to stay flexible and foolish. It had been working thus far, so he had no reason to believe it would stop. He'd been guided every step of the way, so maybe it was time for him to lead.

Sitting at the table with Rick, Billy suddenly asked, "Do you guys play basketball?"

With Rick about to speak, Gina, the dining room manager, burst through the door and yelled, "So, what's the problem? I can't take an afternoon off without getting a call?" right before looking at Billy and saying, "He's not Glen."

"No, he's Billy."

"What happened to Glen?"

"I don't know, but Billy bailed us out."

"Thanks," said Gina. "So do you want a job?"

"I hired him already, but he's going to work in the kitchen—if that's all right with you, Billy?"

"Sure," said Billy.

"So who's going to work the dining room?" asked Gina.

"Glen, I guess," answered Rick. "You need a ride home, Billy?"

"I'd appreciate it. I came here with my girlfriend but she's gone, not for good though, I hope."

"I hope not either. I'd feel responsible."

Rick didn't know the half of it. When he threw Billy that apron, he had no idea what it might mean for him, for the town, or the world for that matter. It could either be really good, or really, really bad.

Calm, cool and collected, Rick had just the right demeanor for the kitchen. He looked to be in his mid-thirties, but he was still fit. While shorter than Billy, he was still pushing six feet. With a backwards cap and a pair of worn-in Air Jordans, he had the air of a shrewd, hardworking chef. Billy knew the look, because he'd once had it. He'd wanted to be a chef, but that was before Rita and before the spirits. He couldn't be a chef anymore, but he could still cook.

Rick drove a Chevy truck—a short-bed, perfect for carting things around and picking up produce from the farmers market.

As he and Billy drove off Rick asked, "So, where you headed?"

"It's off of 54. I'll let you know when we get close."

"OK," replied Rick.

"It looks like you've got some experience. I was watching you work. You're pretty good."

"Yeah," agreed Billy. "I was a cook in a past life, in Florida, before I got run out of town."

Rick laughed, but Billy didn't, which led him to wonder. But he needed help, so he let it slide. It wasn't an industry of clean-cut Wall Street types but of hardened, often invisible misfits who could only exist in a small, hot place, cutting and sautéing their way through life. Billy didn't have to be perfect, as long as he was on time.

"You did say something about basketball, didn't you?"

"Yeah," replied Billy, "you guys play at all?"

"We play at least once a week, maybe more. This here's Tobacco Road, son," declared Rick with a measure of pride. "Basketball's a religion here."

Billy knew more than he let on, but just to keep things rolling he said, "The Tar Heels, right?"

"That's right. Did you see the guy in here with the four other guys, the one with the white hair and a limp?"

"The one that didn't wait in line."

"Yeah," replied Rick, "that's Coach Gene Shatterly, head basketball coach of the Tar Heels, and a close personal friend of mine, I might add."

That was it, the smoking gun. Things were coming together.

"Well, what about Andy, does he ever play?" asked Billy.

"Play? Man, he barely talks. He's in here nearly every day, and I've never heard him say more than three words. But if he ever plays again, I know a few guys who would be pretty happy."

Billy didn't need to ask because he already knew.

"Turn here," said Billy. "Sorry, I'm still learning my way around."

"No problem. Can you show up tomorrow around seven? I know it's short notice, but we'll work out a schedule from there."

It seemed like Billy's life of leisure was coming to an end as he muttered an uninspired, "Yeah, sure."

"Solid player. See ya then," sounded Rick, as he caught a glimpse of Celia and asked. "Who's that?"

"That's my aunt, Celia."

"Hi Celia!" exclaimed Rick with an excited wave.

"Do I know him?" asked Celia as she returned the wave.

"That's Rick."

Billy then tromped into the house to discuss the day's events—and there was a lot to discuss. All things considered, he seemed to have now reached the hard part, even more difficult than being thrown around like a rag doll. The spirits had departed and left it up to Billy, so now he'd have to build the relationships. He'd have to gain the trust and sustain the belief. Billy didn't know if he could do it, but something else thought he could, so now he'd have to. He'd have to get back to his roots. He'd have to get back on the road. In Mexico Billy walked everywhere, so that's what he'd do now.

Facing his salvation as well, there was no room for half measures. This was serious business. This was saving someone. But maybe it wasn't all up to him. Maybe the spirits were still there, but that didn't change the fact that there was zero margin for error.

If Billy tried and it didn't work, they could lose Andy forever. There'd be nothing left of his family, nothing to show that they were exceptional and that they were loved, nothing but the shell of a man with a distant memory of happiness. Billy wouldn't let it happen. For the first time he wasn't worried about himself. If he had to perish for something greater, he'd do it, but he wouldn't go quietly.

Andy wanted to get out, he just didn't know how. He'd gone so far down he didn't know which way was up. But every now and then, he'd feel a kind wind on his face; and every so often he'd see a pretty bird flutter by. He'd look at his hands and wonder what they could have done. He'd feel his legs and wonder if he could still jump, and then he'd go back to accepting his fate. There was still a chance that Andy could come back, but it was slim.

Billy couldn't know the pain that Andy had endured, and he couldn't pretend to. He'd been down and out, on a beach with everything else hundreds of miles away. He knew how it felt to scratch and crawl, but this wasn't about getting down, it was about getting up. It wasn't about the past, it was about the future. It was about moving mountains and parting oceans. In short, it was about working miracles.

With Billy still winding down, Celia asked, "So who's Rick?"

"I'll fill you in when Gwen gets here, if she gets here. I kind of left her hanging today."

"In true Billy fashion," replied Celia.

"I had a good reason."

"Don't you always?"

The remark stung, but he guessed he deserved it. Wondering what Gwen had done with the rest of her afternoon, he called, she answered, and then he hit the shower.

Downstairs and ready to discuss the afternoon, Celia feverishly asked, "So what happened?"

"Something just freaking amazing!" replied Billy.

Celia waited as Billy stalled. He had the goods. He knew the story. It was a done deal. He'd be out of here in no time. And then there was Gwen. Watching her pull into the drive, he suddenly didn't feel so transient. He felt connected and wanted everyone to feel that way. It was a relief that he still carried the weight of the world.

Billy opened the door to see Gwen's pretty eyes sparkling through the dim yellow porch light.

"Hello again," she said.

"Hi, sweetie. I'm sorry."

"What the heck happened?" bellowed Celia. "I've been waiting all afternoon."

"Billy ran out on our date, that's all,"

"Oh," muttered Celia.

Billy finally said, "I found the son we're supposed to save. When we passed that restaurant, I had a feeling."

Then to catch Celia up, he added, "I got a job today, at the same restaurant where we ate lunch. That guy who dropped me off, he's the chef."

"He's kind of cute," added Celia.

"Whatever," continued Billy. "Anyway, I tried to go to the bathroom but instead walked into the kitchen, and then Rick threw me an apron. He thought I was the new guy. The new guy's name is Glen, by the way, and he never showed."

"I was wondering," said Gwen.

"So with the apron in hand, I had a choice. I could either give it back or put it on, so I put it on. There was something in the air; it seemed preordained, or arranged. That's when I came out and cleared the table."

"That's when you came out and blew me off."

"But it was for a reason. At the end of the shift that kid came in, the tall one I saw at the basketball court, in the distance. I got to see him up close this time, and then I heard the story of Andy Völler."

"Andy Völler?" repeated Celia.

"Yeah, who is Andy Völler?" asked Gwen.

"Thought you'd never ask."

With the girls sufficiently hooked, Billy told the tale of Andy Völler; that he was a brilliant junior basketball player from the area, a one-of-a-kind talent who was sure to go pro. He told of how, on a dark and stormy night, disaster struck. Andy's family perished in a car accident and then Andy, riddled with guilt, suddenly dropped out of society. Billy went on to say how the head coach of the college basketball team is his godfather and how he took care of him and made arrangements for his well-being.

"There were plenty of families who offered to take him in, but he didn't accept. Andy actually quit speaking. He doesn't say much now. He only eats at the restaurant where we ate today, and to add to the growing set of circumstances, the coach frequents that same restaurant, and now I work there."

"Unbelievable," said Celia. "This is completely unprecedented."

"It's so sad," added Gwen. "You have to do something, Billy."

"*We* have to do something. It was given to us, a ragtag unit of specialists, an unaffiliated group of spiritual warriors with a top-secret mission."

"When you put it like that," said Celia.

"It is like that. It's nature at work. It's divine wisdom. It's the things we can't understand but are compelled to complete. It's mystical and beautiful and deadly and sad and then one day happily over."

"Why happily over?" asked Gwen.

"I guess that's when we're perfect. When we've weathered our storms and conquered our fears and learned our lessons and then maybe given something back. Maybe those who leave in an instant are the lucky ones? Their beauty never fades. Their laughter is never hushed. They live forever in our hearts cherished and unchanged."

"But what about the people left behind?" asked Celia.

"We continue. We sustain their memory. We honor their lives. We use them to make something better. It's supposed to change us, but not for the worse. It's supposed to make us stronger so we can make someone else stronger. If not for that, then who are we?"

"But what about Andy?" asked Gwen.

"What about Andy?" repeated Celia. "What about Andy?" she said again, walking toward the stairs while Gwen and Billy stared.

As Celia wandered throughout the second floor, they wondered what was up, and why she'd left muttering, "What about Andy?"

Was she losing it too? It couldn't happen to both Billy and Celia. At least one of them had to stay sane. With Billy and Gwen still at the table, Celia returned in a tizzy, holding a deed of some sort.

"I knew that name sounded familiar!" blurted Celia, waving a piece of paper. "Take a look at this."

All eyes then turned to the document. On the top line it read, "From the Völler Family Trust."

"This is Andy's house!" exclaimed Celia.

With the startling declaration, they were completely mystified. Whenever it seemed like nothing more could surface, something else happened. Thoughts swirled as they wondered whether the house was a portal into a parallel universe. There was something very strong at work—the unstoppable power of redemption—and Billy was fascinated.

As they reflected on the latest reveal, Billy said, "And that must have been his basketball."

Gwen recalled how she felt in its presence, like there was a sadness but also hope, and she wondered why.

The deed to Celia's house rested remarkably in the middle of the dining room table. Still processing the new information, Celia surmised that maybe she was just holding it until the real owner arrived.

As Billy's mind continued to spin, he quickly exclaimed, "Follow me!"

Trailing Billy into the front yard, Celia and Gwen looked curiously around as he said, "Look at that spot above the garage doors."

Billy then pointed to some splintered wood as Celia said, "Oh yeah, it needs to be patched."

"I see it," added Gwen.

"What do you think it was?" asked Billy.

"I don't know," they both said in unison.

"It must have been where the basketball hoop was."

"So what happened to it?" asked Celia.

"He ripped it off."

Something about that statement hit home, the thought of a distraught kid with nothing else to do but to rip, tear, and destroy. There was no manner of control other than to take something he loved and trash it and then walk away.

So this was Andy's house, and that was his basketball. This is the place where he was lost, and perhaps where he'd also be found. With the sudden realization, everything changed. It seemed like something came together but also fell apart. It was confusing, to say the least—either a hugely intricate design or just another coincidence.

"It's a special house," said Billy. "I feel like it's here to help, not hurt us."

"There was joy here," added Gwen. "A lot of good things happened in this house."

"I'm just a little emotional," replied Celia. "It suddenly hit me, the fact that there's something so unresolved."

"We'll resolve it," declared Billy. "One way or another, there will be closure."

Celia then put her long arms around Billy's wide shoulders and said, "Thanks Billy," before slowly trudging back into the house.

"So what now?" asked Gwen.

"I've got another hunch," answered Billy as they walked quietly into the garage. "Call the ball."

Gwen wasn't sure it would work, but nevertheless, she said, "Basketball, basketball, where are you?"

To Billy's surprise, the ball popped cheerfully out of the loft and rolled straight over to her. Beaming from ear to ear, Gwen cradled the ball against her chest as tears ran slowly down her cheeks. Her head then fell beneath the weight of even more tears as her delicate white skin reddened.

Billy watched but didn't intervene. He remembered she could feel things, and that she held a distinct attraction for items of interest. That was another one of his suppositions, that she was connected in a different way. Something was there, he just didn't know what. Gwen didn't know either. With a hand on her shoulder Billy asked, "Do you want me to take it?"

"No," sobbed Gwen. "It's OK. It's just something I had to get out of the way. I'm not sure why, but there's a strong pull here."

Billy had a clue, but for the moment it was unconfirmed. He had to remember that he was but a servant, a means for things to work through, a medium, so to speak. But that didn't dislodge the feeling that something was pulling her away from him.

"Hold on to the ball while I check out the loft then," said Billy as he scaled a ladder.

Now in the loft, he discovered a few more artifacts, one of which was the basketball hoop he suspected had been torn from the garage. Examining it for bends and breaks, he found it a little dinged up but otherwise fine. He'd restore it to its former glory. Moving further back, he saw clothes and yearbooks and also a shiny square item showing a large white swoosh. It appeared to be a really big shoe box. Billy cautiously opened it, and found a brand-new pair of blue-and-white high-tops that sat curiously unused. *Somebody's missing these*, thought Billy as he stacked them by the rim.

Billy didn't know how the chips would fall; all he knew was that he needed to get this basketball rim back on the house so he could get the ball working.

"Can you grab this rim?" asked Billy.

"Hey, you found it!" exclaimed Gwen.

Ducking a healthy swath of dust, Gwen took the awkward object and placed it on the ground beside the ball. With the basketball and rim now side by side, it seemed like something was being rescued or getting fixed.

Now on the ladder, Gwen noticed Billy carrying the huge shoebox.

"What's that?" she asked.

Without a word, Billy simply opened the box to display a glowing pair of brand-new blue-and-white high-tops.

"They're beautiful," said Gwen, "and they're new."

"Yeah," agreed Billy. "It's strange. They must be Andy's, but they couldn't have fit him then. These shoes are for someone who's around six eleven or more."

"Is he that size now?"

"I guess we'll find out."

"We will?"

"With any luck," answered Billy, now eyeing the interesting collection of goods.

With Billy carrying the rim and ball, Gwen followed with the ladder.

Celia then walked up and exclaimed, "You were right!"

As Billy made his way back into the garage, he softly chanted, "Power drill, power drill, where are you?"

A power drill obviously wasn't going to jump out and smack him in the head, so he was going to have to search. Scouring the various boxes, Billy found some screws and anchors but still no drill. Celia poked her head in and said, "Maybe you could tidy up while you're at it."

"Hmph," sounded Billy as he went from drawer to drawer only to find more junk. "I know you're here," he wheezed, sifting through a dusty closet. Then pulling a black plastic box from the clutter, he said, "There you are! Now please tell me that you've got a power cord."

"I sure do," said Celia as she ran into the house.

"OK, Gwen," ordered Billy, "I'm going to need you to hand me that basket once I get everything prepped."

"Sure thing, boss," answered Gwen.

So with the extension cord plugged in and the drill fully functioning, Billy put on his safety glasses and went to work. With Gwen holding the ladder and Celia the safety expert, they were cooking with gas. Billy drilled and screwed and tightened, and as the smoke finally cleared, there was a basketball hoop once again mounted on the Völler garage for all to see.

"That's nice," remarked Gwen.

"We're going to have to get Andy over here," added Celia.

"That's the idea," replied Billy as he returned the drill to the garage and walked back out with the big orange box.

"What's that?" asked Celia.

Without answering, Billy simply opened it up to reveal a huge pair of high tops as Celia's jaw dropped.

"Andy's shoes," she mused. "Where is Andy?"

"Where is Andy?" repeated both Gwen and Billy as the ball popped readily into Gwen's waiting hands.

She then hoisted it toward the basket for a perfect swoosh. Billy then fielded the ball and passed to Celia, who—to everyone's surprise—hit a towering shot. It was then Billy's turn. He dunked with considerable force just to test his work. The basket held, and the ball again went to Gwen. She and Celia, of course, played keep-away, laughing the whole time, with the ball seemingly happy as well.

Everyone's spirits were lifted. It was the beauty of sport, bringing people together and putting smiles on their faces. It was the ultimate redemptive force, and they needed more.

Wondering what Billy's next move might be, Celia asked, "So, what's next, Billy?"

"I'm going to get out there again."

"Billy's the bait," added Gwen.

"Yep," agreed Billy, "I'm the bait."

THE TEAM

With their game finally over and the day quickly moving into dusk, Gwen and Billy took a walk. She didn't know what they'd become, but in this time of change, all she could do was hope for the best.

The reason for Billy's arrival had strangely materialized, and Gwen wondered where she fit in. She also wondered if he'd forget about her when it was all said and done.

Remembering Billy had gotten a job, Gwen asked, "So how do you feel now, Mr. big man with a new job?"

"Inspired but also a little worried. What if I'm not up to the task, what if this thing's too big for me?"

"Not a chance, Billy. Just like the spirits, you materialized. You're of our ilk, you're one of us. You can't fail."

"I can fail just as good as the next guy," said Billy.

"But you won't," replied Gwen giving him a deep, reassuring hug.

Tomorrow was a new day, sure to be full of surprises, but tonight would be quiet, just as a night should be. Wrapped together in the comfortable covers, they drifted off to sleep beneath dreams of things to come.

Waking to an obnoxious alarm, he knew today was the day. It was the first day of the rest of Billy's life, whatever that meant. He tried to be optimistic, but regardless of his actual purpose, he was still going to work.

"Morning, sugar," whispered Billy. "I'm heading into the office."

"Ah, do you want a ride?" asked Gwen, still half asleep.

"Not today, babe. Today I'm walking. I'll call you later."

"Ugh," was all that Gwen could muster before rolling over and going back to sleep.

Unassuming in a T-shirt, a trucker cap, and a pair of shorts and shoes, Billy headed out. Nothing ever materialized when he was driving, so on he walked valiantly into an uncertain future. Ray obviously wasn't going to pick him up, but he still kind of wondered.

With roughly a four-mile round trip ahead of him, Billy would probably get there early. It was his first day, so at least he'd make a good first impression. After all, he wasn't sure how long he'd survive.

It reminded Billy of his last kitchen job. He'd been on assignment then, and he seemed to be on assignment again. He couldn't help but wonder if that assignment had led to this one. Maybe the spirits had seen Billy fumbling along and then running away to Mexico? He would have seemed disposable enough, and who knows, he might just succeed. But if he didn't, there was no harm done, they could just bring in the next dummy.

But Billy was off to a pretty good start, and he was also excited to get back into the kitchen. At least that's how he felt now; he wasn't sure how he'd feel later.

Rounding the corner and with the restaurant in view, it seemed like a nice place. It had a quaint patio, adequate outdoor seating, and from what he could tell, a pretty good menu. With his feet still beating the pavement, Billy wanted to enjoy a few more minutes of peace before jumping in.

As if a regular job wouldn't be challenging enough, Billy also needed to get a kid who hadn't played basketball in years to play again and then get a prestigious coach to take notice. No problem.

He'd just have to see how things went. Billy couldn't come on too strong, because he was supposedly there to work. There was something else brewing as well, but he couldn't tell anyone. They'd find out soon enough.

Finally at the Friends Café, Billy paused. At least now he knew where the kitchen was as he walked in to see Rick walking out of the cooler with a stack of boxes.

"Billy, you showed. I know yesterday was kind of hectic, with you not really here for a job and all," said Rick.

"Yep, came back for more punishment," replied Billy.

At a glance, the configuration made sense. There was a cold side for salads and sandwiches and a hot side for fried food, steaks, and sauté dishes. The dish room was around the corner with stainless steel sinks, a dish machine, and some counters for storage. There was adequate prep space with plenty of cutting boards, sharp knives, and even a slicer. The walk-in cooler was clean and packed with perishables as Billy prepared to rummage through it.

"We supply the kitchen shirts and aprons. Shorts are fine for the summer. You got nice legs, anyway," said Rick with a wink.

"Damn," replied Billy, "that was quick."

"You haven't seen anything," continued Rick as he walked into the dish room.

"George, meet Billy. Billy, this is George."

"Pleased to meet you," said Billy.

"Oh, bullshit," replied George. "What you say, Rick, he's got nice legs? Show me them legs, Billy!"

Billy then lifted his shorts and flexed as George chortled, "He sho does, Rick. He sho does!"

"Nice to meet you, man," said George.

Billy extended a hand and replied, "Likewise."

"George is the main man. Keep him happy and you'll be fine, piss him off and you probably won't last long."

Billy didn't want to last long, but he didn't say it. He also had a history with dishwashers, but he didn't say that either. This was a new place, so he'd start with a clean slate.

"Thanks for the tip," replied Billy as he buttoned the shirt and tied his apron.

Previously a long-haired hippie freak, he was now clean cut with something to prove. It was really just a disguise, he guessed, as he noticed Rick's backwards cap, chef's pants—and high-tops, of course. Rick had dark, engaging eyes, a friendly smile, and a swift, athletic gait. Following Rick around the kitchen, Billy surmised that he'd found his first teammate.

As Billy filled the cold side and Rick cooked off the bacon, a fresh-faced kid walked in and said, "Hey, ah, I'm Glen. I'm here to work or something?"

"You were supposed to be here to work or something yesterday," replied Rick as he threw him an apron and added, "Grab some glasses and fill up the ice for starters."

"OK, where are the glasses?"

"Around the corner in the dish room," said Rick with a devilish grin as he heard Glen ask George, "Hey, ah, where's the glasses?

"Oh, you the dumbass who was supposed to work yesterday?"

"I guess."

"Well, they're right there, dumbass," replied George pointing to a towering stack of red glass racks.

"The glasses are full. I just sent him back to meet George," chuckled Rick.

"Sweet," replied Billy. Things were starting out pretty good, fast paced and insane, just like he liked it.

"Before I forget, you got a nice place out there in the woods."

"Thanks."

"What I mean is, your aunt Celia is a stone cold fox."

"She's crazy though," replied Billy, just to throw a little water on the flames. The last thing he wanted was to be the middleman.

"OK, well, I was just throwing it out there, I mean, one day if the therapy works out."

"I'll keep you apprised," offered Billy.

"Yeah, keep me apprised," grinned Rick.

As the wait staff filtered in, Gina, the dining room manager, ran into the kitchen and yelled, "Why did you send Glen into the dish room to be insulted by George!"

"It's what George does best, I mean, besides dishes."

"George, you be nice," yelled Gina.

"OK, baby," replied George. To George almost everyone was baby, and there wasn't much that could be done about it.

"So here's the rundown, Billy. We make a lot of burgers and sandwiches. It's not too upscale, but it's good. We do both quality and quantity, so get your running shoes on."

The Friends Café was casual dining at best, not really a dive, though it had certain dive-like qualities. The food was good. It was certainly eccentric, and from what Billy could glean, it had a fiercely loyal clientele.

Scanning the menu, he saw specialty salads and sandwiches. No prob. He saw nachos, fried jalapenos, and grilled ahi. Not bad. He saw burgers and fries and a Philly cheesesteak sandwich. Of course. He then saw a soup du jour listed and realized they didn't have one. Then, from the other side of the kitchen, Rick yelled, "How are you with soups, Billy?"

"Gonna test me right off the bat, eh?" replied Billy, knowing that a good soup was a thing of beauty.

"You know it. No rest for the wicked."

This was new, walking in one day and making a soup the next. The good thing was that he hadn't passed himself off as anything special, the bad was that if he didn't make a good soup, he'd be exposed. But Billy was up to the task, he'd been in hotter kitchens than this.

Looking through the cooler he thought, *A cream soup, not too heavy though.*

"Hey, Rick, you got any plans for those leeks?"

"They're yours, but make it quick. We open soon."

Potato leek soup, thought Billy as he quickly sautéed some chopped leaks with celery and onion and then dusted it with flour to make a light roux. Next came the potatoes and water, which was brought up to a boil and whipped into a luxurious slurry. Billy finally added the salt and pepper, and, as the closed sign flipped to open, he uncapped the soup, added the heavy cream, and mixed it into a delicious creation—a quick one and fully vegetarian, too.

Chef Rick and George then walked over and said, "Time to test the soup."

"Yeah, I'm hungry," added George.

"It's hot."

"Usually I'd say no shit," declared George, "but I was told to be a little more polite, whatever that means."

"Kill them with kindness," said Billy.

"You can't tell a black man to kill someone with something!"

"Not even with niceties?"

"Yeah, not even with that."

Eyeing the thick white liquid, they both ladled out a cup, and through loud alternating slurps, Rick said, "That's really good."

"Yeah, lucky for you, it's all right," added George.

He'd passed the first test, but there was sure to be more. There were always tests in a busy restaurant, and you were only as good as your last dish. There was never any real comfort level other than survival, and then hopefully appreciation. But Billy was ready. He could do this.

The specials board read, "A half Reuben with house-made pastrami and a cup of potato leek soup," and they were selling a lot of the specials. Billy knew they were selling a lot of the specials because he was making them.

Today was the same as when he and Gwen had first arrived. People just kept streaming in. Billy had never made so many BLTs. The servers grabbed the plates as fast as Billy could put them up, and sure enough, the coach and his entourage were also there again.

"You gonna introduce me to the coach?" asked Billy.

"Why don't we play some basketball instead?" answered Rick, as Coach Shatterly wasn't all that approachable.

"Sounds good."

At the close of his first shift, Billy was whipped. With over a hundred orders complete, there was, of course, one more to go. A final ticket came in for two specials, and it was for Andy Völler.

"Hey, Billy, you remember me telling you about Andy Völler?" asked Rick.

"Yeah."

Rick then pointed to the ticket and said, "That's his ticket, man. It's all you."

"They've all been all me," snapped Billy.

"Jaded already, eh? I went out of my way to bring you in, and now look at you."

"Yeah, look at me," muttered Billy as he read aloud. "Two Reubens, heavy on the pastrami, and two soups to go."

"I got the soups," said Rick as Billy heaped two piles of pastrami and sauerkraut on the hot grill and then walked out to the bar to get a Coke. He didn't need one; he just wanted to get another glimpse of his quarry, or more accurately, the spirits' quarry.

Beneath the wear and tear of a rugged existence, Billy saw what Andy had once been. It was still there, but it wouldn't be there for long. He had to act fast.

Andy was tall. At twenty-one years old, he seemed to be nearly six eleven, perfect for a size-18 shoe. Billy didn't talk to him. He didn't want to scare him off. They did lock eyes though. Andy had seen him on the basketball court that day, but Billy didn't know what it meant. Maybe it meant that he wanted to get back out there.

As Andy drifted off, Rick announced, "Cleanup time."

Billy knew what that meant: sweeping, wiping, cleaning, stacking, and then mopping. With elbows swinging and feet moving, the crew drifted gracefully around, each completing a task and moving on to the next until they were ready to go.

"Let's bail," said Rick. "It's time to play ball."

"Yeah," agreed George. "I'll show you what I do to little Ricky dicky."

"Yikes," replied Billy. "But we need one more. We need Glen."

"Who, the no-show?"

"Yeah."

So Billy stuck his head out the door and yelled, "Hey, no-show, you wanna play basketball? Loser buys."

"You're all losers," replied Glen, "but I'll play."

"What he say?" asked George.

"He said he'd play."

With the crew on the move, Billy's intuition told him to get the basketball.

"Turn here, Glen," said Billy as they drove up to Celia's.

Glen waited as Billy popped into the garage and whispered, "Basketball, basketball, where are you?"

Opening the window, Billy again asked, "Where are you, basketball?"

Following a stiff breeze, the ball bounced out of the loft and rolled straight over to him.

"There you are, basketball!" exclaimed Billy.

With the basketball in hand, he gave Celia a thumbs up as she motioned excitedly back. From the look on Billy's face, she could tell things were heating up.

At the park, Glen and Billy neared the court as Rick and George took shots. Most were going in, so it looked good so far.

"The closer you get, the easier it is," said Glen as he inadvertently grabbed Billy's ball and hoisted it high into the air.

Eyes bulged as the ball sailed through the sky and then dropped straight in; nothing but net. It then bounced quickly back to Billy, who drained another long shot to quash any suspicions of a magic basketball, as if they could even imagine it.

"Let me see that ball, Billy," George quickly said.

Billy then passed it to George, whose effort clanked mercilessly off of the backboard.

"This ball sucks."

"It ain't the ball," chuckled Glen as George glared.

Holding his special basketball, Billy watched the guys shoot around. With close-cropped ginger hair, white skin, and freckles, Glen Davis Jr. shot the ball well. From Tarboro, North Carolina, Glen had been recruited by some smaller colleges, but when it came time to commit, he didn't show, hence the name no-show Glen. Billy imagined Glen as the shooting guard, with Rick on the point. He and George would be the forwards, and Andy Völler could play center. If Billy wasn't mistaken, the pieces seemed to be snapping right into place.

As he further studied the court, Billy surmised that he had a decent squad. With a shaved head and a pencil-thin beard, George Penny was heavy, but good, and he was loud. Hailing from Durham, North Carolina, George came from a long line of Duke fans, but he unapologetically wore Carolina blue. Without any formal training, George had a knack for rebounding and blocking shots but struggled on offense. That and issues of conditioning were his only weak points.

From the cold, northern reaches of Maine, Richard Flores, or Rick, for short, basically grew up in a gym. As a four-year letterman and community college standout, he moved south to escape the frigid Maine winters. Not good enough to play for the Carolina colleges, Rick found work in a local restaurant and an affordable rental. Content to exist in the epicenter of college basketball, rather than make the long trip back to Maine, he stayed. More comfortable with the ball in his hands, Rick had the carefree look of a playmaker. Fast and fluid, it seemed like he'd be able to get the ball up court pretty well.

And then there was Billy.

"Hey, Billy," yelled Rick, "are you gonna shoot, or just stand there looking stupid?"

With a wry smile, Billy took a couple of strong bounces toward the rim and then leapt. Soaring toward the basket like a bird in flight, Billy slammed the ball through the hoop and hung for a spell just for dramatic effect. He wouldn't use his powers often, but every now and then they'd have to come out.

"Damn, Billy's got some ups," said Glen. "He's on my team."

"You must have rockets on them shoes," added George.

Rick was suspicious.

"So a guy drifts into town with a nice soup, a thunderous dunk, and a gorgeous aunt. It must be nice to be Billy."

"It's tough to be Billy," corrected Billy.

Rick hadn't seen him losing his love and getting run out of town. He hadn't seen him down and out in Mexico. He hadn't seen him at the temple, getting ravaged beneath the storm and the spirits. He didn't see him driving around with Ray and jumping off of the roof of a frat house into a kiddie pool. He didn't hear the screech of the train or feel the force of being spun out of a deadly chair. Rick knew nothing of the medicine man or the sacred powers or the car that smashed into Billy's legs. He didn't see Billy going one on one with the one-armed basketball player. He didn't know about Gwen and her special powers or the basketball that he now bounced. But in some strange way, Rick knew something was up.

"OK, Billy," replied Rick, "I'm not sure what's going on, but whatever it is, I'm in."

"I'm in too," said George.

"Count me in as well," added Glen. "I'm ready to get paid!"

"We gotta play before we get paid boys," said Billy as he hoisted up an outside shot and followed his miss with a layin. He then passed it to George, who quickly backed him into the basket for an easy lay-up.

"Gonna have to put a little meat on them bones to stop that."

"Don't let him do that to you, Billy," said Rick as he bounced the ball through George's legs on the way to a sweet midrange jump shot.

Glen then rebounded the ball and ran it back behind the key for another towering three.

"Nice shot, Glen," said Billy. He liked what he saw.

Someone else liked it too. As the guys continued to play, the hulking figure of Andy Völler watched from afar. Moving even closer, he was now within striking distance as the action stopped.

"What you know, Andy?" said George, as Andy would sometimes give him a nod as he took out the trash.

"What brings you out this way, Andy?" asked Rick. Andy spoke to Rick every now and then, but nothing more than a short greeting or maybe a weather report, real simple stuff.

Looking fiercely on, Andy stood courtside like a towering figure ready to pounce. Wearing pleated khakis a couple of inches too short and worn-out boat shoes, he looked like an immigrant kid desperately searching for a city of gold. His arms rested easily at his side, and he wore that same empty stare from before.

With things at a standstill, Billy quickly passed Andy the special ball and it snapped firmly into his hands with a thunderous clap. Billy swore that he saw sparks fly as Andy clasped his old basketball and gave it a quick spin. The ball whirled away on his outstretched finger, then curiously traveled up his arm, around his shoulders, and down his other arm to continue its spin.

"Damn, Andy, didn't know you was in the Globetrotters," boomed George with a hearty laugh.

"I wasn't," replied Andy as he dropped the ball and walked off.

Billy jumped for the basketball as it followed Andy away, but nobody really noticed. They were still looking at Andy. It had been quite a show.

George and Glen loved it. They didn't know what was at stake. It meant more to Rick. He knew who Andy was and what he was supposed to have been. He also knew that if Andy was ever going to do anything in basketball, he needed to do it now.

So Billy just happened to walk into the kitchen and then into their basketball game, and now Andy had a ball in his hands again. Something didn't add up.

"Nice game, Glen," said Rick. "I'm glad you made it in today. After yesterday, I wasn't so sure."

"I'd call it a scheduling glitch."

"You a glitch," said George.

"Can you give George a ride home?" asked Rick. "I got Billy."

"I'd be honored," answered Glen.

"You better be," said George as they walked off.

Approaching the truck, Rick said, "You got quite a game there, Billy."

"Yeah, I've been working on it for a while. I played when I was younger and kind of got into it again, first for exercise and then for spirituality, I guess."

"Spirituality, eh?"

"Yeah, to get centered."

"To get centered, huh?"

"Yeah, you know, to tune out all the noise."

Nearing Celia's house, Rick was done with the repetition, but he had more to say. "Look, Billy, I'm not the brightest crayon in the box, but I'm not altogether naïve. I've seen things today that I never thought I'd see, namely Andy Völler holding a basketball that seemed to be alive."

"If you think something's going on, you're right, but if you're looking for answers, I can't give you any. So If you need to let me go, I understand."

"That's not what I meant, Billy. What I mean," continued Rick as they pulled into Billy's driveway, "is that I'd like to help."

"Well let's just say you'll be in pretty good shape because we're going to play basketball tomorrow and the day after that and the day after that as well. So do you still want to help?"

"Like I said before, Billy, I'm in."

As Rick's car slowed to a stop, both Gwen and Celia approached, mostly out of curiosity for the new guy.

"So this is how you live, out here in the woods surrounded by beautiful women?"

"Who, us?" chimed the girls.

"Yes, you," repeated Rick. "I met you the other day. You're Celia right?"

"Right," answered Celia. "But I wouldn't say we met."

"Are we meeting now?"

"I don't know, are we?"

"Yes," answered Billy as he carried a large shoebox. "You have now met."

Rick's eyes then shifted from Celia to the shoebox as he asked, "What the hell is that?"

"It's a shoebox," answered Billy as he opened it up on the hood of Rick's truck.

Now staring at a gargantuan pair of sparkling white shoes, he asked, "Whose are those?"

"I'm guessing they're Andy's. This is Andy's old house, and I found them in the attic along with his basketball. They were probably his to grow into. I think he's probably grown into them."

"Probably has," said Rick.

"I was thinking we could keep 'em in your truck. Maybe he'll put them on the next time he shows up. If he shows up."

Not wanting to wear out his welcome, Rick stowed the shoes behind the seat and said, "So, I'll see you tomorrow, right?"

"I'll be there."

"Well, it's nice to have finally met you, Celia," called Rick.

"Likewise," replied Celia as Rick drove away, thinking of Celia, champagne, and roses. And then of Andy and a living basketball. And then Billy, who, it seemed, had just breezed into town to completely turn it upside down.

But it seemed like his job was to cook and to play basketball, so that's what he'd do. Maybe he could get to know Celia a little better as well.

"He's kind of cute, Celia, and I think he likes you," said Gwen.

"So now you're the little matchmaker, I guess," replied Celia.

"I think Billy's actually the matchmaker, he's the one bringing guys over."

Without further delay, Billy said, "Andy came to the court today."

"No way!" exclaimed both Celia and Gwen.

Billy went on to tell how he'd instinctively passed Andy the ball and how Andy caught it and spun it on his finger.

"The basketball traveled up and around Andy's shoulders just like it did to me. It was incredible. It also tried to follow him away. I had to grab it before it rolled off with him."

"Did anyone notice?" asked Gwen.

"Rick's a little suspicious. I obviously can't tell him, but he's going to help. He's going to come to the court with me until we can get Andy back out there. It seems to be moving in the right direction, but nothing's guaranteed."

"You've come this far, Billy," said Celia, "so finish the job."

"That's the goal," replied Billy as they trailed into the house, still immersed in the majesty of everyday magic.

In Billy's bedroom, Billy was preoccupied and Gwen was aloof. Her strong, shapely legs draped comfortably across the sheets as she wondered about the house and why she was so drawn to it. Billy wondered why the ball had been so attracted to her, and why she'd been so attracted to him.

Billy thought that maybe Gwen's special powers were pulling her in a different direction. If they were, he wouldn't have been surprised. Billy's role seemed to be that of a facilitator, so he'd facilitate. He'd never thought they'd stay together forever, but he hadn't ruled it out. Billy liked the life of coming home to Gwen and Celia, but it was only a time, or a season, and it was bound to change. If it did, hopefully something good would be left behind.

Billy's life had been full of heartbreak, so much so that he thought it his natural state of function. More importantly, he thought that maybe he wasn't living his life for himself. Maybe he was a foil or, better yet, a vessel for different things to work through. It was a heavy cross to bear, but he'd been made strong through his trials, and he was getting even stronger.

As they lay together reflecting on another interesting day, Gwen asked, "So what's it like to be back on the hamster wheel?"

"Tiring," answered Billy. "As if you didn't notice, it's a busy little restaurant. I was on the sandwich station, and of course, everyone ordered sandwiches."

"The punishment begin."

"The punishment never ends."

"Oh, cut it," said Gwen. "You've got it good."

"I've got it some way."

Gwen snickered as Billy smiled a lonely smile.

"Goodnight, sugar," said Billy.

Gwen replied, "Good night, sweet prince."

It seemed like as soon as they fell asleep, it was time to wake. Billy hopped up and donned his new disguise.

In a baseball cap, tennis shoes, and shorts, Billy again headed out. It was a nice walk to work, a good warm-up for whatever would come. Setting his sights on the restaurant, Billy was in a funny place. He wouldn't be there for the next few years. He wouldn't be learning birthdays and meeting families. That made him sad, but he could still make some friends.

Making his way into the kitchen, Billy found Rick and George setting up for another busy day.

"Billy's back," said Rick.

"You late," added George. "Drop and give me twenty."

"I guess you're the coach." replied Billy.

"You damn right."

"He's not the coach," said Rick with an excited stare. "I've just been thinking about a team, you know. After yesterday, my mind was soaring. I was finding new heights and suddenly it came to me: if we're going to have a team, we need a name."

"How about the Trees. There's a lot of trees here," offered Billy.

"That's stupid. We need to be the Saints," replied George, perhaps taking the biblical route.

"No, no, no!" exclaimed Rick, "the Raptors, the Hornets, or the Eagles, something like that, something that conveys strength and power."

"Raptors are long gone, hornets are usually harmless, and eagles are basically extinct," noted Billy. "But it's not a bad idea. It needs to be a team decision though."

"Yeah," murmured Rick, "now you're getting it."

"Who's on the team?" snapped George, obviously wanting to hear his name called.

"I'll have the roster by the end of the day," joked Billy.

"Bullshit. We need it now."

With a pause for dramatic effect, Billy put himself in the coach's shoes. With a steely-eyed stare, he said, "We weren't picked, we were chosen. We were the last in line, but the first to step forward. We didn't start this, but by god, we're going to finish it!"

"What the hell is he talking about?" growled George.

"I think it means you made the team," answered Rick.

Billy then turned to George and, with a hand on his shoulder, said, "Yes, George, you made the team."

"Yes!" exclaimed George before asking, "Who else made it?"

"It's going to be Rick, George, Glen, and me. And with any luck, we'll be able to sign Andy Völler. And until we can decide on a proper name, we'll simply be known as the Team."

BACK TO LIFE

With the team in place, now all they needed was Andy, but as the workday drew to a close, something happened—or something didn't happen. Andy didn't show.

"So, what do you think?" asked Billy to both Rick and George. After all, they knew him better, or they knew his routine better.

"I don't know," answered Rick. "He hasn't missed a day in quite a while. Come to think of it, I can't remember him missing a day, can you, George?"

"No, he's like clockwork, comes in before close, usually."

Glen then poked his head through the door and said, "Come on, players, we playin' today?"

"Maybe," replied Billy. "Let's make some food first."

He had a feeling, one of those overwhelming notions, kind of like when he passed Andy the ball. It seemed like they might have to do something else today.

As George finished his cleanup, the last order of the day sizzled away on the grill. Billy continued to think as both he and Rick wiped up and swept down.

What if today was the day? thought Billy.

He then asked, "Hey, Rick, what if today was the day?" asked Billy.

"What if today was what day?"

"What if today was the day of the accident?"

"What if today was the day of what accident?"

"What if today was the day of the Völler accident?"

"What makes you think that?" asked Rick.

"I don't know, I've got this weird invisible antenna that just picks stuff up."

Rick looked over to Billy and saw that he wasn't joking. He was actually concerned. It was concerning. For someone who was unstable or on the brink, time was of the essence. Rick couldn't remember the time and date of the accident, but he knew someone who might.

Calling Gina into the kitchen, Rick asked, "Hey, Gina, do you have any idea when the Völler accident might have happened? Andy didn't come in today, and we're kind of worried."

Gina knew more about the comings and goings of the patrons than anyone else. She knew birthdays and children's names, and she was on a first name basis with Coach Shatterly. The dining room was actually a testament to the café's place in the community, adorned in Tar Heel memorabilia and featuring snapshots of customers near and far. If there was a local happening, Gina would know about it.

"Ah, I don't know. Let me check the ledger. From what I remember, he usually comes in on that day. It's the right month though."

With the ledger in hand, Gina looked down and then solemnly announced, "Yes, today was the day."

"That's what I thought!" exclaimed Billy. "Where does he live, Gina? We've got to get his order to him."

"It's the right thing to do," nodded Rick.

"Yeah, we gonna go get him," added George.

Gina had mixed feelings. She wanted to see Andy again, but she also wanted to give him his space. She didn't want to pressure him, because if he couldn't go up, she sure didn't want him to go down.

"But what if you scare him off and we never see him again?" asked Gina.

"How do you want to see him? Do you want to see him broken down, limping in here every day until he's eventually gone for good, or do you want to see him better?" asked Rick.

Giving it some thought, Gina finally answered, "I want to see him better."

"So give us the address so we can get him his food Gina, it's getting cold," ordered George.

"OK, OK," said Gina as she went back into the dining room and returned with a piece of paper. "This is the only address I have. If this isn't it, then I can't be of any more help."

"Thanks, Gina," added Rick as the rest of the guys nodded on their way out.

Hopefully it would pay off.

It was an amazing turn of events: Billy had been on his back, under the elements, battling the spirits, and now he was working with them.

Scrambling quickly into their cars, they'd do it as a team, a team that didn't have a name, but a team all the same. They were off to get Andy Völler and to bring him back to life.

Maybe it wasn't the right day to roust him, but maybe it was. Maybe it was time for him to finally move on. Maybe Billy and the guys would be able to do what the others couldn't. Maybe they'd be able to save him.

They pulled into a red-brick apartment complex with white sidewalks that all led to identical doors with identical hardware. Billy spied Andy's number and knocked. A low-frequency buzz emanated from the apartment, but nothing else as Billy quickly knocked again.

"George, you ready to bust this thing down?" whispered Billy.

"You know it," answered George.

"Why don't you just try the doorknob?" asked Glen.

"Even better," said Rick, gently opening the door to reveal the hulking figure of Andy Völler lying on the ground in a fetal position.

They thought it was a crime scene or some other kind of gruesome discovery, but as they stared, Andy turned and said, "You came."

"We sure did," exclaimed Billy. "We're here!"

Andy sounded an extended wail.

"Quick, get him onto the couch, George," ordered Rick as both George and Glen gingerly moved him onto the couch.

"We didn't see you today, Andy, so we brought you some food," said Billy, somehow ignoring the fact that he'd been lying on the ground writing in pain.

Andy looked suspiciously around and suddenly felt like a caged animal. He could have run, and almost did, but he was weak and hungry. On the ground, in the dark, he wanted to die, but then the door opened to Billy and the others. Andy knew them from the restaurant. They were pretty good guys, and he'd seen the basketball yesterday, the day before this dreadful day.

"We've got some food for you, Andy," offered Rick.

Carefully studying their movements, Andy took the food and started to eat. He was tall and thin, and he ate like he hadn't eaten in days, getting stronger with each desperate bite.

With the food gone and the people still there, Andy suddenly asked, "What are you doing here?"

No one spoke. This was Billy's territory, and they all knew it.

"We came to pick you up, Andy. We're going to play."

Rick then threw a huge shoebox to the ground and said, "I believe these are yours."

Andy's eyes lit up as he carefully opened the pristine box. Soft and white with light-blue trim and an Air Jordan emblem, Andy's sacred shoes rested peacefully among the layers of crinkled tissue paper. The shoes had been a gift from Coach Shatterly; something to use when the time was right.

"But I don't have any shorts."

"Take your drawers off," said George.

"Huh?"

"Go ahead, Andy, get in the room and take off your drawers," continued George as Andy quickly exited and sent the pants back out. With a sharp knife firmly in hand, George then went to work. He punctured the side of one long pant leg and ripped. Doing the same to the other leg, George somehow made a perfectly measured pair of cutoffs.

"Man," said Glen, "If that dishwashing thing doesn't work out—"

"Shut up," replied George as he threw the shorts back to Andy.

Wearing his new cutoffs, Andy sheepishly emerged to the eager stares of the crew. It felt almost like Christmas morning; trying on a new shirt or a new pair of pants and wearing them for the rest of the day.

There was a different mood in the room. Looking curiously around, Andy actually felt something. Maybe it was love or kindness or acceptance, but regardless, he thought it the perfect time for a joke as he muttered, "But those were my only pair of pants."

"Dammit," remarked George to the sudden stares of the guys.

"I'm just kidding," said Andy with a wide grin.

"Man, you really had us going," and, "You got us good," were a couple comments from the crew as Andy continued toward the couch.

Still shirtless, he was all skin and bone. Like an emaciated cyclist, his cheeks were completely sunken in as he took a seat and eyed the shoebox.

"Are you going to try them on?" asked Billy.

He didn't ask where they came from, because he knew. He'd had dreams too; of a big blond guy walking shirtless down a dirt road in the rain. He also had dreams of car crashes and one-armed basketball players and then Billy holding his basketball. At first, Andy thought they were just random horrific images. He figured it was more punishment from above, but then he was drawn to the court, and Billy was there and so was the one-armed basketball player.

"See if they fit," said Rick.

It was like Cinderella's slipper in a way, if they fit then everything else would. But what if they didn't? Would they get to try again? Would they be able to buy another pair or would Andy simply slip back into the depths? The tension was palpable as he reached for the closest shoe. Picking it up, he eyed it from top to bottom, feeling its heft and balance just as a samurai would his sword. And then with a startling efficiency, Andy slipped on the shoes and sprung high into the air.

"I take it they fit then," said George.

"Yeah," grinned Andy, "they fit."

Still in a daze, Andy bent down to tie them as Billy said, "Grab a shirt and let's go."

"Where we going?"

"We're going to play," said Rick.

"Ah, I don't know."

"You don't have to know," said Billy. "It isn't about knowing, it's about doing. You're not sitting out today, Andy. Today you're playing."

The words were powerful. It was almost like a message from above and Billy was the messenger. Andy looked down at his hands, and they were no longer shaking. He felt his legs, and they were solid. The shoes felt soft, and Andy suddenly remembered game day. He had butterflies, the same butterflies as before, the ones that followed him onto the court and then disappeared once he touched the ball. It felt good, and he was ready.

With a shirt in hand, wearing pleated cutoffs and a glowing pair of shoes, Andy tromped out with the rest of the guys to claim their city of gold.

"We've got a team and everything," said Glen.

"What's the name?"

"The Trees," answered Billy.

"No, it's the Saints," said George.

"The Eagles," added Rick.

"Ugh," sounded Andy as he, Glen, and George piled into Glen's car with Rick and Billy in the truck.

Driving off, Billy and Rick had an errand to run. They needed to get the ball.

"We did it!" said Rick.

"We did something," replied Billy. "Now we need to get to the court before anything bad happens."

And by bad, Billy meant Andy losing his nerve. He wasn't only thinking about Andy, he was thinking about himself as well.

The house looked deserted as they motored quickly up the drive. Running hurriedly into the garage Billy said, "Basketball, basketball, where are you?"

"Come on, basketball," he continued as something moved.

Opening the window for added effect, the ball dropped heavily to the ground and before it could do anything else, Billy grabbed it and ran.

"Let's go," ordered Billy, jumping back into the truck.

Rick then slammed it in reverse, spun around on the gravel driveway, and sped toward the court. As they approached, Glen and George played while Andy just watched. Walking quickly toward the group, Billy yelled, "Andy, here's your ball."

Billy flung the ball to Andy, but instead of spinning it, he took a shot.

After not playing for a while, most people might get a little closer, maybe do a couple of lay-ups or something, but not Andy. Carefully eyeing the basket, he hoisted the ball from half court and watched it fall perfectly through the hoop.

"You still got it!" yelled George.

"Yeah," added Glen, "but let's see you do it again."

With a wry smile, Andy shot from the same spot and nailed it for a second time.

"Lucky," hissed Rick as Andy again launched from distance and again watched his ball sail straight through the basket. He was surprised to have hit his first three shots. It seemed like the time off had done him good.

In awe of everything, Billy just watched. Angels were everywhere, but above all else, he sensed the spirits.

"Hey, Billy," said Andy with the ball in flight, "heads up!"

After all, Billy had passed the ball to Andy, so it was only fair that he should return the favor.

"Show us what you got, Billy," yelled George.

"Yeah, Billy, throw it down," added Glen.

With the ball now in his hands, Billy took a couple of strong bounces before surging skyward and thrashing the hoop with a forceful tomahawk dunk. Not to be outdone, Andy rushed forward for a complete 360-degree slam, rattling the basket to its foundation for a second time.

"Wow!" exclaimed Rick. "We've got a team."

"Take a shot," said Andy as he threw Rick the ball.

He felt good being back on the court. It felt natural but also different. Andy's family used to watch him play, and now they couldn't. But he was a different player. He was stronger and faster, but he'd never be happier. He had to play though, that much was evident, and there was still joy to be had. He was having fun now.

Still passing the ball around and shooting, Andy was getting more and more comfortable. Being as tall as he was with a good outside shot, he'd be tough for any team to guard. He also moved well and had since gone through a growth spurt. With his added height and dexterity, Andy was sure to be formidable.

As the day moved further into dusk, the team took a few more shots and then called it quits. Tired and content, there were smiles all around as they walked slowly off the court. Both Billy and Andy seemed to have superpowers, and Rick, Glen, and George were all solid players so everything was good. For Andy, getting back on the court had been a healthy distraction, but now that they were done, he had a few questions.

In a halting, almost timid fashion, Andy asked, "I was wondering, where did you get that ball?"

"I can show you, if you'd like," answered Billy.

"OK."

In a somewhat euphoric state, Glen, George, and Rick were star struck. They'd played a lot of basketball but never like that. It was the same for Billy. Even with his special strength, Andy was still stronger. Billy wondered if maybe he had special powers as well.

"Can you give us a ride, Glen?" asked Billy.

"Sure thing," replied Glen.

"You know where we're going?"

"Yup."

And as they turned onto Pleasant Drive, Andy knew where they were going too.

Gwen's little yellow car was in the driveway and Billy wasn't surprised. It must have been fun for her and Celia, waiting around to ambush whoever showed up. Billy imagined he and Andy must have looked pretty funny stuffed into a tiny car teetering into the driveway, but it wasn't about optics. Billy had a job to do.

"What did you bring us today?" asked Celia.

"Yeah," added Gwen, "Who are the new guys?"

"My name's Glen," shouted Glen, "and my phone number is—"

"Thanks, Glen," interrupted Billy, "but this is a home, not a singles bar."

Billy then opened Andy's door and said, "Come on, Andy, it's one small step for man."

"And one giant leap for mankind," finished Celia as Andy smiled and then peeled himself out of the car.

"I'll see you all tomorrow then," added Glen.

"You bet," said Billy as Andy and the girls waved a friendly good-bye.

Standing in the driveway with his basketball in hand, Andy now had to face his fears. He recognized the dark-stained wood and the high-pitched roof of his old house. The basketball hoop was back on the garage. It looked good. Billy wondered if it was too soon to bring him back, but it had to be done. To move forward, Andy would have to make peace with his past.

But it wasn't just happenstance; Andy had been having dreams and visions as well. He knew that he needed to come back; he just didn't know how to do it.

In his former front yard Andy felt like an intruder, but maybe it was new, and he was new, and rather than an impostor, he was a guest. Tall and handsome with brown hair and blue eyes, Celia kindly said, "Hey, Andy, I'm Celia."

"Hi, Celia."

In awe of the tall stranger, Gwen also moved forward and said, "And I'm Gwen."

"I'm Andy," replied Andy as their hands attached like two strong magnets.

Billy had noticed a change, and it was just as he'd suspected: Gwen had been working her way through the channels as well. When he saw how the ball was attracted to her and how she'd been touched by it, he knew things were different.

"Would you like to come in for a drink, Andy?" asked Celia.

"I'd like that," answered Andy as they all filed into the kitchen.

And just like that, instead of three, there were now four.

With the drinks poured and ready to go Billy said, "Gwen, maybe you could get the drinks for us."

Gwen looked suspiciously around as Celia whispered, "Go ahead, Gwen."

The glasses then miraculously lifted and eased slowly down, each one perfectly in front of its target.

"You no longer live in the sensible world, Andy," declared Celia.

"I haven't lived in the sensible world for a long time."

It was a table unlike any other, and the energy was bouncing off of the walls. With two huge handsome guys and a couple of beautiful women, who would have guessed there was so much pain? But pain wasn't exclusive to this place, and now it was important to figure out how to get rid of it.

For the first time in a while, Andy was inspired. He'd also felt the pull of the paranormal, and now he knew why.

"I've had dreams, dreams with you in them Billy, at a temple somewhere after a storm walking around shirtless. I've seen the one-armed basketball player and also relived my family's car accident."

"I saw you at the court," said Billy. "He came and we played. Did you watch?"

"I did, and I've never seen anything like it. It seemed like a duel rather than a game."

"It felt like a duel, I can tell you that."

Tears then fell from Andy's eyes as he said, "If this is all for me, I'm not worth it. I deserve to be where I was, on the floor, ready to die."

"Don't say that," said Gwen.

There was something about the day or about the night. Maybe it was the joy or perhaps the sorrow, but in his former kitchen where he'd had so many good meals, Andy started to speak. Looking affectionately around the room, he said, "This is my old house. My sister, June, and I used to play outside until dark. I'd shoot baskets, and June would steal the ball and throw it into the rafters. I'd always look for it and say, 'Basketball, basketball, where are you?' My mom took up most of the backyard with her garden. We'd have kale, collards, and lettuce all winter long and then peppers, tomatoes, and zucchini in the summer. My dad was a tinkerer, he could fix anything. He grew up on a farm and then joined the service, that's how we ended up here. Instead of fixing farm equipment, he started programming computers. He was super smart. He was a war hero too, a Purple Heart recipient. He saved one guy's life and recovered a couple more. He didn't talk about it much though. I really miss him. He's the one who actually taught me how to play basketball, and I was good. I was always getting offers for things, for tickets and shoes and for everything else under the sun. I wanted to take them, but my father wouldn't let me. He told me to wait. The night of his accident we had a blowout over something stupid, I drove a car home from a dealership, and he made me drive it back. I was hurt and embarrassed and I told him I hated him and that I never wanted to see him again. And I never did see him again. Nor my mother or my sister. They all perished," continued Andy with his head held low, "I've never told anyone that. I never told anyone anything, I just quit talking. It was too painful, but now not talking is painful, and I've got nowhere to go."

"You could have been in the car that night, Andy, but you weren't. Because of that fight, you stayed alive," replied Billy.

"I should have been in the car!" yelled Andy, now red-faced and in tears.

"If you should have been in that car, you would have been. You owe it to them to carry on and to make them proud."

"I don't owe them anything. They left me."

"They didn't leave you, man, they saved you," said Billy. "Look around. There's peace and friendship here. We need you. We're here just for you, and that's a pretty powerful thing. We came a long way for this."

Drying his eyes Andy added, "Whenever she left, my sister June would say, 'We'll be back soon,' but I don't know if she said it that night."

"She did," replied Gwen. "I said that very same thing holding this basketball, and it flipped out."

"It did?" asked Andy.

"It did," answered Gwen.

"So let me get this straight, you can levitate things, and the basketball is alive?"

"Yes."

"And your father is still looking out for you," added Billy. "I've got it on good authority."

If Andy could believe everything else, he guessed he could believe that too, but hearing the words didn't make it any easier.

There was a strong silence as they all absorbed some of the anguish. Little by little it was being portioned out until maybe it would one day be gone.

Andy's back was against the wall, but he had a choice. He could walk away, and there wasn't a thing they could do about it. But he had to bow to the spirits. There were some powerful forces at work, and it wasn't all about him. Billy had put in a lot of work as well, but he wasn't done.

"You said it, Andy, but you didn't mean it."

"But I said it," replied Andy in a defeated tone.

"Kids say things, people say things and not everything makes sense. The people sitting at this very table are a perfect example. None of this makes any sense, nothing but you and me and Gwen and Celia and what we can do. It's not what we get, it's what we give. And you've got a lot to give, so don't waste it."

"I said it," said Andy, "but I didn't mean it."

"You said it, but you didn't mean it," repeated Billy.

"I said it, but I didn't mean it. It was late and they hadn't come home yet so I waited downstairs like a kid. I would have given anything just to see them walk through the door, but they didn't."

"And it's not your fault."

"And it's not my fault," Andy finally said.

There wasn't a dry eye in the house as Andy finally made a breakthrough. There was still a lot to do, but at least he was talking.

"It's gonna be a long way back," said Billy, "but it's worth it. You've had a lot go against you, but you've also got a lot going for you, and not everyone gets that."

"Well," replied Andy in a sad but hopeful voice. "If I can accept everything else, I guess I can accept that as well."

"Then you're on your way, Andy."

"Yeah, Andy," said the girls, "you're on your way!"

"I'm on my way, but I don't know where."

"That's for you to decide, but we've got a team and we could sure use some help at the center position."

"Sounds good to me," replied Andy, as Gwen and Celia let out an ecstatic cheer.

Andy just grinned. It brought him back to the schoolyard, where he was relieved not to be the last one picked. It felt like he was starting over.

There was peace in the room and in the house, for the matter. Billy, on the other hand, had yet to feel any real comfort.

With the day winding down, something else needed to be done. Billy couldn't see it any other way. It made him sad, but sorrow and joy were all equal in the grand scheme of things, which lately had been dictating Billy's actions. So he'd have to act.

"Maybe Andy would like to see the house, Celia," offered Billy.

"Oh, well, how about a tour then, Andy?"

"That would be nice."

With the two traipsing upstairs, Billy turned to Gwen and said, "I think I know what's going on."

"Is that why you asked me to move the glasses?"

"Yes. I wanted Andy to see you for who you really are. I don't want you to have to hide anything ever again."

"I had such a strong reaction to the ball, I just can't explain it."

She didn't need to, Billy already knew. He understood her powers of attraction, and he sensed their run had, most likely, come to an end.

"I think it's right," affirmed Billy. "Of things that don't make sense, this actually does. You helped me. I couldn't have understood this without you. I couldn't have taken the next step, but I also don't know what's next for me. Things aren't finished here either and Andy is still raw, so be his friend and be my friend and be Celia's friend. You need stability, and I'm unstable. You need family, and I need to be free. It's the only way I can operate."

Through tears of both joy and sadness, Gwen said, "Thank you, Billy, I don't know if I could've found my true self again without you."

"I couldn't have come this far without you either. And it wouldn't have been half the fun. It's a pleasure to have met you, Ms. Gwen Reynolds."

"It's a pleasure to have met you too, Mr. Billy Winslow," replied Gwen, with their hands still intertwined. "Don't be a stranger."

"I won't," said Billy, and as Celia and Andy came down the stairs, their hands slowly fell apart.

"Gwen's going to give you a ride home, Andy, and I'll see you tomorrow, at the restaurant. We've got our first practice. Five o'clock sharp," announced Billy through a light sniffle.

"OK, Coach—Billy."

"Billy's fine, but coach sounds good too," replied Billy as they all chuckled.

With the evening's revelations finally complete, Andy and Gwen walked toward the door as Billy said, "Bye, Gwen."

"Good-bye, Billy."

"Bye, guys," said Celia.

Andy and Gwen both said, "Bye, Celia."

And just like that, as quickly as she'd arrived, Gwen was gone.

Wild-eyed and somewhat confused, Celia asked, "What's going on, Billy?"

"Well, for lack of a better term, Gwen and I broke up."

"Really?"

"Really."

"Why?"

It was hard to explain, because Billy didn't really understand, but maybe explaining it would help.

"I loved Gwen, but I could never really say it, and I think it was the same for her. I've always felt like things were working through me rather than for me. What I'm trying to say is that it seemed Gwen was less for me, and more for the experience, if that makes any sense."

"It does," replied Celia. "But how did you know?"

"The ball was the first clue. It came on Gwen's first call, almost like June's spirit had inhabited the ball and then latched on to Gwen. It was astounding but also telling. I knew then that she wasn't for me."

"So, Andy's sister's spirit inhabited the ball and took a liking to Gwen, and Gwen in turn took a liking to Andy."

"That sounds about right, but it doesn't make it any easier. The only consolation is that maybe she'll be with Andy, and together they can right some of the wrongs. It doesn't mean I like it, but I can live with it. After all, I came here on a mission and it's almost accomplished."

Hearing that gave Celia chills. She'd stuck with Billy through the whole thing, and if anyone ever doubted his resolve, they needn't look any further. Billy Winslow Junior had truly arrived.

"Well, finish it up then," said Celia.

"I have a feeling you'll be seeing Gwen again. You two were good together," added Billy as he walked off to write. It had been a while and he needed to get something down.

With his notepad opened to a clean sheet of paper, Billy wrote,

Once there were two and now there was just one.

But that's how it started and that's how it would end.

He wasn't looking for anything more than a friend, or maybe something new.

Maybe a new beginning, or a new place, but with all the changes, it was hard to stay safe.

It was hard to know what was real in a world where everything moved and felt and flew, but it all came down to a simple smile and the feeling that anything was possible.

He'd miss the girl with auburn hair, but more than missing her, he knew her and he felt her, and in a way she'd always be there. In the sky that constantly changed and in the clouds that bring the rain and in the sun that never sets would be her, wondering where he'd been and wanting to go for a walk down a long country road with the wild flowers in bloom and the darkness sliding down.

Good-bye, Gwen.

With a tear in his eye, Billy slid the notebook to Celia, who read and also cried. Billy figured that would get him a pretty good grade.

RITA RETURNS

Billy woke to an empty bed and felt strange. But the birds still chirped an inspired song, so he figured he'd be all right. He'd been in awe for quite a while and listening to the intricate sounds of dawn, he was still amazed. It seemed like every time he walked outside, something incredible happened.

But he couldn't get too emotional. At face value, it seemed like he'd shuffled his girlfriend off or pushed her away, but it wasn't like that. Billy knew that Gwen was meant for Andy, and Andy for Gwen. He didn't know for how long, but judging from their needs and challenges and from the way they could complement one another, Billy guessed it could last a lifetime.

It would be hard to see Gwen with Andy but also encouraging. There had been lessons for Billy as well—on attachments and how to finally let go. He'd been forced to abandon all conventional wisdom and embrace a new understanding. He'd spoken words he didn't think he could speak. He'd found strength where he was weak and harnessed a hidden power from deep within. Billy lost Gwen, but he gained a lot in the process.

She hadn't just run off with stars in her eyes, anyway. Andy was in a precarious position, and Gwen was sure to proceed with caution. She wanted to help Andy. She wanted to help Billy as well, but he was too far into the stratosphere. He'd come down one day, but who would be there when he did? He wasn't sure.

It felt different though, almost like a new chapter, or maybe even a final chapter. Billy needed to put aside his romantic concerns and get back to being the bait. There was more to do. He just wasn't sure what.

Getting dressed, Billy was excited to get back out there. Things were moving right along. But what if Andy didn't show? What if the guys didn't want to play? What would happen to him? Billy imagined everyone ready to go, and it gave him strength. He didn't have a girlfriend, but he had a team, and hopefully they were up to the task.

Jogging down the stairs to see Celia's long graceful form at the dining room table, everything seemed new. Billy was energized, but Celia was sad. He knew the problem and also the solution, as he'd considered something for her as well.

"Good morning, Celia," said Billy, as he gave her a light hug.

"Morning, Billy. Did you sleep well?"

"Mostly, how about you?"

"Honestly, no. I'm kind of sad. I was getting used to having Gwen around, and last night was just so emotional."

"But it was amazing, wasn't it! All sadness aside, people are healing, and things are getting better. People are getting better."

"People are getting lonelier."

"Just hold on," replied Billy. "Something big is on the way. I don't know what it is, but I can feel it, and it's not just for me, it's for you too."

"I hope so, Billy."

"I know so, Celia."

Anticipating the grand finale, Billy had an extra spring in his step. Walking down the road, he wondered what Andy and Gwen had done after leaving Celia's. Billy wondered how Andy felt after going back to his old house and talking about the accident. Was he better or worse? Had it been empowering or just a mistake? There was no way to know. Billy didn't have any regrets though. He'd done what he was supposed to do, and now he was alone. Maybe he needed help? It couldn't have been a bad thing though. It seemed like something Andy wanted to do. He just needed a way to do it.

All Billy needed to do was to finish the job. No matter the circumstance, he needed to stay focused and press on. There was still work to do, and more importantly, as Billy walked into the Friends Café, there was still cooking to do.

"Hey, champ," said Glen as Gina offered a sweet, "Morning, Billy."

"Hey people," replied Billy. He hadn't worked there long, but strangely enough, it felt like home.

"Billy!" yelled Rick as Billy walked into the kitchen.

"Billy!" yelled George as Billy grabbed his apron.

The guys were cool, and they lifted Billy's spirits. He imagined keeping in touch after everything wrapped up.

"Hey Rick, do we have time for a quick meeting, in the dining room maybe with Gina and Glen?"

"If you make the soup, superstar."

"I got it, but grab George if you could."

"Team meeting, everyone. You too, Gina. You're on the team as well," announced Billy.

"Wow," said Gina, "but if I have to be the equipment manager, I quit."

"We don't have any equipment to manage. But how does a coaching position sound?"

"Yes!" hissed Gina with a clenched fist.

"OK, team, the reason I called everyone is to say thanks for yesterday. I also want to be clear when I say that in some ways this is an intervention. When we picked Andy off the floor and brought him out to the court, we started something, but we didn't finish it. What I'm trying to say is that we can't act any differently. We don't want to spook him. We need to let him come out of his shell. Andy's coming back, and this team is what's doing it, so let's stay focused and keep our eyes on the prize."

Billy then put out his hand as the others added theirs to a raucous cheer of "Go team!"

"Man," said Rick, "when I threw you that apron, I had no idea that all this was going to happen."

"There's more to come," replied Billy. "Practice at five everyone. Andy's supposed to play, but we'll see. We need to be available just in case."

"You need to make some soup," yelled George, bringing Billy back down to earth.

"Where's the carrots and celery? How does chicken vegetable sound?"

"Sounds good," answered Rick. "Just don't use all the rest of the chicken."

"You think you're talking to a rookie?"

"He thinks he's talking to a dummy," sounded George.

"Hmph," muttered Billy as he started to chop.

With the dining room beginning to fill, it wouldn't be long before the tickets came in. Sure enough, the first order was a club sandwich, so Billy had to restock the frill picks before starting the assembly. It was sure to be an interesting day.

Making a chicken vegetable soup for a tuna salad combo, Billy was reminded of his first kitchen job, at an air force base in Florida. Something about cooking lunch brought Billy back to where it all started, slicing cold cuts for the lunch rush and then working the omelet station for Sunday brunch. The day had a strange nostalgic feel to it. As Billy slathered a piece of rye toast with tuna, he was in for another surprise.

With Rick pushing out the burgers and the sauté dishes, Billy worked the cold side. Grilled Caesar salads along with their house-made Cuban sandwiches were flying through the window. With his skills honed to perfection, the volume didn't scare Billy. But just as they conquered the lunch rush, Gina poked her head through the doors and asked, "Can you handle a ten-top, boys?"

"Bring it!" yelled Rick.

"Damn," hissed Billy because he knew what it meant: more salads and sandwiches and, sure enough, the tuna salads and soup orders started streaming back. Turning and burning, Billy couldn't help but wonder about the large table of stragglers. Taking a peek, he not only saw a fancy bunch drinking cocktails, but he also noticed someone familiar. With a sexy voice, long shapely legs, and dark, curly hair, it could have only been one person. In a short, fashionable skirt and high heels, with a dark seam running up the back of her stockings, she stood next to a handsome guy who was holding court.

"No freaking way!" exclaimed Billy.

"What?" asked Rick.

"It's her!"

"It's who?"

"It's Rita."

Billy knew he'd be saying her name again, he just didn't think it would be here. But with the way things were going, Rita was bound to come out of the woodwork.

"Who is Rita?" was the next question as they swarmed the kitchen, pushing out the final orders.

"Rita's my ex. She left me down and out in Mexico, and then went on to marry a millionaire."

"That's not fair," replied Rick.

As the shift wore on, Billy had two choices: he could let the moment pass or he could own it. There was no blueprint for this kind of thing. It was all experimental at this point, so there was really nothing to lose.

Ready to strike, Billy said, "I need you to cover for me, Rick. I'm going in!"

"You ain't goin' nowhere," yelled George. "Get yo ass back on the line."

"Shut your trap and make some sandwiches," hissed Billy on his way out.

Billy didn't know what to do. He didn't have a plan other than to be himself, which didn't always work out too well, so he had to be careful.

He was reluctant to disrupt the party, but it was obviously what that the spirits wanted, so Billy wouldn't disappoint. It might be his last chance to see Rita as well, so he didn't want to spoil it.

Deciding to enter the fray, Billy waded into a sea of shiny hair and fancy clothes, dirty apron and all. Making his way over to the dazzling couple, he had mixed feelings. For Rita to go and get married when he was hiding out in Mexico left something of a bad taste in his mouth, but maybe he'd left a bad taste in her mouth too. She'd actually reached out to discuss a settlement on the *Kidnapping Steve* novel, but Billy refused and thus ended up with a house. It was a tidy deal, but it also left something unfinished. Walking forward, Billy aimed to finish it.

Moving toward the striking brunette, Billy announced, "Now if I'm not mistaken, Chapel Hill, North Carolina, seems a bit too far south for a couple of slick New York socialites."

Surprised but not shaken, Rita turned and replied, "I guess that depends on how you define socialite."

And just like that, Rita got him again. Suddenly speechless, Rita chuckled and said, "Corbin, meet Billy Winslow. Billy, this is Corbin."

"So you get the girl, and all I get is a firm handshake," winced Billy as Corbin let up.

With his superpowers in full swing, Billy wasn't worried about Corbin, but he seemed formidable nonetheless.

A little shorter than Billy, with square shoulders and sharp blue eyes, Corbin said, "I've heard a lot about you, Billy. It's nice to finally put a face to the name."

"Hope I didn't disappoint," replied Billy, "but then again, I usually do."

"I'm not disappointed."

"This is an interesting way to meet though," added Rita as Corbin and Billy engaged in a mild stare down.

Rita was every bit as enticing as Billy remembered, maybe even more. He really had no interest in idle chatter with Corbin, but it had to be done.

Following a short pause, Corbin asked, "So how did we all end up here?"

"Well, I'm working," answered Billy.

"Isn't your work back there?" asked Rita pointing into the kitchen. She didn't feel sorry for Billy. He did what he wanted to do. He lived life on his terms, and that kind of freedom comes with a price.

"Ah, yeah," muttered Billy, "just kind of on a break."

"Do the other guys know that?" smiled Rita.

Rita's smile lit up the room, and for a moment, Billy was back in Florida on the beach at low tide. They'd walk for hours and then jump in the ocean to cool off. That's when she'd just left Chicago to be closer to her sick father. He'd go back if he could, especially now that he'd lost another girl, but he couldn't. All he could do was remember that they'd once been together, and that they'd been in love.

"They've been advised."

"Same old Billy," replied Rita, "still large and in charge."

"Still large, maybe."

"So, Billy, how are you enjoying the house?" asked Corbin, referring to the house they'd bought Billy in lieu of payment for his book.

"I'm not. I haven't really had the chance. When I got back into town I was suddenly called up here, so I had to go. I appreciate it though."

"You make it sound so official Billy. What exactly are you doing here?" asked Rita as the other customers began filing out.

"Slaying dragons and rescuing damsels in distress, same old thing. What about you?"

"Nothing that heroic," replied Corbin. "We flew in for a conference at the business school and just decided to catch a lunch with some of the group."

"Corbin went to Duke," said Rita, obviously doing a name drop, reminiscent of her days at Northwestern, before Billy caused her to drop out.

"I heard they had a little school over there," replied Billy.

"It's actually not that small," said Corbin.

"That's what they all say," muttered Billy with a wink.

"Ah, you got me, Billy. Anyway, Rita, looks like the guys are taking off. Are you coming or should I send the car?"

"Just send the car, love."

Then, without a care in the world, Corbin gave Rita a kiss, patted Billy lightly on the back, and said, "Nice to finally meet you, Billy. Maybe we'll get a drink later, on us."

"Sounds good," replied Billy, watching Corbin leave. The guy had swagger, that's for sure. He was just Rita's type: strong, assertive, and not too squeaky clean.

As he and Rita made their way out to the patio, Billy said, "I don't remember you looking this glamorous when we were together."

"I was a beach bum when we were together."

"You say that like it's a bad thing."

"It's a good thing, but it's not a thing that lasts forever, especially living with my mom. It was fine for a while, but we started to get on each other's nerves. Things had to change," continued Rita, "and you just happened to be one of the changes."

That was cold, and it definitely put Billy in his place. He was cooking at a restaurant and Rita was flying in jet airplanes. She was going places and doing things, and she wasn't about to succumb to the arrogant charms of a traveling gypsy. Those days were long gone.

"So it was just that easy?"

"No, it wasn't just that easy. It wasn't easy driving you to the airport while the police pulled Steve, bound and gagged, out of our neighbor's yard. It wasn't easy missing you and worrying about you and waiting for you to call and having the sheriff in my house asking questions about you. It wasn't easy writing a book with a lost love and an uncertain future, but you helped me, Billy, so I tried, but in the end, it just didn't work out."

When she said "it just didn't work out," it almost sounded like she said it wouldn't work out and that it won't ever work out. It sounded final. He'd once held some hope for the future but talking to her now, it seemed rather hopeless.

"No, I guess not," conceded Billy. "But it's nice to see you, and you look gorgeous as usual."

"You look great too, Billy. I like the haircut; it makes you look more serious, and also a little more handsome."

"You don't say," said Billy.

"Of course," replied Rita. "I wouldn't lie about something like that."

Billy knew she wouldn't lie about that, because she never lied about anything. He'd never known anyone graced with so many gifts. Rita was intelligent, funny, graceful, and of course, beautiful, and not only on the surface. There was still a weakness though, in her heart, for the time she'd spent in Florida with her father and with Billy.

Beneath the striking sunsets and soaking rains of the glorious peninsula, Rita lost something, but she found something as well—herself and the way she wanted to live. It wasn't easy, but it was necessary. And now, at a restaurant talking to her ex-lover, Rita wasn't about to be vulnerable.

"Well, I'd be lying if I said that I wasn't at least a little let down, but I wasn't really surprised, and I'm glad to see that you're happy and healthy and that your book was such a success," offered Billy in reference to *Kidnapping Steve*, Rita's novel borrowed primarily from Billy's notes. "And congratulations on Corbin, he seems like a great guy."

"Thanks," said Rita. "I wanted our time together to speak for something other than failure and fleeing. It's not what we deserved."

"I should be thanking you. It was really generous of you and Corbin to buy me the house as well. I didn't deserve it."

"Nonsense, Billy. But what are you working on now? I sense more to this coincidence than meets the eye."

"Ah, you know me too well, Mrs. Rita Polli."

"It's Rita Flake," said Rita as Billy let out a slight chuckle. "I laughed too, but the joke now seems to be on me."

"It's no joke, and you won't believe what's going on."

With Rita's tight skirt shimmering, and Billy handsomely defeated, they seemed strangely connected. There was no book and no Corbin and no planes or spirits or teams; it was just them, and it was nice.

"So what's happening, Billy?" asked Rita.

"In Mexico, when I was on the run, I was contacted by the spirits."

Now if anyone else had made such a claim, Rita would have scoffed, but it was Billy, so she listened.

"Stranded at an ancient temple, in the throes of an epic storm, I received a message to save someone. Ancient voices echoed through the thunder and lightning, and then everything just blew up. I had signs and dreams and it all led me here, to my aunt Celia's. I'm in the final phase now, but it's been quite a ride."

"Should I be worried?"

"Not especially. Concerned maybe."

"Are you writing about it?" asked Rita.

"I am, but I'm also living it, just like before," answered Billy.

"Is there anything I can do?"

"Funny you should ask," announced Rick, as he and the kitchen crew stormed their table. "We're starting a basketball team for a special redemption project and could sure use a donation from a stunning young lady such as yourself, maybe some uniforms or something. And by the way," he continued with an outstretched hand, "I'm Rick."

"And I'm George," said George as Glen raised a hand and added, "Glen Davis at your service."

"Hello Rick, George, and Glen," replied Rita in a sexy drone.

"These are my boys," said Billy.

Rita then set a devastating gaze on the crew and said, "I remember beating your last gang back in a dark beachside apartment."

Surprised, Billy sputtered, "Yeah, well, not these guys."

"Yeah, not us," repeated the guys in a confused unison.

"We'll see," sighed Rita as she rose from the table, pulled a card from her clutch and laid it in front of Billy.

The card simply read:

Flake Industries and Entertainment:
Don't Fake it—Flake It!

Rita then gave Billy a kiss on the forehead and said, "It was great seeing you again, Billy. My number's on the card, and I'd like to see what you're working on, it sounds interesting."

"Oh, and Rick," continued Rita as she strolled out to the sidewalk, "contact my office with the information on the uniforms. I'd like to help."

Then, like an apparition, Rita floated away in perfection. With her shapely body wrapped tightly in a sequined skirt, her thick hair bounced a final good-bye as a Bentley pulled smoothly up. Nearing the curb, Rita's chauffeur hopped out, opened the door and whisked her quietly away. With Rita gone, a little yellow car arrived, and Billy was relieved.

Tracking Rita's Bentley down the road, Billy got to Gwen's car only to hear, "You sure don't waste any time, do you, Billy."

"I could say the same for you," replied Billy. "But seriously, Gwen, thanks for getting him here today. It's important."

"He wanted to come. He was actually excited about it."

Gazing into Gwen's pretty eyes, Billy couldn't believe that he'd had, and then lost, two such exceptional women. It was also strange to see them both on the same day, but he could reflect on that later. Right now, he had to get back to the guys.

With the cooks shutting down the kitchen, Billy yelled, "Hey, Andy, you need something to eat."

"No, Billy, I'm fine, thanks. Gwen and I actually went somewhere different. I rode in a car today instead of walking."

"We didn't lose a customer now, did we?" asked Gina as she breezed by with the afternoons deposit.

"No, Gina, this is still my favorite place."

Andy looked different today, and Billy knew why. Instead of cut-offs, he was wearing a pair of shorts and a nice new T-shirt. Gwen was working her magic, and Billy was glad. The finish line was in sight.

With the restaurant closed, the guys got into their cars and headed for the park. Billy and Andy rode with Glen, while Rick got George. Driving up to the court, it was a surprise to see people playing. Aside from the one-armed black man who nearly bludgeoned him to death, Billy had yet to see anyone else there, yet there they were, running and jumping, and Billy was suspicious. It was almost too perfect. Billy, of course, suspected the spirits.

As his friends got out of their cars and limbered up, Billy studied the other players. His team definitely had the size, but the other guys were also big and good, and they didn't look like kids. Bouncing his ball, Andy was first to the court followed by the others. They didn't know what was going on, but Billy did. Rick also suspected something.

"So, I guess we're supposed to play these guys?"

"It seems that way," replied Billy. "And they look pretty tough."

It wasn't the perfect day for Billy to play an actual game. He was sapped, both physically and mentally, but people were counting on him, so he needed to step up.

Clapping his hands, Andy gave Billy a strong pass, and Billy drained his first shot from the three-point line. He then turned to the other crew and yelled, "Hey man, you got any basketball players over here?"

"Sure do," said one of the guys. "How bout you?"

"We got it," yelled George. "Now you gonna get it."

"Oh, tough talk already. Hopefully the man can back it up."

Meeting in the middle, Billy said, "We're only talking a little trash. You know, we just took up the sport, kind of like a hobby, but if you kind gentleman would be interested in a game, we could make it happen."

Billy's counterpart scanned Billy's squad and replied, "I don't know of any casual teams with a seven footer. You all wouldn't happen to be hustlers, would you? Because I kind of feel like I'm being hustled."

"No, sir," said Rick, "we can barely bounce the ball."

"Yeah," added Glen, "and don't mention shooting."

"And I'm tall, but I can't jump," said Andy, adding his two cents.

"Speak for yourselves," said George. "I got the moves. Flash Gordon ain't got nothing on me."

"OK, Flash, you take the ball out then. We play to twenty-one. Call your own fouls and no three-pointers, sound good?"

"That's straight," said George as he took the ball and handed it to Rick.

Rick was the obvious choice at point guard, with Glen lined up as the shooting guard. Billy and George would be the forwards, and Andy would play center.

Perhaps because of the afternoon, or possibly the unknown, it felt like a big game. It needed to be friendly as well, so Billy said, "Before we get started, please allow me to introduce the guys."

"Please do," replied the mystery player.

"I'm Billy. The guy with the ball there is slick Rick. The skinny ginger is no-show Glen, Flash Gordon over there is George, and the big man is Andy."

Hearing the names, he scanned Billy's team, almost like he was extracting information or plugging in coordinates. He then stepped forward and said, "I'm Rod, and the guy to my right is Sam. Dillon and Will are on the wings, and Han is the man in the middle. Let's have a good game."

Rod's voice had a strange resonance to it, a deep, unearthly drone that chilled Billy to his core. It was something wild, like the roar of a lion, or the shriek of an elephant before a deadly stomp. Built like a middleweight boxer, he looked fast and strong. They all did. With ropy muscles wrapped in a dark, imposing sheen, Rod's partner, Sam, looked like a pure shooter ready to score. Dillon and Will were the hired hands. Tall and physical, they'd have to scramble for loose balls and jump tirelessly every single rebound and then maybe they'd get a few points. Moving even higher into the stratosphere was Han, a large Asian center who stood out above the rest. As an exotic offering from above, he was the perfect player to round out an already intimidating team. Indifferent to the brutal task ahead, they looked like a group of mercenaries rather than a basketball team as Rick started the game with a quick inbound pass to Billy.

Billy's team hadn't played full court basketball in a while, but he was still hopeful. He and Glen were in shape. Andy walked almost everywhere, so he had some legs. Rick played a couple of times a week, and George was George. But as the ball started moving, they were at least a step behind, maybe more.

Billy passed the ball back to Rick, and Rod promptly slapped it out of his hands. Three passes later, it found their center, Han, for an easy point, and then possession.

The ball sounded that same hollow pop from Billy's game with the one-armed specter. This game seemed kind of unreal as well, and Billy started to get the picture.

They passed with precision and ran with purpose. The ball had barely hit the court, and there was Sam making a towering outside shot to make it 2–0.

Bouncing the ball through Rick's legs, Rod then found a soaring Han for a brutal slam dunk over a dazed Andy.

"Three to none," growled Rod.

Sweating profusely and still chasing the specters around, Rick was just lucky enough to knock the ball to Glen, who was equally lucky to hit a shot to at least get them on the board.

As the game wore on and the points piled up, George suddenly doubled over.

"What's up, Flash Gordon, your spaceship run out of gas?" yelled Rod.

"Spaceships don't use gas, dumbass," wheezed George as he some-how snatched the ball from Rod and hurled it to Andy for a brutal slam dunk. Billy was reinvigorated as well, and he started running the court like a champion. With lost loves looming and his life in the balance of a basketball game, Billy flew. He threw the ball to Rick, who was able to shake Rod and get it back to Billy for another precious bucket.

Rick then took over and started shredding the defense. With no-look passes and kickbacks to Glen, the outside game started working and the specters fell behind, but as George went down again, the specters surged. They started going inside to Han, and Andy was taking a beating. But the harder it got, the better he played. His passes were crisp and clean as he snagged a rebound and threw a perfect strike to Billy for another point.

With Billy playing like a man possessed, Andy kept swatting balls away, Rick kept passing, and Glen kept shooting, but it wasn't enough. As George limped up and down the court, Andy hissed, "These guys are good."

"There's a reason for that," said Billy as the opposing forwards started making shots. Rod was barely bouncing the ball anymore; he just seemed to be passing, flinging it from one side of the court to the other. Rick was merely a spectator at this point as a final searing pass hit Han for twenty-one. Game over.

With Billy's team taking long deep breaths, Rod seemed ready for another game.

"You guys wanna run it back?"

"Nah," answered Billy. "It's been a long day. I mean, it's been a busy day, waddaya think guys?"

"I'm done," said George. "My legs kind of hurt anyway."

"I gotta run," added Glen.

"I can play," said Andy.

"Later," said Billy. "It's time to go."

As the other team sauntered off, with Rick in earshot, Billy asked, "I trust you'll be here tomorrow."

"We'll be here whenever you are."

Rick was floored as the players crept quietly into the darkness, and one by one, just kind of evaporated.

"Where'd they run off to?" snarled George.

"They didn't really run," answered Rick.

"Yeah, they just kind of walked, real slow like," added Glen.

"There's something strange about them," noticed Andy.

"Yeah, they're strangely good, and they're going to be our competition for the next few weeks, or until we beat them. So it's time to get going."

Billy didn't want to divulge anything more, because it couldn't really be proven. It was more a feeling or a notion or maybe even a perspective from the other side. It wasn't something to be openly discussed, because not everyone could handle it.

"They're a good team, but we stayed with them, so nice job. You looked really good out there, Andy, and keep shooting, Glen. Rick, you kept a lid on Rod for a while. And just stick with it, George, it'll come."

"Screw you, Billy," replied George.

"Let's go, Billy boy!" exclaimed Rick, ready to move things along.

There were two reasons Rick always gave Billy a ride home. One was so that he could see Celia. The other was to find out what was going on.

"So what the hell was that?" asked Rick.

"What was what?"

"What was that? I mean, who in the hell were those guys?"

Rick had never played a team like with their speed, efficiency, and flat-out effectiveness. They moved in angles and designs, way more advanced than anything he'd ever seen.

"And why did Rod say if we were there, they'd be there too?"

"I don't know," answered Billy.

It was the kind of "I don't know" that meant I know but I'm not going to tell you, and Rick wasn't buying it.

"Well you need to know, or I'm going to quit."

That was unexpected—and also a problem. Rick was here so Billy surmised that he was supposed to be here. If he left, Andy might leave, and then George, and then Glen might follow, and then what would happen to him? The spirits were unclear on these matters. For the most part, Billy had been exercising restraint, but when faced with a mutiny, he'd have to relent.

"You're not a quitter."

"I'm not an idiot either," replied Rick. "So what's up?"

Billy smiled as he prepared to blow this guy's mind. If Rick ran off into the distance screaming, it would be his own fault.

"We were playing the undead, Rick."

"We were playing the what?"

"The undead, the not dead, we were playing a team of apparitions, of specters, of ghosts."

Rick was flummoxed. "Well . . . are you a specter?"

"No," answered Billy. "I'm undeniably, unmistakably, indisputably here. I do have some special powers though. It's one of the perks of the job, I guess."

"And this is all about getting Andy back on the court?"

"It's about getting him back into life."

It was a strong statement, and Rick wouldn't have believed it if he hadn't seen it with his own eyes. One day Andy was toast and the next he's playing basketball and riding around town with a cute girl. It was a lot to digest, but it was slowly sinking in.

"So you're working with them?"

"We're all working with them."

"So that's why all this stuff's happening!" exclaimed Rick. "Remarkable, unbelievable, outstanding! You are my best damn friend right now, Billy."

"We'll see," said Billy. "I don't know where this is going, but they were here for a reason. Every single thing that's happened, from me coming to North Carolina to walking into your restaurant to you throwing me an apron has been for a reason. I don't know what's happening now, but whatever it is, it's going to be big."

Getting back to the team of specters, Rick asked, "So do you think we'll be able to beat them?"

"Not with skill. They're too good. My guess is that we'll have to beat them with effort, with sheer will. They have the power, but without any emotion, they don't have a second gear, so to speak."

"From the looks of it, they don't need a second gear."

"Maybe not."

With the sun going down, they rode the rest of the way in silence. Easing into the drive, now Billy had a question.

"You wouldn't have quit, would you?"

"No. I was just bluffing."

"Ha," laughed Billy as he saw Celia through the window.

"Hold on, Rick."

Billy then walked into the house and walked back out with Celia.

"Maybe you can tell Celia what happened today, and don't forget Rita."

"Rita?" repeated Celia,

"Yeah!" exclaimed Rick. "She came in looking like a real Hollywood movie star, had Billy eating out of her hands."

Free from Rick and Celia, Billy walked calmly into the house to finally rest. His blue eyes shone through the darkness, and his tall, muscled body was sore. He'd seen both of his lost loves today, so in a quest to make some sense of it, Billy needed to write.

Grabbing a pen, into his favorite old notebook he scrawled:

With the sun setting into a cosmic blur, something almost made sense until he wondered where things went.

Where did love go when it left? Did it move on with a purpose or slink off into the distance?

If it left, would it return? And if it returned, would it be as good? Would it be as pure as it was in the beginning, when the skies were blue and the sun was shining and the days seemed to last forever?

Questions of love were infinite and the answers hard to find. Where did it reside and how did it grow? When would it come

*and when would it go? Who had the most and who had the least
and where was the love that never leaves?*

*But love wasn't a thing, a name or a badge. It wasn't a mood,
a phase, or a fad, it wasn't in something else, it was in everything.*

As Billy finished up, Celia walked into the house raving about the day's events.

"So now there's a whole team of them?"

"It looks that way. There was definitely something in the air. Their basketball had that same hollow pop, and they had those same empty eyes. They were all there, yet none of them had any cars. They played like professionals and only one of them spoke; he said his name was Rod, for whatever that's worth. I mean, alive or not, it was a pleasure playing them. I asked if they'd be there again, and Rod said they'd be there whenever we would. My guess is that they're getting us ready for something. I just don't know what."

"That's what Rick said. He was really keyed up. I think you've got quite an advocate there."

"I hope so. He was getting suspicious, so I took a chance and let him in. I couldn't divulge everything, but I filled him in on the things that were happening now. You can explain the rest later, I guess."

"And what about Rita, how was that?"

"Bittersweet," replied Billy. "She was pretty unapologetic."

"Does she have anything to apologize for?"

"No, but it would have been nice to hear anyway. We had a moment though, where it was just her and I. I remembered what it was like in the beginning, when everything was new, when there was love rather than resentment. So maybe it's good that Gwen and I ended how we did, as part of a grand celestial bargain."

"Maybe," replied Celia. And then, eyeing his notebook, she said, "So let's have it."

Almost, but not quite tired of the charade, he slid his work into the waiting clutches of his benevolent aunt Celia. With her soft eyes trained on the pages, rather than a searing response, in three words Celia wrote: "It's beautiful, Billy." A large glowing A graced the top of the page, and Billy finally smiled.

PRACTICE

So what kind of crazy, emotional, incredible events await me today, wondered Billy as he brushed his teeth and went downstairs. By now he was a little shell shocked. It could have seemed miraculous and wondrous to the others, but for Billy it was intense.

The kitchen was empty. Celia had gone back to work. With her little hiatus ending, Billy thought that maybe things had returned to normal, whatever that was. He hadn't seen normal in quite a while.

Wondering if they'd play today, he also wondered whether the team had any chemistry. They seemed good enough, but they needed to get better. It was funny that in the kitchen where he used to be a cosmic traveler, he was now a coach. Coaches needed to make decisions. Billy needed to decide when and how hard to work the guys. He couldn't ask them what they wanted to do; he'd have to tell them what to do. He was ready to speak; he just hoped they were ready to listen.

Alone at the dining room table, Billy resolved to keep the pedal down. If a couple of players fell off, he'd just need to find some more. But maybe there weren't any other players. Maybe only certain pieces would fit. If so, Billy would have to employ the talents of a real coach. He'd have to exemplify strengths and minimize weaknesses, all the while gaining the respect and trust of his players. It was a complicated task, one that wasn't so obvious amid the game day gesticulations of a topflight coach.

Billy wasn't a real coach, but he still had a job to do, and he needed to figure out the best way to do it. Walking back to the restaurant, his thoughts began to coalesce. He needed a team, which he thought he had. The team needed a name, which they didn't have. He needed the uniforms that Rita promised, and he also needed an assistant.

Going to work now was basically a technicality, but Billy still needed to show up. If he ditched his shifts, he wouldn't be able to keep the respect of the guys, so he'd simply play his part.

The dining room was empty and quiet. It was unnerving, always having to trust that everything would line up. Rather than play defense, Billy would have to go on offense. Rather than wait for something to happen, he'd have to make it happen. For the last phase of this little outing, Billy would have to employ the unbridled enthusiasm of a celebrity coach.

The kitchen had a different feel to it that day. Rick was different. Billy was different. But George was pretty much the same. He hadn't changed.

"It's good to see you, man," whispered Rick, like they were on some kind of a secret mission.

"Good to see you too, Rick, but you don't have to whisper. It's kind of freaky."

"What you dummies whispering about?" yelled George.

"If we wanted you to know, we wouldn't be whispering," replied Billy.

"Screw you."

Switching gears, Billy rounded the corner and said, "So how you feelin today, George? You ready to play? No rest for the wicked."

George thought it strange to have a schedule. They used to just play whenever, but now they were playing an actual team, and he had to run more. He wasn't sure he was up to it.

"I'll play, but that Rod guy better not piss me off."

"I'll take care of Rod," said Billy.

"I'll take care of Rod," repeated George.

Doubt that, thought Billy as he walked over to Rick and asked, "Are you all right, Rick?"

"Yeah, I'm all right. I'm also in love with Celia. Did she mention me?"

"No, but she didn't say anything bad about you, so that's a plus."

"I guess."

As the kitchen came up to speed, Gina poked her head in and said, "Hey guys," followed by Glen's not-so-agreeable greeting of, "Hey losers."

"We all lost," said Rick.

"Not me," countered Glen. "I played good."

"There's no individual stats here," said Billy. "We're a team."

"Speak for yourself," muttered George.

Now if ever there were an example of what a team shouldn't be, there it was.

Needing to nip this thing in the bud, Billy ordered everyone into the dining room.

"I just wanted to make sure we're on the same page," started Billy. "We work as a team at this restaurant, and we need to work as a team on the basketball court. We're here for Andy. We all saw him rolled up in a ball on the living room floor, and now he's blocking shots and dunking the basketball. That's powerful."

"But we're not only here for him," continued Billy. "We all need to accomplish something. We all need to win something. We all need to get to a better place. We've all been selected for this, and that's powerful!"

"Come on, Billy!" cheered Glen. A stern "shut up" came from George as Billy geared up for the finale.

"So what's going to happen is that we're going to play today. We're going to play tomorrow, and we're gonna play the day after that, and then we'll play some more and then after we put the work in, we will win!" exclaimed Billy. "And that's powerful."

The staff was suddenly on their feet as they simultaneously cheered, "Let's go team!"

George then gave Glen a pat on the back, Rick high fived Gina, and Coach Billy just smiled. He let the feeling sink in before adding, "But I want everyone to understand that there's something else on the horizon. This is the first challenge, but it's not going to be the last. So if you're out, you're out. But if you're in, you need to be all in."

"I'm all in," said Rick.

"In," said George.

"Of course," added Glen.

"Me too," replied Gina.

"And we also need to get our sizes in to Gina for the uniforms. Rita offered to buy them, so I'm gonna take her up on it. It's the least she can do."

"Cool," said the guys.

Gina exclaimed, "Hey, I told you I wasn't going to be the equipment manager!"

"I know," replied Billy, "but you're the assistant coach too. We're going to need your organizational skills on and off the court, and your brains and beauty as well."

"Of course, cutie. When you put it like that, how can I refuse?"

With shoulder-length blond hair, cute dimples, and wide hips, Gina was a force to be reckoned with. Being a single mom, Gina put her child first in every regard. When she was a pregnant teen, the father flaked out, but Gina persevered. Shown the door by her conservative Southern parents, she started out in government-subsidized housing before finally being able to afford a small house.

It was tough, but it made her sharp as a tack. Her wit and wisdom always rubbed off on the customers, especially on Coach Gene Shatterly of the Tar Heels. Billy figured that was enough to get her courtside. She was also a rabid basketball fan. Most everyone in Chapel Hill was.

Making their way back into the kitchen, everyone seemed committed to a higher purpose. Rick liked the idea, and it was fine by George, he needed to get into better shape anyway. Playing with those jokers from yesterday would be the perfect way to do it.

"Can you make a soup today, Billy?" asked Rick.

It's funny that the first day Billy walked in they were telling him what to do, and now they were asking. If Billy wasn't mistaken, he'd made quite a mark. He just hoped it would translate onto the basketball court.

"How about a zucchini soup with pasta?"

"Sure," replied Rick, "we can serve it with a chicken parmesan sandwich."

"Sounds like another fun day for me."

"Would you have it any other way?"

"Uh, I guess not," answered the reluctant cook.

It was another busy shift and Billy wasn't surprised. They all loved the special, of course. Billy knew that because he made about forty of them—a fried chicken breast on a crispy roll covered in tomato sauce with a slice of mozzarella and a bowl of zucchini soup. Bellissimo!

There were still concerns for the team though. Everyone at the restaurant was in, but he still needed Andy or Andy needed Andy or the world needed Andy. Billy wasn't sure which.

Billy wasn't sure when or where it would end. He wasn't sure if he'd get credit for a job well done, or if he'd have to keep going. Sinking deeper into the scenarios, Billy guessed that the real mystery was in the unknown, and the chance to let it happen.

As the last few orders went out, Andy sure enough appeared and this time, Gwen was with him. Seeing her through the window, Billy walked out and greeted the two.

"You hungry, Andy?" asked Billy to the towering patron.

"Yeah, Billy, I haven't had anything today."

"Guys, can you make something for Andy? I've got to duck outside."

"Sure, boss," answered Rick.

Billy wasn't sure, but he had a feeling that someone would follow him out, and she did.

As she stood on the front patio, Gwen's pretty red hair shone like a burning flame beneath the afternoon sun. Her eyes sparkled, and Billy made it a point not to look into them. He wasn't ready yet.

"So was that Rita yesterday?" asked Gwen.

"Strangely enough, it was. I didn't expect it, but I'm not surprised."

"She's something else. I'm surprised you had anything to do with me after her."

"You're no slouch either," replied Billy. "You've got a more earthly beauty, more comforting and nurturing. I like it."

Gwen didn't expect the Mother Nature comparisons, but she'd take it, especially after leaving Billy high and dry.

"Well, you're a handsome guy, Billy. But you already know that."

"I guess. It hasn't really helped me though."

"It helped you meet me."

"And look how well that worked out."

Gwen understood the disappointment. She felt it too. It took something strong to pull her away, and something even stronger was making her stay. Somewhere in time, a bond had formed between her and Andy, and perhaps the family.

"Like it was supposed to, I guess."

Billy was impressed that Gwen could see things so clearly, but it was more than that. Gwen was something special, but the only way she'd survive is with another broken hero. Only someone who'd seen the ugliness of the world could realize the beauty in something so strange. Only a soul who'd been saved could appreciate such special power without any pretense. Only a man who'd come back from the dead could see such a thing and not be scared. Billy also thought that Andy might be hiding something as well. Most people were.

In a sudden moment of honesty, Billy said, "Throughout my whole entire life, I've only wanted what was right. I only wanted what was right for Rita, and I only want what's right for you. You came to me at the right time, and I can't thank you enough."

"I miss you guys though. I miss Celia."

"She misses you too. You should give her a call."

"I will," said Gwen.

"So how are things going?"

"They're going well. I'm just kind of driving Andy around right now, getting him acclimated and being there for him. As you can probably understand, we've got a pretty strong bond."

"If you could keep getting him here in the afternoon, it would be a great help. I don't know what's going on yet, but it seems like we're getting ready for something, and we don't have a lot of time."

"No problem," replied Gwen as the guys spilled out of the restaurant. "He's been asking to come."

"Outstanding."

"Yeah, outstanding," mimicked Rick.

With the guys joking around and cutting up, Billy felt like he just might have a team. He hoped he did because the other guys really did have a team. Unhinged and on the move, they were something primordial, they were murky and misty, and they were heading straight for Billy.

Billy's short drive to the park was filled with angst. Each day seemed more demanding than the next, and today was no different. He always wondered if things were still working. He wondered if the pipeline was still operational and as they neared the basketball court, they saw that the team was there.

From a distance, they looked more dangerous than before. They shot flawlessly and moved mechanically around the court in a quick, robotic fashion. Billy wondered why they couldn't have started off against a lesser team. They seemed to have skipped college and gone straight to the pros.

As his guys laced up and straggled onto the court, Rod walked over to Billy and said, "You showed."

"I was about to say the same to you."

Rod just sounded a deep hollow cackle and added, "The team looks ready."

"You all do too. Did some of the guys go through a growth spurt or something?"

"No, we're the same. We're always the same," replied Rod as he trotted back up court.

Billy swore that Rod was an inch taller and a bit bulkier as well. Sam, Rod's partner in the backcourt looked like a fighter jet with arms and the two forwards, Will and Dillon, seemed to have just walked out of a weight room. With a big black eye and a headband, their towering center, Han, looked like a bouncer at a South Beach nightclub rather than a basketball player. It was sure to be an interesting day.

Heading back over to his team, Billy said, "Be ready today, Glen. if you get an open shot, take it. We're going to need some easy points."

"Sure," replied Glen as he feigned a couple of imaginary shots.

As Billy and Rick walked to center court, Rod and Sam approached as well.

"Same as yesterday," barked Billy, "play to twenty-one by one."

"How's Flash today?" asked Rod.

"Flash is fine," yelled George, "and he's ready to go to your ass."

"He-he," chuckled Rod. "Let's go."

"Your ball," said Billy.

Scanning the court, Rod quickly inbounded to Sam, and the game was on. Working the ball around, they took a few passes before going back to Rod for an easy lay-up.

"My fault," said Andy before facing up Han.

Then, as Glen passed in to Rick, the specters forced a turnover and scored another quick basket.

"Two nothing," said Rod as he shuffled the ball back to Rick.

Rick then threw the ball to a speeding George, who somehow forced the ball into the basket for their first point.

"Two to one, sucka!" yelled Gorge.

"Ahh," sounded Rod, "Flash is on a hot streak."

But the ball kept moving, and the specters kept scoring as Billy's team struggled. Running back and forth, Rick finally wrestled the ball from Rod and went back to George for another bucket.

"Top that, son," snapped George as Rod let out a low growl.

Passing the ball back inside, Andy blocked a weak shot from Han, and then the game sped up.

The specters blasted around the court trying to drop Billy's team, but the guys held. George kept their forwards away from the basket as Andy started to take over. He stripped the ball on one end and found Billy for an easy basket on the other. Then Glen made a shot, stole an inbound pass, and threw it to Andy for another dunk.

"You got yourself a player there," noted Rod, before going straight through Rick for an easy lay-up.

"Take notes up there, big man," said Rod as Andy just nodded.

Then the other guard, Sam, started to get hot. He hit one shot and then another as Glen said, "Man, you can sure play some basketball."

"I thought we was playin' tiddlywinks, mate," replied Sam in a thick English brogue.

"No, ya daft bugger," countered Dillon, "It's called ring around the rosie."

"A pocket full of posie," added Will.

"Ashes, ashes, we all fall down," finished Han.

"Things get a little messed up in the afterlife," explained Rod, "confused, I guess you could say."

"I guess," agreed Billy, as it seemed like a crew of Englishmen had somehow inhabited Rod's basketball team.

Glen just stared. Not sure if they were messing with him, he picked off another pass and quickly threw it to Andy for another point. Billy then noticed George starting to slow, so he picked up the pace. Making eye contact with Rick, Billy jumped toward the basket, caught the ball in midflight, and then slammed it forcefully through the hoop.

"Lucky," said Rod, and his team then took over.

And on it went, with the teams trading points until George finally took a knee.

"What happened, Flash, your motor broke?" laughed Rod.

"I'll show you Flash," said George as he staggered to his feet.

"You don't want to do that, George," warned Billy.

"No, George!" yelled Rick as he moved deliberately forward.

Now within striking range, with a raised fist, George swung harmlessly through Rod's shifting form.

"That was a right good swing, mate," said Dillon as George again swung for the fences only to fall flat on his face.

"Give it another go, old chap," cheered Will as Han added, "He's a crafty little bugger."

"No, George," said Billy, "don't give it another go, we need you. Team, remember?"

Still breathing heavy, George repeated, "Yeah, team."

Rod then walked over and said, "I'm sorry, brother George, I was just tryin' to get under your skin."

"You're a fast little dude," chuckled George. "I'll get you next time though."

"I know you will, George,"

"I know you won't, George," said Rick.

"Shut up, Rick. Just take the ball out."

So, with order restored, Rick passed to Billy, who shuffled the ball off to Glen, who then passed it to Andy for another slam dunk. If Billy wasn't mistaken, Andy seemed to be having a pretty good time. His game was also improving as he moved outside of the arc and started to hit long-range shots.

Billy wasn't playing at full speed, but that was deliberate. He wanted to see what his team had. Aside from the temper tantrum, George was running better, and Andy had found another level. Rick was moving the ball well, and Glen was dangerous from the outside. But the specters still won. They were too solid, too fast, and they didn't make any mistakes. Billy's guys would need a few more outings before they could crack the code.

"You guys were better today, but still not good enough," said Rod as they moved away from the court.

"Rome wasn't built in a day," replied Billy.

"It was fun while it lasted though," affirmed Rod.

As the rest of the players milled around and shook hands, Will said, "Cheers mate, you fancy a spot of tea?"

"What?" asked George.

"Tea," repeated Rick, "you know, iced tea, sweet or unsweet?"

"Iced tea," muttered the players, "sounds horrid."

"Who would ever think to put ice in tea?"

"Looks like it's tea time, so we gotta split, but we'll see ya around," said Rod.

"We'll be back," replied Billy, "sooner rather than later."

Then, as the specters moved into the darkness, Billy wondered if they were ever really there.

"We got better, but tomorrow's another day."

"Yeah," said Andy, "we'll get them next time."

Yeah, next time, thought Billy as he was hit by a sudden wave of sadness. Watching the guys drive off, Billy sensed things were coming to a close. He'd once wanted it finished, but faced with the prospect of an actual end, Billy was glum. But it was too early to reflect. There was still work to do.

"So what do you think?" said Rick. "I've played a lot of games but never one like that, with George swinging at air and American players with English accents. What a trip!"

"There's more to come," said Billy. "Don't ask me what, but there's something else."

"How does this stuff not completely blow your mind?"

What could he say? Billy's mind was blown long ago, at the temple in Mexico and then on the plane ride back to Florida. The spinning chair at Celia's also threw him for a loop, as well as the mystical journey with the medicine man. There were too many ways to count.

"You're new to this, Rick, but you need to hang in there. There's more to the story than you know. One day it'll all make sense, or it might make sense. You're part of the story though, and you deserve to know, I just don't have the time to tell you. Celia can fill you in later."

Billy just threw it out there to get Rick's mind off of the anomalies. He needed Rick to stay productive, and hopefully sane. Billy wanted to give him the whole story, but he needed to focus on getting the team ready.

"Sounds good," replied Rick, especially the mention of Celia.

It was effective subterfuge, but it seemed like all that Rick had was questions. It wasn't surprising though, because he'd never met anyone like Billy Winslow, and he probably never would.

There were more stories as well, stories about Rita and the kidnapping. Billy wanted to spill the beans, but he just couldn't. They were making progress, and Billy wanted it to continue, because of all the people who wondered how it would end, he was the most curious.

"Well, what about Rita?" asked Rick as they drove to Celia's.

"What about her?"

"She was something else, man. She was like an executive. She had power. And don't even start on the looks. She was smoking."

"She used to be a model."

"Used to be? In case you didn't notice, she still is a model, champ."

Billy laughed. At the time, life with Rita seemed chaotic and dysfunctional, but in retrospect, they were the best of times.

"And what about Gwen. I thought you and her were an item?"

"We were."

It was a short answer, and Rick knew not to press. As Billy thumbed Rita's business card, his head was somewhere else. He needed to talk to her about the uniforms anyway. Why they needed them, he couldn't say. He didn't want to; he just wanted to let things unfold.

Coasting back up the drive Billy said, "I'll send Celia out so you can fill her in on the game."

Walking into the house, he saw Celia, who excitedly said, "I got a call from Gwen!"

"Did you set something up?"

"Yes, we're having coffee on Saturday."

"Great," replied Billy, "now I'm more alone than before."

"Oh please, it's not like you to feel sorry for yourself."

"That's easy for you to say," said Billy before adding, "Rick's waiting to tell you about the game."

"Oh, exciting!" exclaimed Celia as she ran outside.

Billy then took a seat at the dining room table and wondered what to do. The end of the day always felt different, especially when he was alone. He hadn't expected to meet anyone. He didn't really want to, and then when he did, he thought maybe something had changed. Billy thought that maybe he could settle down, but it now seemed like everyone else was.

But Billy served a higher purpose, and it was in the rarefied air where he'd operate. Celia was right; it wasn't like Billy to feel sorry for himself. So he wouldn't. Taking Rita's business card out, he dialed the number and then waited. Hearing the long, lonely ring, he suddenly remembered the first time they'd met. Rita was at the bar with a migraine and Billy offered an aspirin. He actually wondered if he should be calling. He wondered if she'd extended her card as a mere gesture or if she really was interested in what he was doing. There was only one way to find out.

As the phone continued to ring, Billy wasn't sure why he was calling. Was it to tell her what was going on or was it to proclaim his love for her? He couldn't possibly do that as Rita's sexy voice slid through the line and said, "Hello."

What he said was, "You actually answer your own phone. I'm surprised."

"It is my number."

Man, she got him again. There he was, tongue tied and twisted. Rita was the only one who could do that—her and every other woman he'd ever been with.

"I just thought at this point you'd have an assistant."

"I do."

"Well, I figured you did," snickered Billy. The other end of the line stayed quiet, so he added, "But I guess you can answer if you want. After all, it is your phone."

"Yes, we've already established whose phone it is tonight. Is that why you called, Billy?"

"Well, you did say you were interested in what I was doing."

"I am," replied Rita. "Are you finished doing it?"

"No, but I will be," said Billy. "But I was actually calling about the uniforms. You did offer to buy some, didn't you? It's for a good cause."

"Yes, I did say that I would buy them, but for that I'll be directing you to my assistant. I'd assume there will be some sizes and things of that nature to consider. She'd be better equipped to handle that."

More finality, thought Billy as he asked, "Should I take her number?"

"Of course, it's Constance Cavalleri at extension 336. Call early, she's very busy."

"Sure will, Rita, and thanks again. It was nice seeing you."

"You're welcome, Billy. It was nice seeing you as well. Take care."

"Bye," said Billy as the phone went quiet.

Celia then raced into the house and said, "It just gets better and better! You've got British basketball players and George fought a ghost. That's awesome."

"Yeah," Billy weakly agreed.

"What's wrong?"

"Nothing, really. I just talked to Rita and it brought back memories."

"Why did you call her?"

"I'm not sure. On the surface it was to discuss the uniforms, but I don't really know the deeper purpose. I don't think I want to know."

"You can still be in each other's lives. It'll just take some time. What will be will be."

What will be will be, thought Billy as he grabbed his notebook and wrote:

"It'll take some time," she said, but it still messed with his head.

The things he'd wanted done, he now wanted undone so he could try again.

It was strange that in perfection there was imperfection and in nature there was destruction and in all things held dear, there was danger and sorrow.

But he was lucky and tortured and she was beautiful and fortunate, and the things that put them together had also torn them apart. She'd landed on her feet, while he just landed. She'd soared through the sky, while he just sputtered. She'd found herself perched on high, while he was still on the bottom. But it was his bottom, and the sky was his, and there was still a great beyond with secrets still to reveal.

Handing the notebook to Celia, she quickly read, and then wrote, "It's sad and inspirational. You've finally got it, Billy. Nice job. A+"

Finally an A+, thought Billy, *it's about time.*

PROGRESS

ollowing the usual progression of the afterlife, Billy's days were a blur of work and play and then more work. He was getting more comfortable at the restaurant, Rick was getting more comfortable with Celia, and Andy was getting more comfortable in his new skin, which was actually his old skin, but he was in a better place. Gwen was still strong, cute, and functional, and she was certainly functioning.

The basketball team was getting better. George had finally made it through a whole game without folding, and as Sam from the specter team put it, "The lads are coming along quite well."

Gina had Constance Cavalleri's phone number for the uniforms, and the guys had all furnished their sizes. They still didn't know why they needed them, but they soon would.

"That Constance is a piece of work," said Gina. "She seems to know everything. She knew that the uniforms were supposed to be black and gold before I even told her. She actually told me what color they were supposed to be."

"Sounds like a good assistant to me."

"True, but there was something else."

"There's no telling," replied Billy.

With the way things were going, he wouldn't have been surprised if she were a superhero as well. Rita had also changed. She was harder, more complex. He'd heard it in her voice; she was more guarded and mysterious. Billy didn't know what she had going on, but it was sure to be interesting. And what about Corbin, was he just a tagalong or was he the real thing?

Following the kidnapping, Billy had pretty much fallen off the face of the earth, but as soon as he finished this project, there were a few things he'd look into, namely Flake Industries. It sounded kind of flakey to him, but Rita looked good, and she seemed happy so there was no real cause for concern. After all, Billy had enough to worry about on his end. He was still a short order cook at a local dive. The future wasn't exactly looking bright, especially with the prospect of being bossed around by Rick and George.

Make a soup here. Make a sandwich there. Rick hadn't even let him work the grill yet.

"You're too good at the other stuff," he'd say.

But Rick was a good guy, and he'd been a lot of help. Just think what would have happened if someone else had seen and heard the things that Rick had. They'd either be committed or they'd be blabbing all over town. Rick hadn't done either; he was solid.

"Listen, guys," grinned Billy, "we've got some uniforms coming."

"Rita came through," replied Rick.

"She sure did."

"Tell me they're light blue," bellowed George, thinking in terms of the Tar Heels.

"Even better," said Billy, "they're black and gold."

"Black is better than blue?"

"Wouldn't you rather be a Knight than a Tar Heel?"

For George, it wasn't even a question as he glaringly said, "Tar Heel born and Tar Heel bred and when I die, I'm a Tar Heel dead."

"Ingrate," scoffed Billy as they all got back to work.

Changes had definitely taken place though. From playing every afternoon, they were all stronger, and George had actually gotten thin. It hadn't helped his disposition, but he'd taken quite a liking to the specters. They hadn't had tea yet, because George still wanted to put ice in it, but other than that, they got along pretty well.

Customers came and went, but there was still one Billy needed to talk to. When he first toured campus, Billy had seen Coach Gene Shatterly walking up the hill. It was strange that even then he seemed to be part of the story. He looked approachable enough, almost friendly, but it was too early. In these parts, the head coach of a championship basketball team was nothing to trifle with. Share a smile, maybe a couple of words of encouragement and then move on, but Billy would need more than a couple of words.

Billy used to joke with Gina about introducing him to the coach, but when he said it today he wasn't joking. He'd been moved. His life had been upended, and now he was about to upend someone else's.

With the regulars arriving early, Billy of course had to make a soup and then get ready for the constant barrage of sandwiches. Rick hustled him right from the start. Rick didn't want to make soup, so Billy made the soup. Rick didn't want to make sandwiches, so Billy made the sandwiches. After everything wrapped up, he was most definitely going to take a break from the beloved sandwich.

Already busy, as the tickets piled up, Billy started to move. Seeing the special table set for a special guest, he knew the coach would be there soon. It was a good day for Billy to engage, because he didn't have time to think. He couldn't rehearse anything; he was just going to have to wing it.

Still pushing out plates, with the lunch rush coming to a close, Rick asked Billy if he'd help Glen on the patio. Normally he would have said no, but not today. Today his quarry, white haired and unsuspecting, was right where Billy wanted him.

Gina usually wouldn't have introduced someone to Coach Gene Shatterly. There was nothing good that could come of it, only bad. After all, Gene was making introductions, taking phone calls, speaking, scheduling, and coaching all day long. Gina didn't want to bother him at lunch, but something was happening and she figured the coach would want to know.

With Billy cleaning and the coach on his way out, Gina said, "Gene, before you leave, there's someone I'd like you to meet."

"Really," replied Gene with a raised eyebrow. She'd never made such a request. It was bold.

"It'll be worth it, I promise."

"Well, lead the way then."

And with that, Gina summoned Billy over to the coach and said, "Billy, meet Mr. Gene Shatterly. He's the head coach of the Carolina Tar Heels, and an all-around good guy as well."

"It's a pleasure to meet you, Gene," offered Billy, studying Gene's steely eyes and no-nonsense glare.

"Likewise," replied Gene.

"The team's looking good this year," said Billy as Gene's crew moved in a bit.

"Yeah, they're coming along," replied Gene in way that said Billy's time was just about up.

"I've got a pretty good squad myself," declared Billy, beginning to feel the strain.

"Really," remarked Gene, now moving away.

"Yeah," continued Billy to the back of Gene's head. "I've got Andy Völler back on the court."

Hearing Billy's stunning announcement, the coaches stalled their speedy exit. Coach Gene Shatterly then turned back to Billy and said, "If this is your idea of some kind of a sick joke, you better leave now and never show your face in this town again."

Billy felt the weight of Gene's words, and it was real. He meant it. Billy had dealt with ghoulish one-armed basketball players and dead limo drivers, but the coach had an intensity to rival even the strongest of forces, dead or alive. Billy stood firm though, because he knew it was right.

"It's no joke, Gene. Andy's back on the court and he's looking really good."

The coach took a second to process the news. He didn't think Andy would make it through the year, never mind back onto a basketball court, and he didn't know this Billy character, but he was about to set him straight.

Limping gingerly over to a clean patio table, Gene said, "Take a seat, son. I've got a quick story for you."

Gene's stories were never quick, but they were always effective. The rest of the crew sat as well. They were riveted.

"I was gung ho as a youngster. I joined the service to protect Lady Liberty and all she stands for. Whether it be the jungles of Southeast Asia or the mountains of Afghanistan, I'd go. But we didn't go to any of those places. We went to the desert, Operation Desert Storm. During Special Forces training at Fort Bragg, I met a tall skinny kid from Indiana named Kurt Völler. At first, I thought he was one of those stuffed shirts. He always had his head in a book or under a piece of equipment. He was always reading or fixing something."

"Kurt was a good soldier, but where he really shined was on the basketball court. See, we all liked to play, me and a few of the other guys. There was this black guy from New York named Lewis and another guy called Ray who used to challenge me and Kurt. We were young and aggressive, and the games were tough, but they created a bond between us, one that we eventually took into battle. We were loud and proud Americans in the desert. But not Kurt. He was always reserved, studying maps, planning escape routes, and even learning the language, whatever it's called."

"Arabic," said one of the assistants.

"That's right, Arabic. And he was getting pretty good. You see, we were one of the first teams over there, and our job was to scout it out, reconnaissance, so to speak. We'd basically lay low during the day and then patrol at night. Ray drove with Lewis in the passenger seat and they always joked about transporting the noble King Völler of Prussia. On a routine patrol somewhere in Kuwait—I remember it as an unusually dark night—for some reason, we took a different route, and by the time Kurt noticed, it was too late. A strong blast ripped through the cab of our vehicle, instantly killing Ray and Lewis and lodging a piece of metal deep into my calf muscle," continued the coach, lifting up his pant leg to reveal a mutilated calf.

"Well you can probably imagine the kind of problems that created. Not only was the disintegrated cab littered with the remains of our good buddies, but our eyes were burned and our ears were ringing. I was DOA, dead on arrival. I couldn't move, but Kurt yanked me out of the burning truck, tied off my leg and stuffed a belt in my mouth to shut me up. Kurt knew they'd come, and they did, but he couldn't blow them up. We needed a ride. We needed to get Ray and Lewis back to base, so Kurt took my weapon and moved down the ridge. Using the little Arabic he knew, he summoned the soldiers. I think he said he found something of value, gold or something like that. When they rushed toward the voice, Kurt started shooting. There were four of them and not long after that, all four were dead."

"In a mad dash to get the hell out of there, Kurt stuck me in the Iraqis' jeep, grabbed what was left of Lewis and Ray, and somehow got us back to the base. It was the end of my military career, and definitely the end for Ray and Lewis, but Kurt stayed on. He started working on computers and things like that. It was the perfect job for him, and he stayed with it, even after the war."

"But that's not the end of the story," said Gene as his assistants started to get fidgety. "After he left the desert, Kurt moved here, to work in the Research Triangle Park for IBM. That son of a bitch wouldn't ever take anything from me," continued Gene, his eyes watering up, "said that I helped him, that I got him out of the cornfields or something like that. Man, he had the nicest house, I mean it wasn't big, but it was fresh, just like a mountain stream. His wife, Ingrid, had this beautiful garden in the back and the kids were as healthy as could be. The only problem was that they took a car ride one night and never came back. One of them stayed at the house though, and he instantly became an orphan."

Coach Gene Shatterly then pushed his tan face into Billy's and said, "You see, Andy Völler used to be Kurt's son, but since Kurt's no longer with us, Andy's my son, and if you're out there telling tall tales about my son, we're going to have a real problem."

Billy was finally and utterly blown away. Lewis, the one-armed basketball player, and Ray, the deceased chauffeur, were both in the desert that night. It was their last night on earth.

Of course Billy couldn't tell that to Gene, but returning Gene's stare he said, "He's got a deadly outside shot, good instincts around the basket, and a pair of size-18 white-and-blue shoes that fit him perfectly."

The coach remembered giving Andy those shoes. It was the only thing Kurt would allow. He wouldn't take anything that Andy could use as a junior, only something he'd grow into. Billy couldn't have known about those shoes unless Andy was wearing them.

"It's true, Gene," added Gina. "Andy's been playing every day, and he's got a girlfriend, or at least a girl that's a friend."

Gene mulled it over and finally said, "So you've got a squad, eh, son?"

"Sure do," replied Billy, "and we're tough."

With his assistant standing by, Coach Gene Shatterly said, "Go ahead and schedule us a game against, what did you say your name was, son?"

"Billy."

"Yeah, Floyd, schedule us a game against Billy's team if you would. Call it a scrimmage, but it'll be a full-time game with referees and all."

Floyd then looked at Gene and said, "No way. There's no possible way. I'm not going to put our guys against some ragtag squad. These are highly trained athletes with hundreds of thousands of dollars invested in their health, training, and well-being. I'm not putting them out there to be stomped on and injured by a bunch of hacks!"

"I guess you'll be looking for another job then; tomorrow."

"OK, then," agreed Floyd. "I'll schedule the game."

With a pen quickly in hand Gina asked, "When's good for you?"

Billy then strolled back into the kitchen like the cat that ate the canary.

"So what did he say?" asked Glen.

"Yeah, Billy, what's up?" said Rick.

"Speak, Billy!" ordered George.

That was part of the problem: Billy was actually speechless. He couldn't tell them about the war, the casualties, and how the coach stared him down. What he did say was, "Hold onto your hats, boys. We're going to play the North Carolina Tar Heels in a full-court, full-press, full-fledged basketball game in the Dean Dome of all places!"

There was no immediate reaction from the guys until George's booming voice exclaimed, "I knew that I loved you, Billy!"

"You did it, Billy," added Glen, giving Billy a high five.

Rick simply said, "You're amazing, Billy."

"It's not me," replied Billy. "It's Andy."

"We playin the Tar Heels. We playing the Tar Heels," sung George as he popped into the dining room and yelled to Gina, "Hey Gina, you hear we playing the Tar Heels?"

"I heard about it, George. It's already on the schedule. We've got two weeks to get ready."

"I've been ready for this my whole life," beamed George, still dancing around the dining room.

It was like Christmas Day, New Year's Eve, and every birthday in between all rolled into one, but as George continued his victory lap, something was missing. In the majesty of the moment, something had been forgotten. In their excitement, the fact that there was a game to play, and that it was against one of the best teams in the country was completely lost. Billy thought it could be a good thing or that it could also be a really, really bad thing. If they showed up and got embarrassed, it wouldn't change anything for the guys, but it might for Andy. The coach believed in them, though, so Billy would as well.

"I thought Coach Shatterly would just want to have a look at Andy or something. I didn't think our team would be playing his team in his house. I had no freaking idea."

"Be careful what you wish for," said Rick.

"Shut up," said George. "I'm going to shut that place down, man. I'm gonna turn off the lights in that joint."

"OK, Flash," replied Rick.

"So what do you know about the team, Glen?" asked Billy, getting started on the scouting.

"They're stacked. They've got a couple of starting seniors matched with the usual All-Americans, real tough."

"You gonna make it for the big game?"

"Wouldn't miss it for the world."

"What about you, Rick?"

"You bet, Billy."

Billy didn't have to ask George, he was ready. But they all looked good. Billy was in the best shape of his life, not to mention his special abilities. At six five, with at clear, determined stare, and the spirits overhead, he was ready. With shoulder-length hair and an impish grin, Rick could cause some trouble as well. Glen had the vacant look of a shooter, and Andy was by far their best player. Billy just needed to get him on board.

"Take the afternoon off, guys; I'm going to have to talk with Andy. I don't really know where he stands on it yet. He doesn't know anything about it. I didn't tell him I was going to talk to the coach. If he says no, we're sunk. There won't be a game."

"You better make sure there's a game then," said George, "or it's your ass."

"Yeah," added Rick, "make it happen."

He was expecting Andy to show soon. In fact, Billy checked the clock just as the little yellow car pulled up.

Gwen and Andy looked almost as funny in the car as Gwen and Billy had, one short and one tall, one big and one small—although

Andy wasn't just tall, he was huge. He barely fit, but he seemed content nonetheless. It seemed like he and Gwen could have driven around town for the rest of their lives and been completely happy.

It was strange that Andy had found such an overwhelming calm. It could have been a wisdom gained from suffering or perhaps the dark days were finally turning light. Billy hoped they were.

"Where's everyone going?" asked Andy

"We've got the afternoon off," answered Billy. "I've got some exciting news."

"Oh," sounded Gwen.

Andy was a little less enthused. In his world, announcements weren't always good.

"Listen, Andy," started Billy, "I had a talk with Gene Shatterly today."

"Hmm," sounded Andy, "I haven't talked to him in a while."

"It was an interesting conversation, to say the least."

Billy, of course, couldn't tell him about the firefight and about Lewis and Ray, but he did tell how Andy's father, Kurt, had saved Gene's life.

"Did you know your father saved Gene's life?"

"I had no idea," answered Andy. "My father never talked about the war, said it wasn't important."

"Well it was important to Gene. It was so important to Gene that he's scheduled a game for us. We're going to play the Tar Heels for a full forty minutes, under the lights at the Dean Dome in Chapel Hill, North Carolina!"

Gwen quickly grasped Andy's arm as he said, "We are?"

"We are. Everyone else is in."

Andy didn't answer right away. His thoughts drifted back to his sister, June, and when she used to hide his basketball. She'd like to see it. His father, Kurt, used to talk about the day Andy would go pro, if he kept his grades up, that is. Kurt secretly wanted Andy to play for Gene. Andy's mother, Ingrid, used to let Andy stay out after dark playing on the gravel driveway, dirty and grimy, hitting shot after ecstatic shot. Everyone told her Andy would be great one day. She said that he already was.

With Gwen's hand still on his wrist, Andy said, "I'll play."

"Yes!" exclaimed Billy as Gwen sounded an enthusiastic, "Yay!"

With the roster complete, Billy had some unfinished business. They needed reserves, and he knew where to find them.

Walking back to Celia's, Billy wondered where the hell Rick was.

Billy found out where the hell Rick was as he approached Celia's only to see Rick's truck in the driveway.

"Oh, ah, hey Billy, I was just here to give Celia the news."

"I know why you're here," said Billy, "and I also know where we need to go."

"Where?"

"We need to go to the park."

Rick wondered why, but he figured Billy had a reason. Billy always had a reason, so, as usual, he went along with it.

"We're not playing today, are we?"

"No," answered Billy, "but we need reserves, so I'm gonna get the specters."

"Don't you think that's a little risky?"

"Yeah, but this whole thing is risky, so what's a little more risk going to hurt?"

Could hurt a lot, thought Rick, but he didn't say it. He just did what he was supposed to do, which was drive.

When they neared the park, the court was empty and Billy wondered why. He thought maybe the specters had moved on to the next basketball court or soccer pitch or wherever else they might be headed.

Rick and Billy shot around on the court until they heard a familiar voice ask, "Where's the lads?"

"Yeah, where's old rocket man Flash?" asked Rod as the team, one by one, emerged from the darkness.

Unshaven, with one blue eye and a clear orb wedged neatly into his other eye socket, Rod looked spookier than ever. The glass eye looked more like a crystal ball, and Rod seemed to be staring straight through them. The others stood steadily by like all they wanted was a game. They still weren't sure what they were playing, but they liked it.

"Rather than run around here, we came to see if you wanted to play in a real game."

"Now you're talking, big boss."

"Since you've been getting us ready for the big game, we were wondering if you'd like to play in it."

"Absolutely," said Rod. "I've been waiting to get a crack at those guys ever since they beat my Hoyas in eighty-two."

"You're a Georgetown fan?" asked Billy

"I was," grinned Rod.

"Bring it, then."

"You know it."

Surrounded by Rick and the specters, Billy was instantly present. Feeling the cool breeze against his face, he suddenly felt secure. All he'd worked for was finally coming to fruition, and it felt good. He needed to keep pushing though, because there was still more to do.

The days became a strange mix of celebration and concern. The guys weren't concerned, but Billy was. He'd started this thing, and now he needed to finish it. He knew what needed to happen; he just wasn't sure how to make it happen. People had tried to manipulate sporting events for hundreds of years, mostly unsuccessfully. It was difficult enough to guess or even to pick a winner, not to mention actually win. But he didn't need to win; he just needed to show, and that was going to be the hard part. He'd pledged not to use his special powers unless completely necessary, but as game day grew closer, Billy was beginning to feel the necessity.

For the most part, everything else had remained normal. Coach Gene Shatterly hadn't shied away from the restaurant. For the coach and his crew, it had been business as usual. He mentioned the game to Gina in passing, but had largely passed it off to his assistant coach, Floyd Gaines. He wasn't only testing his team; he was testing Floyd as well, and this was the perfect way to do it, against an unwieldy opponent with nothing to lose. The coach couldn't get too invested, because of the personal implications, but he was excited as well.

Andy thought of the consequences too. After cutting Gene out, he didn't really know how to get reacquainted. He guessed that's what the game was for. They could take a beating and then Andy could retire, or maybe not. Maybe they'd win. They'd been staying with the specters, but on an outside court with no pressure or expectations. This was going to be the real thing.

With the game rapidly approaching, the guys were starting to wonder about the uniforms.

"Rita wouldn't have forgotten, would she?" asked Rick.

"No," answered Billy. "She may have decided not to get them, but she definitely wouldn't have forgotten."

Then in a loud, thundering bluster, something landed in the dining room. It was a woman. Wearing high heels, plaid overalls, and black horn-rimmed glasses over a radiant pair of blue eyes, she looked like Rita, only more manic. With the stunning resemblance, it seemed strangely like a Rita bot had delivered their uniforms.

Rolling a big cardboard box through the dining room, she excitedly announced, "The uniforms are here!"

"Who are you?" asked Gina as the restaurant instantly surrendered to the new, interesting intrusion.

"I'm Constance Cavalleri," answered Constance, "and you're Gina Bell, the mild-mannered dining room manager of this quaint local eatery, and the assistant coach of the team as well."

"Coach," corrected Gina with a look of surprise.

As the guys began filtering into the dining room, they noticed the spectacle of Constance and were instantly curious. It was Billy's operation though, so they deferred to him as he obviously stalled. They expected uniforms but not a sexy, wild delivery lady.

Suspiciously eyeing the Rita look-alike, Billy asked, "Who are you?"

"I'm Constance Cavalleri, and I'm also Rita's personal assistant. She sent me to ensure the delivery of the uniforms, and also to review the proceedings."

To Billy it sounded like she'd be sticking around.

"Well, I'm Bill."

"I know," interrupted Constance. "The great Billy Winslow, an uncommon commoner walking the earth to somehow cleanse the ills of humanity. I'm Constance Cavalleri, and for some reason, I know everything. It's a strange defect that seems to have made my hair frizzy."

"Really?"

"No," answered Constance, "but you fell for it. I knew you would, I think it's more the humidity."

"What about him?" asked Billy, pointing to Rick.

"He's Rick Flores, the good-natured chef of the café, and also your aunt Celia's boyfriend."

"He is?"

"We've got a date," affirmed Rick.

"Well, what about him?" said Billy, pointing to Glen.

"Who, no-show Glen?"

"How bout him, then?" Billy finally asked, pointing over to George as Andy and Gwen entered the dining room.

"Oh, the big-hearted, big-mouthed teddy bear."

Then with the other two in earshot, Billy asked, "Well, since you know everything else, are we going to win?"

"I said I knew everything, I didn't say I'd tell everything. What fun would that be?"

"Hello, Gwen and Andy. It's such a pleasure to finally meet you," said Constance, giving them a big hug.

It didn't faze Andy, but Gwen had a few questions.

"And you are?"

"I'm Constance Cavalleri, and I—"

Before she could finish, Billy said, "She seems to know everything. It's another anomaly."

"He's marginalizing it, but that's no surprise."

"Sounds like their first fight," said Gwen. "How cute."

"Yeah," added Constance, "maybe you could put him in his place again."

"Silence," yelled Billy. "There's bigger fish to fry. The game's a day away and we still don't have any uniforms."

"They're right here." Constance pointed.

Opening the big, brown box, rather than sleek black and gold uniforms, the ones that Billy revealed were a brilliant purple and white.

"What!" exclaimed George, "I'm not gonna show up to the big dance wearing purple."

"It's not a dance," corrected Constance. "It's actually a game in which you're woefully outclassed."

Stepping forward, Andy picked up one of the kits and said, "They're cool. Kind of reminds me of the Northwestern Wildcats."

"Yeah," added Billy. "Rita went to Northwestern. She never lets me forget it."

A note simply read: "Thought you'd look better in purple. After all, it is quite a royal occasion. May the spirits lift you to new heights. Love, Rita."

But how did she know about the spirits, and where did Constance the sexy medium come from? And what was next? Just when Billy thought things were wrapping up, new mysteries were being unveiled, and he was still amazed.

Sifting through the uniforms, they seemed to be numbered accordingly. Andy had requested the number four to represent the four members of his family. George requested twenty-three, which was promptly rejected in favor of forty-five. Billy took the number three for its special properties. Rick took number five to stay in line, and

Glen got number six. They were sure to be one of the strangest looking teams, but they wanted it that way. They didn't want to make sense.

As the uniforms were doled out and the restaurant went quiet, there was a genuine feeling of accomplishment. Looking around the room, they knew they'd done something remarkable: they'd become a team. Billy just hoped they'd play like one when the time came.

The game was scheduled for a Saturday, and it was a closed-door event. Only close family and friends would be admitted, most of whom would come for the visiting side—Billy's side. There wasn't much excitement from the home team. They figured they would just deliver another drubbing and then be back to the showers.

"Let's meet tomorrow to go through some formations and assignments, sound good?" asked Billy.

"Sure thing," said Glen before a couple of cheers ensued.

"So how are you feeling about everything, Andy?" continued Billy. Andy was playing well, but he hadn't checked on anything else.

"I feel good, Billy. It's great to be playing again. I couldn't have come back without you and Gwen and the rest of the team. I mucked up my first chance, but I'm not going to ruin my second."

"Hell no," said George. Rick added, "No way."

Gina simply said, "We're here for you, Andy."

Constance added, "You've come a long way, kid."

How did she know that? thought Billy before remembering that she somehow knew everything.

With the restaurant closed and everyone moving on, Billy asked, "So where are you staying tonight, Constance?"

"Normally I'd stay in town, but knowing you'd insist that I stay at Celia's, I didn't bother booking anything."

Piling into Rick's truck, Billy further inquired, "Is Glen going to show?"

"He is, but it's gonna to be close. And if we're going to hang out, you're going to have to get a car."

"Who said we're going to hang out?" replied Billy before turning to Rick. "So you and Celia have a date?"

"I was going to tell you. I was just waiting for the right time."

"You're adults," replied Billy.

"He's still a little distraught though," said Constance.

"Distraught? Don't you think that's a little strong?"

"OK, disappointed maybe."

"Better," agreed Billy as they pulled into the drive.

Out of the truck, Celia was surprised to see a Rita clone in the front yard.

"Has anyone ever told you that you look kind of like Rita?"

"I get that a lot, but she's a lot more glamorous than me. She's smarter and a lot more important too. And no, I'm not going to sleep with you tonight, Billy. Only maybe if you guys win," added Constance as Billy showed her to her room.

"That's rather presumptuous," answered Billy.

THE GAME

It was another busy day at the restaurant. George was chomping at the bit, while Rick was supposedly visualizing his game. Gina and Glen were there too, and Billy had some special instructions. In the event of a close game, he asked Gina to pull Andy.

"It's the final step," he said. "I don't want Andy to feel like it's the last game of his life. I want him hungry for more."

Gina agreed and they planned tomorrow's shoot around to start at twelve thirty for the one o'clock game. Billy didn't want to overstay his welcome. He wanted to show up, take care of business, and then leave.

With Andy on the way, it was then on to the park for their final practice as Rick, George, and Glen loaded up. The specters also appeared, and Billy commenced a light-hearted scrimmage.

"Andy, show 'em what that ball of yours can do," yelled Billy as Andy raised a long finger and gave it a strong spin. The ball then quickly traveled up one arm, down the other, and then ended up spinning away on his opposite hand.

"Brilliant, mate!" exclaimed Sam.

"That's live," added Rod.

"You guys gonna show tomorrow, Rod?"

"We'll be there."

"You gonna make it, Glen?"

"Yeah, but if you keep asking . . ."

"You ready, George?"

"You know it, Coach."

"Bring your bag of tricks, Rick, we're going to need them."

"They're packed up and ready to go."

"OK, basketball fans," said Billy. "Tomorrow, twelve thirty sharp at the Dean Dome. It's time to wrap it up."

And with that, they said good-bye to the park and hello to a brave new world, one where they'd fight for their lives—and hopefully survive.

Sleep didn't come easy for Billy, especially with Celia and Constance downstairs yucking it up. The more wine they drank, the louder they got, until he finally passed out.

Suddenly awake, a single, solitary beam of light broke through the bedroom blinds and Billy knew it was morning. The birds were unusually loud, which he took as a good sign. At least they were cheering for him.

With everyone else still asleep, Billy took a walk. Scanning his surroundings, the things that were once so unfamiliar were now familiar, and he loved them. It would be hard to leave.

Beginning a light jog, Billy remembered his exile to Mexico and then the enlightenment. Reflecting on all that had happened since, he picked up the pace. Now at a full sprint, he thought about Ray and the flying car and then about Gwen. That was all the inspiration he needed. Billy was ready.

As Billy stood in front of the house, toweling off, Rick coasted up the driveway and said, "You're sweating already."

"You're not?" answered Billy.

"Not yet," replied Rick, exiting the truck in a brilliant purple-and-white blur.

"Now that's what I'm talking about," said Billy. "You're looking sharp!"

Walking into the house, the ladies cheered at the sight of a man in uniform.

"Yay number five," said Constance.

"Yeah, he's kind of cute," added Celia.

"You're too kind, girls," replied Rick as Billy went upstairs to dress.

Now with his uniform on, Billy looked in the mirror and saw something new. His eyes were different. There was a belief and a strength that wasn't there in the beginning. It reinforced the notion that it hadn't all been for Andy. Billy had made a splash, and the ripples were traveling far and wide. He couldn't have been happier.

When he eased down the stairs, he saw that the girls were ready as well. Constance looked spectacular, accentuating her ample curves in a tight purple jumpsuit. With her hair pulled back in a slick ponytail, wearing a pair of Carrera sunglasses, a thick gold chain, and matching earrings, she'd surely turn some heads.

Celia was equally sexy in a white skirt, with her shoulder-length hair gracefully brushing her tan, square shoulders.

"Even if we don't win, at least the girls will," said Rick.

"We didn't get all dolled up to watch you lose," replied Celia.

"Ah, actually—" started Constance.

"Hush," said Billy. "It's time to go."

With the ladies in Celia's car, Rick and Billy once again got into Rick's truck. It had kind of become their good luck charm, and they'd need all the luck they could get.

As they rode through campus, the Dean Dome slowly emerged like a glowing mother ship calling them home. After parking, they ran into Andy and Gwen, and the girls immediately broke off into an excited trio. Andy walked along like it was just another day, and Rick started into a light jog.

"There it is, Andy," said Billy. "It's your birthright. It's yours to conquer. Today's the day."

"Yes, it is," replied Andy. "I just hope the guys in there know it."

Then, out of nowhere, a booming voice yelled, "Hey, you're not going to walk in there without me."

"Hurry up, George, the game is just about to start," said Rick.

"You look damn good in purple," added Billy.

"Don't remind me," snarled George.

It was just about twelve thirty as they made it to the court. Varied in their styles, they all looked good, and suddenly, Billy's team at least had a little credibility.

Walking into the Smith Center was like entering a different world. The hardwood floors shimmered like a clear sheet of glass, and retired jerseys and national championship banners hung heroically from the rafters. It was hallowed ground, and being able to play there was an honor. But they might not be able to play—there were only four of them, and the other team noticed.

As the Tar Heels slowly filtered onto the floor, assistant coach Floyd Gaines studied the opposition. With Andy and Billy on the court, they definitely had some size, but they didn't have a full squad. It would be a quick game if no one else showed.

"So this is what we dressed out for?" asked Dante Carter, the second-year center who was already a top draft prospect.

"It's a favor to Gene."

"Oh, so now we're in the favor business," added Jevonte Smith, the first-year All-American with a brutal crossover and deadly outside shot.

"Today we are."

As Billy's team stumbled around in awe, more Tar Heels hit the floor, and it was time to go. After stripping down to their uniforms, Andy took a first shot, and luckily it went in. He was off to a good start. Gina then arrived with a clipboard, her son, and a few extra basketballs as George yelled to the opposing side, "Hey, you gonna give me one of those pretty blue jerseys?"

"No chance, pops," answered Dante, "you gotta earn these."

"So that's how it's gonna be."

"It's always been that way, man," added Jevonte.

Twelve more Heels were now on the court. With pinpoint passes, long outside shots, and thunderous dunks, they were putting on a powerful display of basketball, perhaps trying to end the game before it even started.

Rick also began limbering up and taking a few shots. He hoisted the ball toward Andy, who snatched it for a thunderous dunk of his own. The girls cheered in delight as the Tar Heels turned up their noses, but there was another interested party as well.

While the guys warmed up, a friendly voice said, "Hey, Coach, it looks like you've got quite a team there."

"Hey, Gene." replied Gina. "We're light a few players though. I don't suppose you'd have any to spare."

"I don't know, you might be able to win with what you've got."

"I'd have to jump in," joked Gina.

"Even better."

As Coach Shatterly and Gina joked around, Andy sauntered over and said, "Hey, Gene."

"Hey, son. I'm glad you could make it."

He then looked down at Andy's shoes and asked, "How do they feel?"

"They're the best I've ever had."

"Well take it easy on my guys then."

"I will," assured Andy with a laugh. And then with a light tap on Gene's shoulder, he said, "Thanks, Gene."

"Oh, it was no problem at all," replied Gene with a wide smile and a single tear running down the side of his face.

Billy watched but didn't speak. It was Andy's business, but they also had a more pressing issue: their team. At the moment, they didn't have one.

"Hey," heckled Celia, "how come the other team has so many more players?"

"Yeah. You guys need help?" continued Gwen.

"They most certainly do," added Constance.

"You can cheer for us, if you want," said a Tar Heel player. "You might have more to cheer about."

Now they were going after the girls. Billy had to do something. And where was Glen?

Things were about to get ugly, but something was also stirring. There was a twist in the universe and suddenly, out of nowhere, a group of guys wearing the same purple uniforms strode into the building and onto the court. Long and lean, the specters looked more dangerous than before. Wearing new cuts and abrasions, they stared across the court at the guys in white, and suddenly there was a game.

"Rod, you made it!" exclaimed Billy.

"I told you we would," replied Rod with that same eerie eye.

"Cheers, mate," said Sam. "It looks like a right cracking match."

"Never thought I'd be happy to see you guys," added George.

"Back at ya, Flash. We teammates now."

As Billy's team finally took shape, Floyd Gaines was concerned. They were buzzing around the court like a swarm of killer bees, and something told him it could be a busy afternoon. Coach Gene Shatterly studied the court from above and had the same feeling. He was elated.

It was nearing game time as the clock sprung to life, and the referees slowly emerged.

Billy ran over to Constance and hissed, "I thought you said Glen would make it."

"I did."

"Where the hell is he then?"

And then in an excited unison the girls said, "He's over there!"

"Come on, Glen, get a few shots in and then let's go," ordered Billy. "And another thing."

"What?"

"It's good to see you, Glen."

"Nice to see you guys too. Sorry I'm late."

Billy ran over to Gina and said, "Here's the deal. The first team is going to play the bulk of the game. When one of the guys on the bench stands up, you'll know he's ready to come in. I'll give the signal, and then we'll switch them out. And remember our plan for the end of the game as well."

"If the game is close, pull Andy."

"That's right. And use the time-outs wisely."

"Sure will."

Billy then gathered the troops and said, "As always, Glen, if you've got an open shot, take it."

"Stay on your man today, George. Don't worry about offense. Concentrate on defense."

"Don't turn it over, Rick, I'll be an easy outlet. And Andy, don't hold back. You're the stars and the stripes so let it fly! This could be the most amazing thing we ever do, so let's freaking do it!"

"Yeah!" cheered the guys as they broke for the game.

"You're definitely going to get some playing time, Rod, just stay patient and wait your turn. I'm saving you for the second half."

"Solid," said Rod.

As Gina collected the extra basketballs, there was a special one that stood out from the rest. With Celia, Constance, and Gwen all feeling the butterflies, Gwen raised her hand as Andy's basketball slowly started to move. Celia saw it first, and then nudged Constance as the ball trailed through the players and into the stands to snuggle comfortably in next to Gwen. The girls then snickered at their innocent game and at the fact that no one else had noticed. There was definitely something in the air.

Floyd Gaines also huddled up with his players as the starters separated from the reserves.

"Here's the deal, guys. It's time to shine."

"Yeah," said Dante, "I can feel it."

"Does anyone else out here feel it?" exclaimed Floyd.

"Yeah, coach, we feel it," echoed a few of the other players.

"I can see it," added Jevonte.

"It looks good on you," continued Floyd. "Just remember: patience and persistence. If it's there, take it. But if we have to work for it, were gonna grind it out."

"Don't forget that we're the Tar Heels. We're the good guys. We wear the blue and white, so let's go!" yelled Floyd.

So, with the Heels sufficiently lathered up, the teams met at half court as the referees looked to Billy and asked, "What's the name of your team? We need a name."

The guys then looked to one another as George muttered, "Ahh, Purple."

"Team Purple it is," said the ref as Rick glared and Andy chuckled. The Tar Heels laughed as well.

The referee then threw the ball high into the air, and the game was suddenly on. Andy jumped, but Dante edged him out, knocking the ball squarely into a streaking Jevonte's hands. Having to cover a real live point guard, Rick was instantly off as Jevonte shook him for an easy layin and a quick two points for the Heels.

The ball then went to Team Purple as Andy inbounded to Rick, who passed it to Glen, who somehow lost it to Dante, who then slammed the ball forcefully through the basket for another two and a foul. So with the free throw converted, it was now 5–0 and the ball went back to Billy.

Shocked into reality, the pace of the game was quicker, and they weren't practicing anymore. With the opponents ready to pounce, Billy threw the ball to a darting George, who got it to Andy, who passed to an open Glen for a high, arching shot that miraculously went in. Team Purple then cheered like they'd won a championship, but they hadn't won anything.

Incensed to have given up a basket, the Tar Heels went on a tear, scoring six more unanswered points for a comfortable 11–2 lead with fifteen minutes left in the first half.

The ball then went back to Team Purple as Rick again faced Jevonte. It wasn't a fair fight, but as Jevonte jumped in, Rick spun away and found a soaring Andy for a spectacular slam dunk and two more points for Purple.

The Heels then got the ball back and started to put on a clinic. They had superstars all over the court. A sophomore All-American named Nick Pike had taken on George and was having his way with him. Nick was sinking shots and making decoy runs to pull George away from the basket so his teammates could rebound and get the occasional slam dunk. Billy wasn't having much luck against his guy either. He'd drawn a local prospect named Melvin James. Melvin was going straight through him and had four points already. The ball seemed to be bouncing off Billy's hands right into Melvin's. As Melvin scored another two points, Gina called a time-out.

"What's going on out there, guys? We're better than this."

"We're tiring them out, coach."

"Yeah, we're just about to get them."

Andy simply smiled and waved over to Gwen. He was having a heck of a time going against the big dogs. It was nice being on a court again and not being the star.

"Do I need to start subbing you out?"

Probably, thought Billy but he said, "Not yet Gina."

Floyd simply told his guys to stay the course, but he did kind of wonder why Team Purple hadn't gone to their reserves. He would have. It wasn't his team though.

So as the guys again took the floor, Rick pushed the ball up, passed it to Glen, who found Billy on the perimeter for a shaky midrange shot that somehow went in. With every point being a celebration, Billy excitedly pumped his fist. After everything he'd been through, he finally scored. It was long overdue.

The Heels still had their skates on though, and they worked the court like a geometry quiz. Their passes were sharp and straight, and they came from all different angles. Like a real team, they found the right players at the right time for point after painful point.

Team Purple had 6 points to the Tar Heels' 20 as Billy found Andy in the corner for his first three-point shot to make it 9–20. It was still a pittance though as the Heels then opened up another ten point run to make it 9–30.

Rick took the ball out again, and somehow keeping it from the clutches of Jevonte, fed it to George, who pushed it through for a hard-fought basket and then growled, "I knew it."

"You knew what?" said Nick as he grabbed the ball back and subsequently hit another three. "Talk when you're ahead, not when you're behind, Pops."

Through all the squeaks and sprints of a proper basketball game, Team Purple was down but not out. Everyone had scored besides Rick, and it increasingly seemed like he wouldn't. But as he fed the ball to Andy, the Heels converged, and Andy quickly passed it back to Rick for an easy two points. Finally on the board, the girls excitedly cheered as Rick showed a wide, ecstatic smile.

Now 33–13 with five minutes left in the half, Andy grabbed another rebound and threw it up to Glen for another two to give Purple a hard-fought fifteen. The Heels then reeled off another seven points to make it an even forty, and as they switched out a few players, the Purple team did the same. Glenn went off for Sam, Andy went off for Han, and Will came in for Billy.

Floyd looked at the new players and sensed something different. Their passes were quick and intelligent, almost mechanical, and Rick instantly took advantage of it. He hoisted the ball to Sam, who cut straight through the middle for a jarring slam dunk, putting the Heels on notice with a polite, "Cheers, mate."

In the final minutes of the first half, with the Purple team starting to click, Rick rolled his ankle and went down. As time expired, he was helped off of the court, and his race was run. He had done what he needed to do though. He'd kept Team Purple in the game.

"I'm not gonna lie," said Gina. "We're not done, but we're pretty damn close to being done. Rod, you're in for Rick, and the front court stays the same with Billy, George, and Andy, so let's get it going!"

"Team!" cheered the guys, even though there wasn't much to cheer for.

"You're in, Rod!" said Billy.

"I'm ready," growled Rod.

And as the teams milled around, Billy heard the slam of a window and felt a stiff breeze fill the building. The sudden push of wind sent papers flying, and people scurrying, and then in an instant, it was gone. While the spectators gazed up and around, Billy didn't wonder. He knew. The spirits had arrived, and they wanted to see a game.

Billy then walked over to Andy and said, "Be ready, Andy, it's coming your way."

Andy simply nodded as the new and improved Team Purple took the floor.

The starting five for the Tar Heels were also on the court, poised to put the final nail into a purple coffin.

The second jump ball went to Andy, who swatted it over to Billy, who quickly passed to Rod, who was then picked up by Jevonte. As they faced off, Jevonte noticed something strange. This new guy appeared to have a glass eye, and he was also growling. He was stronger than the first point guard and seemed to drift rather than run. Moving seamlessly up the court, Rod passed to his partner, Sam, who hit a towering three to cheers of "Brilliant," as he handed the ball off to Dante for the inbounds.

As Jevonte tried to do the same, Rod quickly knocked the ball to Billy, who then made a long bounce pass to Andy, who laid it in with a foul from Dante. So with Andy at the foul line, he easily sunk the free throw to make it 23–40, and the Purple squad was on a roll.

In a frenetic, zig-zag fashion, Jevonte moved the ball up, but again, Rod was just too strong. This time, he simply grabbed the ball out of Jevonte's hands and found rocket man George for an easy two. They were still fifteen points down though, as the Tar Heel guards went to work. Jevonte simply facilitated, picking on George as Nick Pike started to heat up.

Gina then quickly called time and subbed George out for Will. She also pulled Andy in favor of Han, so it was now an all-specter squad with Billy being the one mere mortal. On the sidelines, Rick just grinned. He knew what the guys could do.

Seeing the subs for the purple team, Floyd quickly made his own substitutions, and on the game went. But it didn't go well for the Heels. Rod and his guys just turned up the heat. With his head curled to the side like a ram, Rod ran the floor with authority. The ball was almost invisible beneath his bent shoulder until he'd fling it with perfection to whoever was open. Billy turned it up too. He broke for the basket, and on a lob from Rod, leveled a punishing dunk over the Carolina reserves.

It continued on, with the Purple reserves taking a deep cut into the Tar Heel lead. Han was dominating the boards, with Sam and Will raining down twos and threes. Rod kept the pedal down, finding Billy in the corner for another three and with the Tar Heel lead cut to two, Floyd called time.

With two minutes left in regulation, Gina yanked Han for Andy and Billy for Dillon, who had yet to get any minutes.

With new players, it was the same game as Jevonte faced up against Rod and quickly poked the ball away to Dante for a dunk over Andy. With the Heels now up four and a minute to go, Rod grabbed the ball and said, "Is that all you got, junior cheeseburger?"

"Get it then, Big Mac," answered Jevonte as Rod unfortunately got it. He flung the ball to a breaking Andy for a towering three-pointer and the foul, giving him a chance for a four-point play. Things were getting interesting.

On the line, Andy converted the point for the tie, and then the ball went back to the Heels. Jevonte swung it around to Nick for a final shot, but out of nowhere, Andy tipped the ball into his own hands and fell to the ground as time expired.

The girls cheered wildly as Team Purple did the same. Floyd was suspicious, and the Heels wondered what the hell had happened. They were supposed to be heading for the showers, but instead they were in a dogfight against a mystery team, heading into overtime.

Floyd was going to end this now. He left his starting five in and instructed them to "Finish the job!"

Gina sent Billy back in for Dillon. Rod and Andy stayed in with Sam and Glen also on the court.

Andy again poked the jump ball to Billy, and back to Rod it went. With Rod still against Jevonte, the teams were now on equal footing. Team Purple worked the ball around to perfection as Glen found Andy, who again muscled the ball in and went to the foul line. Easily making the free throws, Andy finally, and for the first time, put the purple team ahead.

As the teams furiously traded off, there were interested parties in other corridors of time. In a faraway cave, an Indian medicine man waved his knotty cane and the grainy image of a basketball game suddenly materialized.

Ray, the deceased limo driver, heard the cheers through his broken car radio and at a neighborhood court, Lewis, the one-armed basketball player simply watched it play out. From a place high in the stands, Gene Shatterly also enjoyed the game. He'd watch the team from above at times to spot things that weren't quite visible courtside.

With both teams playing at a high level, as the first overtime lapsed, there was still work to do. Locked into a second overtime, Team Purple surged as the Tar Heels backed off a bit. With Rod taking the ball up, Glen and Sam played strong on the wings with Billy and Andy now dominating the paint.

Andy scored a quick six points as the Heels scrapped for the same. Billy then slashed to the basket for a thunderous dunk as Rod said, "Nice."

As the teams continued to trade off, Glen hit a three-pointer to put Purple up three. Jevonte then took the ball, and with Rod snarling away, shifted one way, broke the other, and then laid the ball in for two points and a foul. Converting the three-point play, Rod let the time run out. They'd have to play a third overtime.

Trapped in combat against an unknown team, all Floyd could say was, "Keep playing. We can get these guys, just stick to the plan."

It sounded good, but at this point, they were kind of wondering what the plan was. As they took the floor, it kind of seemed like they needed a new plan.

Team Purple stayed the same, as did the Tar Heels.

Andy then won the tip as Rod scooped it up and threw to Billy. Billy again found Andy for another three points, and as the Tar Heels frantically brought the ball up, Gina forcefully yelled, "Time-out."

"Andy," said Billy, "she's subbing you out."

Andy simply nodded and ran for the sideline. He never would have let something like that slide before, but he was a different player now and he knew it was just a game.

"Nice game, Andy," they all said as he again waved to Gwen as she feverishly cheered.

On the bench, watching the game play out, Andy was happy. There'd be more games and more close finishes, but he'd always remember this one as something special, something otherworldly, actually.

With Andy out and George back in, the purple team went small, and the Tar Heels surged. They took it up to a five-point lead and then coasted to a hard-fought win, with Floyd wiping the sweat from his furrowed brow.

As the teams shook hands, Coach Floyd Gaines found Gina and said, "You've got an interesting team there, Gina."

"Likewise, Coach," replied Gina. "It's been an honor."

Shaking his head, Floyd wouldn't get any answers, but he did learn something about his team. He learned they had heart, and he was proud. He wasn't sure who they'd faced out there, but the Purple team seemed to have come straight out of Marvel Comics. He wouldn't have been at all surprised if they could fly. After all, they had played most of the game in the air. Floyd had first refused Gene's request, but he never would again. This had been one of the greatest games he'd ever been a part of.

"Hey, glass-eye man," yelled Jevonte. "Where'd you play your ball?"

"Mostly at the rec," sneered Rod.

"Well, you're pretty damn good."

"You too," replied Rod, and that's about all Jevonte would get. As Billy could attest to, the specters usually didn't say much.

Beneath the gently sloping sides of the dome, it wasn't the building that mattered, but the space inside. It wasn't the wins that made it special, but the cheers, the smiles, and the hard-fought battles both won and lost. Feeling the intensity of the atmosphere, Billy smiled as well.

Rick and George clowned around as Andy sat comfortably next to Gwen. Coach Gene Shatterly congratulated his players as Glen and the specters shared a few final laughs. Gina and her son, Taylor, walked gingerly toward the Tar Heels, pen and paper in hand, while praising Team Purple's heroic efforts as well. Beautifully radiant beneath the artificial light, Celia and Constance illuminated the room. Shining in every direction, they gave Billy an excited wave as he waved back and blew a kiss.

As they headed for the parking lot, the chuckles and random chatter sounded a fitting conclusion to the day. Simplistic in its beauty, it reminded Billy of the chirps and whistles of dawn, and even though it was approaching dusk, something felt new. Billy felt new. He wasn't the same guy who'd arrived in an electrified flying car. He was different. He was changed and walking out, for the first time in a while, he was calm.

As the Purple team gathered at the exit, they took a last look around to savor their brief brush with fame. Some would go on achieve it while others would just go on, but they had all changed as well. The hulking form of Andy gently brushing against Gwen had the look of a beginning instead of an end. With Celia and Rick paired up, it seemed like something was there as well. The specters made a straight purple line and drifted into the distance until there was only one left.

Walking over to Rod, Billy said, "Thanks, Rod, you really came through."

"So did you, Billy, but I'll be seeing you again," replied Rod, intensely flashing his glass eye and instantly searing an image of a snowcapped peak into Billy's consciousness. Constance then took her place beside Billy along with George and Glen. They didn't walk away friends or acquaintances. They walked away as a team, and although they didn't win, they took it into triple overtime.

EPILOGUE

The Tar Heels weren't quite sure what they'd been thrown into. They won, but rather than victory, it felt more like survival. There was a different force on the court that day, and they all sensed it. It seemed like they were playing something wild, something immovable and they held on just long enough to prevail.

Going forward, it served them well, because if they could beat the spirits, they could pretty much beat anyone, which they did. They went on to win a national championship behind Jevonte's story of the growling glass-eyed man from another planet who once stalked their court. Of all the games they played that year, their secret game against Team Purple might have been their best.

Following their championship win, Coach Gene Shatterly's decision to allow the game was ultimately vindicated. He wouldn't have cared either way, but with a debt still largely unpaid, he'd just have to keep trying.

Gene wasn't quite sure what had happened. He'd largely suppressed the Völler accident, along with that night in the desert when his leg was blown to bits. Surviving such tragedy, he still hadn't given much thought to a higher power, but with the recovery of Andy Völler, that all changed.

Seeing such grace arise from utter devastation, Gene discovered a world of intervention and redemption with a greater wisdom in play.

Sitting comfortably in his backyard the sun was shining, and he finally felt the glow.

George Penny was on top of the world. He'd taken his favorite team into triple overtime so, for the next few weeks, his feet didn't touch the ground. He was now a season-ticket holder, and the Tar Heels regularly heard George's booming cheers—and, of course, jeers when they weren't doing so well. He eventually became the pit master at a barbeque joint in Durham. He and Rick still played basketball every week, and George never forgot his friend from Florida named Billy.

Glen so enjoyed the game that he promptly enrolled in a junior college to finish his studies and to play basketball. As an eventual starter for the UNCW Hawks, with a girlfriend and a place at the beach, Glen was never again considered a no-show.

Pooling their resources, Gina and Rick finally bought the Friends Café. Expanding the dining room, Gina, of course, kept the UNC memorabilia, along with a framed and signed portrait of the famed Team Purple.

Coach Gene Shatterly and Floyd Gaines were still loyal customers, and Floyd always wondered why the reserves for Team Purple weren't in the photo. Still seeing them in his dreams, Floyd knew there was something more, but he couldn't prove it.

Following the game, Rick couldn't walk, so Celia conveniently nursed him back to health while Billy grudgingly covered his shifts.

Now officially an item, Celia spent most of her time at Rick's, writing and taking advantage of his cooking. Editing Billy's memoirs was going well, but trying to convince him to stay wasn't. Rick and George threatened to lock him up, but to Billy's delight, he'd retained his special powers, so he was still a handful.

As Constance knew they would, she and Billy slept together. Billy wanted her to stay, and she knew that too, but she had to report back to Rita. There was actually something fishy there. Constance shared such a likeness with Rita that it was almost like being with her, or with her somewhat annoying sister. Billy was intrigued.

In the weeks to come, Billy wrote while Celia corrected. When they were finished, against his better judgment, he sent a copy to Rita. The manuscript was titled *Triple Overtime* and, surprisingly, Rita accepted it. She then put Billy under contract with Constance as his agent. She'd heard they worked well together.

Billy wasn't sure what he'd be doing, but Rita said there was a steady stream of work for someone with his talents. Billy didn't know what his talents were, but he guessed he'd find that out as well. So far, all he'd done was get run out of town and then yanked around by the spirits. Billy actually wondered if he could handle any more insanity. But it seemed that as this chapter was coming to a close another was sure to open.

He hadn't had any strange dreams or visits from any beings in a while, although there was one small anomaly lurking, a clear vision of a snowcapped peak through the glass eye of a specter. Rod said that he'd be seeing him again, and Billy wondered if it was starting over.

Concerned for his safety, everyone pleaded with Billy to stay, but he wasn't worried. What would he do, sit around talking about the game for the rest of his life? Or make sandwiches with Rick and George for the next few years? Billy had an affinity for the place, but deep inside, he knew it was time to go.

With all the teary-eyed good-byes exchanged, Billy pledged to come back soon. He promised Celia he'd stay in touch and that he'd always come home to Carolina. They asked where he was going, and he said he didn't know. They asked how he was getting there, and true to form, Billy said he was walking.

Hitting the pavement, Billy didn't have to wait too long. Beneath a clear, blue sky, a shiny black sedan pulled slowly to the side of the road and stopped. Bathed in electric light, Billy slowly grabbed the door handle and pulled. With Ray at the wheel sporting a new, horrific lesion, Billy was right where he needed to be, alone and at the mercy of the spirits.

"Where we going, Ray?" asked Billy.

"You're going home, for now," answered Ray.

With Billy staring longingly out the window, amidst a brilliant shower of sparks, Ray's mysterious car lifted slowly into the air and blasted off into the stratosphere.

Energized by the game, all Andy wanted to do was play. It almost seemed like he'd been given a second life, and he wanted to live it to the fullest. With Gwen at his side and Coach Gene Shatterly back in the fold, he had a solid head start.

Preparing Andy for the NBA draft, Gene spread the word that his boy was back. Hungry for new talent, scouts from almost every team in the league descended on the Dean Dome to rate the relatively untested rookie.

Playing with an uncommon level of intensity, Andy immediately became a top draft prospect. His performance in the Purple game was just the beginning. He showed his stuff when the specters got him the ball, but he was playing even better now. Still with a competitive edge but without the ego, he was a perfect team player.

Holding their breath on draft night, Andy went to the Charlotte Hornets, which meant that he could stay close to Gwen. He also signed a multimillion-dollar contract, which, fortuitously, meant they could also buy a home.

With Gwen and Celia still the best of friends, Andy and Gwen made an offer on Andy's old house, which was of course accepted, leaving Celia to happily cohabitate with Rick.

With the house, the girl, and the contract, wedding bells were sure to follow. Andy took a knee and proposed. Teary eyed and ecstatic, Gwen accepted, and a date was set. With Celia as the maid of honor and Rick the best man, Gwen and Andy's wedding was a small but festive event. Gene gave away the bride with Gwen's mother unabashedly bawling. The wedding cake somehow floated through the air to each eager attendant as they partied long into the night.

There was something still unaddressed. It was Billy. As things progressed, Gwen started to fill in the blanks. She told of how the spirits had forced Billy into action all for Andy's survival. Gwen explained that she and Billy had been together, but went on to say how she was inexorably drawn to Andy. With the good fortune that had since come their way, they both agreed there was a debt to be paid.

Gwen contacted Celia, and a decision was made. They decided to send Billy a check for an undisclosed amount of money, or more accurately, for a million dollars. It was a safety net of sorts, so that Billy would always have something to fall back on. For everything he'd done, they figured it was the least they could do.

There was one last item of interest, one more redemptive detail to discuss. Moving back into the house, Gwen had a beautiful garden growing and a new set of hands to help. It was a little baby girl, and her name was June.

THE END